A CENTURY
OF STORIES
NEW HANOVER COUNTY PUBLIC LIBRARY
1906-2006

A Christmas Caroline

ALSO BY KYLE SMITH

Love Monkey

A
Christmas
Caroline

KYLE SMITH

wm
WILLIAM MORROW
An Imprint of HarperCollinsPublishers

A CHRISTMAS CAROLINE. Copyright © 2006 by Kyle Smith. All rights reserved. Printed in the United States of America. No part of this book may be used or reproduced in any manner whatsoever without written permission except in the case of brief quotations embodied in critical articles and reviews. For information address HarperCollins Publishers, 10 East 53rd Street, New York, NY 10022.

HarperCollins books may be purchased for educational, business, or sales promotional use. For information please write: Special Markets Department, HarperCollins Publishers, 10 East 53rd Street, New York, NY 10022.

FIRST EDITION

Designed by Susan Yang

Illustrations by Donna Mehalko

Library of Congress Cataloging-in-Publication Data

Smith, Kyle.
    A Christmas Caroline : a novel / Kyle Smith. — 1st ed.
       p. cm.
    ISBN-13: 978-0-06-111987-3
    ISBN-10: 0-06-111987-3
      1. New York (N.Y.)—Fiction.   I. Title.

PS3619.M5895C47 2006
813'.6—dc22

                           2006046658

06 07 08 09 10 WBC/RRD 10 9 8 7 6 5 4 3 2 1

I understand what you mean, Pa, but it's not that. It's not that I care for money to keep as money, but I do care so much for what it will buy!

BELLA WILFER, *Our Mutual Friend*

chapter one

THE THING THAT STARTED IT ALL WAS THAT FURRY boots were dead. I don't mean a little dead. One glance at the woman's shaggy footwear, and it was like, "Where do I send the condolence card for your look?" Or, "Your look is so quaint! I have *such* fond memories of when that was in." Or, authoritatively, "Somebody get me some yellow tape—I'm declaring this a fashion crime scene." Or—sniffing the air dramatically and addressing no one in particular—"Is it just me or does this elevator stink—of last season?"

The other thing was Carly. She was actually kind of dead, too. She had died this very day, Christmas Eve, one year ago exactly, under circumstances that were still too painful to contemplate. So Caroline didn't contemplate them. Contemplation? She wasn't a fan.

Staring in fascinated horror at the furry boots in the last place you'd expect to find them—the center of the heart of the

sun of the fashion universe, the Belle Connerie building—
Caroline felt her heart leap and frolic with a jingly little touch
of Christmas malice, deep under her fox-trimmed Balenciaga
military coat and her blush-colored Chloé tea dress. The BC
headquarters was where, just yesterday, Caroline had swept
into the building wearing her Mantalini sunglasses and had,
personally, gotten a silent nod of approval from the Editrix
heading out the door. The Editrix, who was noted not only for
running the most exclusive fashion book in the galaxy but for
hiding her own aging eyes behind light-expunging discs the
size of hubcaps, did not notice just anyone. With a nod from
her you could practically launch your own fall line. It was the
nod of arrival.

This, Caroline thought as she stood smirking next to the
lady with the unmentionable footgear, has been a very tough
morning. But things are looking up.

That assessment turned out to be as horribly wrong as a
floor-length denim skirt with a big front pocket for holding
your circle-a-word puzzle book. It was wrong as wearing a
T-shirt with a humorous saying on it. It was as wrong as the
Jaclyn Smith collection from Kmart.

The morning had been completely mental. Caroline was in
the habit of beginning each day with vigorous exercise: an argument with her mother. La had knocked Caroline out of bed
with the usual slightly-too-early phone call and the two had,
like a sadistic pair of long-distance workout partners, quickly
fallen into the usual pattern of stretching out their vocal cords
followed by several reps of angry accusations and a session of
emotional kickboxing. Caroline had scored the final points of

the fight, as she often did, by reaching down into the past and pulling up the usual dead weight: the subject of Caroline's father. La never wanted to talk about what had happened to him, and Caroline needed to get in the shower anyway. Conversation over.

The whole time she was on the phone Caroline's face felt as if it had been shrink-wrapped onto her skull by heat lamps. A quick look at the placement of her bathroom creams and essential potions turned up disturbing evidence. She remembered that when she'd finished with the small gray and black bottle of Honeythunder moisturizer she had applied to her face right before going to bed, she had put it next to her Buzzfuzz wax-and-razor relief oil. But next to the tube of Buzzfuzz that morning there was a gray and black sample bottle of Verisopht shampoo. The stuff she had put on her face was not moisturizer. It was shampoo. Result: raisin face.

Her mother. What had gotten into the woman? This morning's fight had really just been a horrible sequel, the *Grease 2* of phone calls. The original problem had begun when La had called to discuss the plan for the holidays. She'd ordered Caroline to guess where La and her boyfriend of the month were going.

"Okay, *Mother.*" Caroline rolled her eyes so vigorously that the motion was nearly audible. "Tasmania."

"Hee hee! No."

"Reykjavík."

"Uh-uh-uh!"

"Okay, London." Duh. It was always London when things were normal. Same old hotels where they tried to make you eat bangers, like it was some kind of quaint Olde Worlde thing to ingest disgusting fat into your pristine bodily ecosystem.

"We thought we'd try someplace new this year," La said. "Branson."

"Bransonne?" said Caroline, her mind scrolling through all the travel magazines she read. New place, she decided: southwest France, maybe?

"Oh Mommy, you know *comme j'adore la France!*"

"It's not in France," said La. "And did you just call me 'Mommy'?"

Okay, then Switzerland. Caroline hoped it would be the cool part of Switzerland, i.e., not the German part. Germans always made Caroline think of *The Sound of Music,* and *The Sound of Music* made her blood ice over. That scene where the poor kids were forced to wear clothes made of curtains? Needlessly graphic.

"We've never done Switzerland before," Caroline said, "but I think it would be fine."

"No no, Caro. It's—" Her mother's cell phone broke up in a cloud of static. "*crackle*—zoor*crackle*."

Zoor? Or Soor? That sounded almost Dutch—or, God, no, so much worse!—Belgian. Belgium was afflicted by packs of government bureaucrats, droopy gray skies, and practical footwear. It made Albany look like Río de Janiero.

"Did you say Belgium, Mother? Can we talk about that a little?"

"Zooree-*crackle*—flight—*crackle, crackle*—day," said Mother's end of the phone.

Caroline brightened. "Branzouri?" she said. "Is that like

Italy? Oooh, I haven't been skiing in the Italian Alps in years! Please say we're going to the Alps!"

"Can you hear me now?" La said, switching channels.

"Loud and clear," Caroline said.

"It's in Missouri."

"I didn't hear that at all," Caroline said.

"Missouri," said La.

Caroline scrolled through her mental database of similar words looking for likely matches. Missoni? Maserati? Moschino?

Caroline gave up. "I'm just not getting this word you keep mentioning."

Caroline's mother sighed. "Branson is in Missouri. The state of Missouri. It's next to Kansas. And, Oklahoma, I think maybe. It's in the middle of the country. You know, Kansas City? Where they have the big arch? Where Daddy got those steaks shipped from last year?"

"Eugene Wrayburn," said Caroline, "is not my father. My father is—"

"Fine, fine," said La, cutting her off. "Kansas City is in the state of Missouri. Branson is there, too."

"Do you really think the skiing is going to be that good in Missouri?" Caroline said. "It's supposed to be flatter than my stomach out there. Isn't it?"

"We're not going there to ski, we're going to eat ribs and listen to country music," Caroline's mother said.

"Mother," Caroline said, "since when does one of the most proper families of Greenwich, Connecticut, take an interest in country music?" Growing up, she recalled vividly, her mother had been vain, snobby, and sarcastic. So: just about perfect, actually.

Childhood had been a blur of days when Caroline lived vicariously through her mother's shopping trips, which had been breathlessly depicted by various glossy magazines and gossip columns. There had been Mother, in huge white sunglasses and matching turban, strolling along the Croisette with Tonio, the professional baccarat player from Malta. There she'd been in suede britches, a loose-fitting embroidered pullover, and unwashed pigtails, getting blissed out on humanity with a turtlenecked vitamin millionaire named Cliff at the Beverly Hills commune known as TG (Transportational Grooviness). Once an interviewer for *Harper's Bazaar* had asked La if she had ever worn the same outfit twice. She'd replied, "Does *Bazaar* ever print the same issue twice?" Some daughters spend their lives trying to prove their independence from their mothers. Caroline wanted to be like her mom, only more so. She kept trying to convince the magazine she worked for that they should stop beginning every third story with a hed that promised, "Not your mother's" dot dot dot. Because what if your mother was an incredibly amazing oh-my-God-can-I-have-your-autograph talent? But no one ever listened. They were the children of nonfabulous mothers.

"You know Daddy wants to try new things," Caroline's mother said.

"He's not my daddy!" Caroline nearly screamed.

"*Doucement,* Caro, *doucement.*"

"Look, Mother, are you trying to punish me in some way? I mean, Mother, Missouri is a place where, I don't know, people shoot animals and then knit sweaters out of the fur. They *go to church!*"

"It's a part of our country, Caro."

"Not my country. My country is like Japan: all coast. Between the Lincoln Tunnel and Santa Monica Boulevard, there's an ocean, as far as I know."

"Caro, I'm trying to make peace between you and Eugene."

"Peace? I can have peace anytime I want it," Caroline snapped, and hung up the phone. And cried.

In the shower, Caroline practiced making mean faces at her mother as she shuffled through her eight shelves of product and grabbed the good stuff: a squat plastic bottle containing a thick three-in-one liquid, one of those combination shampoo/conditioner/desserts. Caroline squeezed out an obscenely huge handful of the stuff and worked it into her hair. The smell of cinnamon buns just out of the oven filled the steaming shower. She was stricken with a crazed desire to eat her own hair. But of course washing her hair was the closest she would come to a sweet snack today. She hoped it wasn't possible to absorb calories through your scalp.

After her shower, she flicked on NY1 News to check the weather (Senator Christopher Casby, that hairy-eared old troll La had once dated and for whom Caroline had once briefly interned, had apparently just been hospitalized), shut the door of her fifth-floor apartment and hurried down the hall. At apartment 5F she pulled up short with a tiny yelp, like a dog at an invisible fence. The ear-assaulting antitune of "Grandma Got Run Over by a Reindeer" burst forth from the doorway like a hazardous waste explosion. No sound was more despicable to

Caroline's ears: not a jackhammer, not the hellish squeal of a subway train, not the dull snap of a $900 heel breaking off on one of those evil New York sidewalk gratings that seem to have been laid everywhere you need to go in a weird conspiracy between the city and the high-end shoe business.

Completely unintentionally, in fact very much without wanting to, Caroline's mind each season kept a running tally of how many times she heard any part of the evil novelty hit pouring out of car radios, at heavy-irony hipster parties, at pathetically "cheerful" little shops, and from the tabletop stereos of sidewalk fir merchants. This year's tally was forty-five, one short of last year's record, and since today was Christmas Eve, two days during which every radio station would be playing nothing but Christmas carols still lay ahead. The song was apparently still growing in popularity. In the postapocalyptic future, the only survivors would be the roaches, the lawyers, and "Grandma Got Run Over by a Reindeer."

This was a crime in progress, and it called for a citizen's arrest. Caroline whirled in her Prada boots and knocked on the metal door right under the tag that read 5F.

A wide-faced, middle-aged woman with black hair, stretchy pink pants, and a mass-merchandiser's cardigan opened the door, making the song even louder. The floor seemed to tilt under Caroline's feet. The noise was like having tiny squirrels munching on her eardrums. Caroline was getting run over by "Grandma Got Run Over by a Reindeer."

"Yes?" said the woman.

That one word was enough: *Mexican,* Caroline ruled, and her verbal-abuse-of-inferiors instinct kicked in swiftly.

"Listen, can't you keep it down? *Comprende* good manners? This isn't Tijuana, you know, you have to be considerate of your neighbors, even if you're just hired help—"

A bolt of horror froze Caroline in place, as though she were a statue called *Berating the Immigrant.* Whirring his way up to the family stereo was a handsome little boy whose eyes shone with determination. He leaned forward in his motorized wheelchair and turned the volume way, way up, from merely fantastically loud to window-buckling. Then he turned and aimed a gap-toothed smile at Caroline as the residents of New Jersey and Connecticut got an earful of the reports of Grandma's reindeer-aided demise.

Caroline hated cripples, the way they took up precious parking spaces, the way they whined and rattled dirty paper coffee cups in your face. Most especially she hated their style, the unintentionally mismatched clothing and their ever-present "Hi, I'm a victim" look.

"The boy likes it," said the woman, gathering the folds of her cardigan around her throat as though warding off the chill in the air that was Caroline. "I'm not a nanny, and we're not from Tijuana. We own some waterfront hotels in Barcelona. *Comprende* luxury real estate?"

The vehemence with which the woman slammed the door in Caroline's face was actually quite rude.

Caroline took a few deep cleansing breaths, but it wasn't helping. She had failed her breathing seminar at the Borrioboola-Gha studio. An angry yogi had screamed at her after class for having knotted up her chakra in a previous life. Caroline had responded that she hoped one of her previous incarnations had paid him in advance, because she had no intention of writing him a check after the way he'd treated her. And by the way, did he know his turban was "tired"? She had barely escaped the building intact after ducking several canisters of aromatic herbs and healing teas, and she hadn't dared walk on Seventy-first between Second and Third since.

On the elevator to the lobby of her apartment building, she was having a pang of preloneliness at the thought of spending the holiday weekend by herself. After her mother's bombshell, she had called Nicole to ask her what she was doing for Christmas and been told "I'm spending it with my family in the suburbs." Claire, Leigh, and Kristen had given exactly the same response.

Of course, there was an issue with Leigh. She and Caroline hadn't really spoken much since Leigh's business debacle. Leigh thought it was a no-brainer. When you go in the drugstore they only sell two sizes of condom: regular and extra large. So she started selling her own line of extra small condoms. She said she knew a lot of guys who would be perfect customers.

Caroline thought there were better uses for the $5 million that Leigh's father invested in the idea. Her strategy was to offer tepid, halfhearted support and slip in a casual mention of the Shoeseum. That was Caroline's dream. She'd give up the magazine and start something totally new and glamorous that was about her instead of some corporation. There were museums full of how-do-you-know-it's-not-upside-down abstract paintings and sculpture resembling car wreckage. They even had a museum for TV. Why wasn't there a museum for shoes? New York would be the natural place for one. Caroline had a plan:

She'd get things started with shoes from her own personal collection, solicit more shoes from celebrities (who would be glad to give up the goods for free in exchange for the prestige of being honored at museum events), use endowment funding to fly to auctions in London or Paris so she could buy up shoes once worn by Jackie O or Marie Antoinette or Eleanor Roosevelt—well, assuming Eleanor didn't wear workboots or nurse shoes or something. She, Caroline, would cease to live on the looking-at side of fashion and take her rightful place on the looked-at side, as the fabulous, the extraordinary, the divine founder and curator of the Shoeseum.

And all she needed was someone to give her ten or twenty million dollars to start.

Caroline got out in the lobby and was about to skulk out of the building when she noticed that the doorman was Mexican and consequently must know the little boy in the wheelchair.

"Excuse me," she said, though she tried to avoid talking to the building staff at this time of year, when they all expected and received tips from every tenant except Caroline, "but do you know the little boy in Five-F?" She looked at the tag on his jacket, which read, "Rudy."

"Of course," said the doorman, who was not from Mexico, or even New Mexico, but rather New Jersey.

"What, um, disease does he have, um, Rudolfo?"

"Oh him?" The doorman chuckled. "He got it bad. Caught the bug when he was a little baby."

Caroline didn't get it. "What's that?" she said.

"Applausiosis. Footlight fever. Uncontrollable swelling of the ego glands. He's in a play tonight," said the doorman.

"You know, that one about Christmas? He plays the little crippled boy. Method acting, they say." He winked.

Caroline's face was turning magenta. "You know, he was playing really loud music this morning. Not just loud, but bad. Someone should do something about it."

The doorman brought his eyebrows together, nodded slowly, and gave her a look of utterly spurious sincerity. "I'll launch a major investigation," he said, and sat down to investigate his doughnut and his *Post*.

On Second Avenue it was another churning, whirling New York City morning. Trucks grumbled, buses swerved, and people hurled themselves in every direction. The big, yummy, fresh smell of newborn doughnuts attacked from the new store across the avenue. Caroline, woozy, felt herself leaning toward the doughnut shop. But she clamped her molars together, put on her Mantalini sunglasses, and walked the other way. She clicked past a dirty Santa with a bell and a grimy gray plastic bucket that looked like it could hold either holiday donations or bait.

"Give to the world," Santa said in a soul baritone. "Give, give, give." He had set himself up in an urban gauntlet; to one side of him there was a long line of aluminum boxes dispensing crappy weekly newspapers and Learning Annex circulars that literally couldn't be given away; to the other there was a relic of a pay phone and a bus shelter. To get to the street where purring taxis awaited, Caroline was obliged to shimmy through the gap between Santa and the nearest newspaper box. Caroline had worn belts wider than this space. As she turned sideways to avoid touching anything, the unwashed Santa stepped right in front of her and glared through his yellow beard slash crumb-storage device.

"Give it up, pretty lady, give it up!" said Santa. "Joy to the world. It only happens once a year. I won't be here in a bunny suit in April. I won't be here with firecrackers in July."

"Let me guess," said Caroline. "Because you'll be back in the custody of the New York State penal system, right?"

"Pretty lady," Santa chuckled, "That's not gonna happen." He shook his head and mulled the future with all the optimism you'd expect from a fat, jolly old elf. Then he muttered something under his breath that sounded a lot like, "Santa got a good lawyer."

"Will you let me pass, please?" said Caroline.

"I'm not asking you to change the world," said the markdown Santa. "I just want your spare change."

"That beard looks flammable," said Caroline. "Maybe you should put out that cigarette."

Santa took a drag of his Kool and sighed.

"Pretty lady," he said, stepping aside and doffing a red and white hat that looked like imitation polyester, "go in peace. But just remember that there are those who want, and that you didn't give even a token amount."

Pushing past him in a tight fury, Caroline stopped so fast she nearly lost her balance on a spot of ice. A phrase of Coco Chanel's flashed on the screen of her mind: *Some people think luxury is the opposite of poverty. It is not. It is the opposite of vulgarity.* She whirled as she flicked off her sunglasses with maximum drama. "Let's get one thing straight, St. Nicotine. I give. I give a lot. I give at the office. I give at home. I give every freaking day. I've just given *to you*."

Santa looked as puzzled as if the elves had just joined a union and started dropping hints about overtime and a pointy-slipper allowance. "How do you figure that?"

"Just look at me!" Caroline commanded.

And Santa was happy to oblige, grabbing himself a good long drink of her from the immaculate strands of her blond hair to the toes of her exceptional black boots. She was perfect, every millimeter, from north pole to south. She may have acted naughty, but she sure looked nice.

Santa smiled. "Keep the cookies and milk. Santa wants something else for Christmas."

"And he's just gotten all he's gonna get," said Caroline. She slipped on her Mantalini sunglasses as she walked away. Then she lit up her fourth cigarette of the day and did some heavy pondering, trying not to furrow her eyebrows as she did so.

If Santa had been worth the effort to upload her most considered feelings on she would have informed him that beauty was a gift people like her gave to the world, and not just seasonally. What good did it do her? She didn't get to see herself, not much anyway, only when there was a mirror handy. And while it was true Caroline consulted various mirrors (vanity, makeup kit, back of bathroom door, back of bedroom door, back of front door, the shiny inside cover of the Altoids box) every day, she didn't do it to bask in her own glow. She did it to spot and take down flaws. Beauty wasn't a positive thing. It was an absence of negatives. It took nine bottles and tubes and vials of various gunks to give her this natural, clean look this morning. Every time she checked the mirror, Caroline therefore became a kind of cop or ambulance driver or superhero, obsessed with detecting and correcting.

Straight boys and unattractive girls didn't realize what a task, what a burden, what a responsibility it was to look fantastic, if of course you happened to be among those fortunate enough to have the potential in the first place. But potential was all it was, until you did something with it. Coco Chanel needed a sewing machine, Isadora Duncan needed a leotard, and Caroline needed makeup. And a personal trainer. And the latest clothes and accessories. And the will to say no every time a doughnut shop loomed in her path.

Looking fantastic wasn't a hobby, it was a calling. Once you were in, you were in for life, like a nun or a mobster. Just the stuff you needed to maintain your hair was so complex you practically needed a Ph.D. in chemistry to track it all. There were potions and unguents and straighteners and curl-makers and curl-killers and things to add shine and take away tangles. Caroline's hair was so full of toxic chemicals it was practically on the EPA watch list.

Then there was the color thing, which was best left to the professionals Caroline saw twice a month. Being blond was like a whole other assignment on top of looking fantastic that involved a four-hour visit to Frédéric, which of course had to happen in the carefully scheduled company of Caroline's mother: if they were going to present to the world a united front of natural mother-daughter blondness, they had to fake exactly the same shade, didn't they? Neither of them could ever let her roots show, even the roots of her eyebrows. It would be such a let-down to everyone. What Caroline spent on hair alone would have constituted a middle-class income in Nebraska, and was the number one reason why she was always, despite the incredible fabulosity of her lifestyle, broke. She had heard it said of certain English gentry that they were land-rich, cash-poor. Caroline was handbag-rich, cash-poor.

So no, she couldn't spare any change.

chapter two

 FIFTEEN MINUTES LATER, CAROLINE WAS SITTING
in Summer's office talking about herself and secretly grading Summer's look: conservative pencil
skirt, low pumps, nothing-special tailored white
Oxford shirt. Cute, but not in a threatening way. Not like the
Thing at work, who could wear the same outfit with ruthless
panache. No, the one-hundred-percent-certified panache-free
Summer Estherson, M.D., Ph.D., faded enjoyably into the background. She was just pretty enough to be worth talking to,
definitely not pretty enough to be competition. Her look said I
am not the star of this conversation. Summer was small, quiet,
and added a decorative accent to the room. She was like a human throw pillow.

Rarely in their weekly sessions did Summer say much of
anything. No matter what Caroline said, Summer never snick-
ered or snorted or "Oh, please"d her. That made this shrink
well worth the hundreds of dollars an hour she must have

charged. Not that Caroline ever saw the bills. The whole thing was taken care of by Belle Connerie benefits, which included full mental health care for routine issues like anorexia counseling (how to escape it, also how to get away with it) or complaining about your boss/boyfriend/mother: twenty-four-hour on-call freak-out repair and ego maintenance. Summer had a forgiving ear, a pleasing smile, and a midcentury modern sofa. Caroline wouldn't stretch out for just anyone but as the months passed she had found herself lounging on it more and more, sensing vaguely that Audrey Hepburn would have draped herself languidly over just such a piece.

"I wonder when they'll promote me," Caroline was saying. "I mean, I'm so clearly the rising star there. After what I did with the January cover, I'm surprised *Vogue* isn't calling me yet. Do you think they're worried that I might be, y'know, *un peu* too good-looking to work there?"

"Caroline," said Summer, "remember the word 'vain'? And how we did a six-week block of exercises on the concept?"

"Ah, see, here's the thing," Caroline said. " 'You're so vain, you're so vain, I bet you think this song is about you?' Right?"

Caroline paused dramatically, flat on her back, her hands balanced in the air like a conductor's. Her life was a symphony. Summer was her rapt audience.

"Yes?" said Summer on cue.

"But, see, the song *is* about them. You get me? The person accused of being vain is correct! 'You' are not vain, 'you' simply see things accurately. They really are so smokin' hot that they're driving the singer of the song crazy. Where's the shame in that?"

Summer had this way of coughing politely, like a butler. Which, along with the tweedy dressing and the Eames sofa, added to the nice retro vibe of Caroline's shrink trips. All that was lacking was a silver tea service, which Caroline kept hinting would make a nice addition to the office.

"You would have been proud of me today," Caroline said. "The new doughnut shop just opened but I totally turned around and walked the other way. It was soooo hard. It's like they're saturating the air with raspberry-filled or chocolate-glazed. I'm going to file a complaint about it. It's calorie pollution."

"Is that the only reason you're thinking about the doughnuts?" Summer asked, a bit intrusively.

"What do you mean?" Caroline said. "Him? Oh please. Doughnut Guy? Get real." She waved her hand like a third-grade teacher at the blackboard, erasing the memory. "And before you ask about the ciggies again, I'm trying to quit. And I will quit. By New Year's. I mean, not this New Year's, of course."

Summer was silent.

"Okay, I know you think I have a problem with guys. But have you seen what's out there? What is happening with the men in this town? Half of them can't talk about anything but sports, and the other half spend more time getting their eyebrows waxed than me."

Summer made an ominous-looking note in her notepad. "Did you hear back from that artist? What'd you call him? Fruit-on-the-Bottom Guy?"

Caroline laughed. "That was one of Mother's, actually." Lately Caroline, with much valuable assistance from her mother, had taken to giving nicknames to her dates to make them more interesting than they actually were. Fruit-on-the-Bottom Guy's real name was Harold Skimpole, a soulful, green-eyed harp-playing painter who lived with five other artists and musicians in a massive, unfinished space in Williamsburg. He had spent three dates with Caroline waxing poetic about his sensitive yet lusty feelings for women but when it came time for the moment of truth—that awkward interlude when you're sitting side by side on the sofa waiting for the guy to get on with it or get out—he always got out. Three consecutive dates, he claimed he had to get up early. Which was odd since he was unemployed. Possibly he was the first painter to ever make this excuse. Anyway, he was far too delightful a conversationalist not to be gay. Also, he smiled a lot: giveaway! The guy was straight on top, Caroline's mother had ruled as they sat side by side getting their biweekly hair fix-up, but Fruit on the Bottom.

"Besides," Caroline said. "I'm the most tolerant soul in the universe, but the man confused Gucci and Pucci."

"What'd you call that one before him? Great-with-Jeans Guy?"

"Ah," said Caroline, basking in the memory of her cruel-but-interesting relationship with Daniel Quilp. With his bushy black eyebrows, his heavy drinking, his shockingly abusive insults and his foul, wet cigars, he was perfectly obnoxious, possibly animal, and very, very sexy. Also, Caroline wasn't prejudiced or anything, but you kinda couldn't help bringing this up: he was a dwarf. Four feet, if that. Not the kind of guy you could introduce to friends, much less your mother. For one thing, he'd probably bite them. He was like any weird pair of shoes, the kind that were such a freaky color and style that you couldn't wear them with any really put-together outfit. They wouldn't go with it. But you bought them anyway, telling yourself, These would be great with jeans! And then you threw them in the back of the closet with six hundred other oddball pairs until it was time to bag them all up and give them to a thrift store for the tax write-off.

"He was kind of like the terror doll in that cheesy seventies made-for-TV slasher flick," Caroline said. "Hard to get out of your mind." She shivered slightly with the memory of his horror allure. "I kinda miss him." Of course she had never mentioned Quilp to her mother.

As Summer sat there—patient, always patient, as quiet and content as a fluffy pet—Caroline talked and talked. Then she took a deep breath, stretched, took a sip of Evian, and talked a little bit more. She went over the story of the infuriatingly charitable Mark Tapley, who put in seventy-hour weeks up at a community development center in the Bronx, insisting all the while that people like him had it too easy. He was some kind of guiltaholic. After a while Caroline started calling him Russian-Novel Guy: he might be good for you, but who had the time to figure him out?

There was also Control-Top-Pantyhose Guy: tall, poker-faced, and overeducated, John Harmon came from "old money," which, as Caroline's mother often said, was often code for "no money." New money was better: New money showed up on Page Six. New money's stock price was up that day or new money got married to some more new money and prepared to give birth to new new money. Control-Top-Pantyhose Guy's money was not only old, it was antique, having come from blacksmithery or stagecoaches or something—John never talked about the source of the family bling—and consequently had a shady air about it. Plus, he had been raised in a stuffy WASPocracy involving forced smiles and shocking abuses of lime green and lavender. Over dinner, you'd try to make small talk with them and someone would say something like, "By law I must not discuss any proprietary or nonpublic information in the quiet period that precedes a public offering." He became Control-Top-Pantyhose Guy when Caroline, after careful consultation with her mother, decided that although he made Caroline look good, she could never breathe when she was around him.

Then there was Ohio Guy. That one wasn't a cute metaphor. He was just from Ohio.

"We're talking Akron," Caroline said.

"And what about that guy you had a few dates with in the fall? Ed Drood?"

"I don't know what happened to him. It's a mystery. I was just getting into him. Then, not a word."

"That's too bad," said Summer.

"I kind of felt like we were starting something, you know? I wanted to see how it ended."

"And weren't you supposed to have a blind date with an athlete six weeks ago? Like in early November? You never told me how that went. Tim something?"

"Ugh," said Caroline. "You mean Neck Face? I totally deleted him from my hard drive. The guy shows up for dinner at Blue Ribbon Sushi wearing one of those sports hats. With logo."

"Well," said Summer, "not to defend him but many men wear baseball caps in casual social settings."

"It wasn't a baseball cap, it was a *football helmet,*" said Caroline. "One of those big, huge, plastic molded things? With some kind of facial grille on the front? It was like talking to Darth Vader's socially maladjusted little brother. Dork Vader."

"I can see how that would be a problem," said Summer.

"He's this huge guy, six foot seven or so, neck like an oak tree, and apparently his job is to kick footballs for the New York Jets," Caroline said. "Only he's really shy away from the ball field. He doesn't like to be looked at. He goes around with this stupid helmet on to conceal his identity, which just makes people stare at him all the more."

"Oh, that's right, they call that guy Tiny Tim in the tabloids," Summer said. "He's supposed to have some sort of mental handicap."

"No question," said Caroline. "He used to be a star player but now he keeps missing these easy kicks. There's all this talk about whether his job is in jeopardy. Nobody can figure out what's wrong with his head or how to save his career."

Caroline was not a football fan. The only sport she approved of was boxing, because the winner got a belt. It was important to recognize that accessories were worth fighting for. Once she was watching a match with Quilp when the announcer said the winner was going to take home a twelve-million-dollar purse, which sounded really exciting.

"He studies Zen Buddhism in between his kicks, I heard," Summer said.

"What a doofus," Caroline said.

In the *Book of Bad Dates* that Caroline seemed to have un-intentionally spent her life gathering material for, the Tim date was worth about six chapters. I mean, the guy tried to eat his sushi with a spoon. When Caroline asked if he wanted some wasabi, he broke into uncontrollable giggling. He couldn't hope to pronounce *edamame* without enrolling in night school. The list of excuses and gestures Caroline could use to get out of dates was not short. Yet on this occasion, she simply wiped the corners of her lips with her napkin, rose from the table halfway through the meal, and said, "Excuse me, but I didn't know you'd be such a dork. Sayonara."

At that point Caroline could have sworn that she spotted a tear in his eye, although it was hard to tell through the football helmet.

She was seated on a banquette against the wall, so when Tim shifted his chair to maneuver his bulk in front of her, she was momentarily stuck and considering, not for the first time, the advantages of keeping a small aerosol can of man-blinding spray in her bag. She had never carried such a thing, but only because she was afraid of confusing disabling weapon with spray-on moisturizer.

"Don't do me like that," said Tim. "Is a nice guy I being. Look, I pay for dinner, you sit down, we have a nice time to-gether. You can check me out any time you want, but you can never seethe."

"Excuse me?" said Caroline.

"Please, Caroline, don't fear the Roper. Come on baby, light my fart."

"Where did you learn English?"

"One-oh-five point two."

"Huh?"

"One-oh-five point two. Classic Rock Kroplochnich. Back in my country. You know, the 'Down Low for Kroplo'? Sometimes when I am being nervous I forget how to say what is I try. Is sometimes helping to think of one-oh-five point two. They songs say everything I try to say, say, say to you."

"Will you let me go?" Caroline said, snapping open her bag with great viciousness.

"Please, no," said Tim. "Is a tough time I am having with the life. The confidence is none, you know what I'm saying? Help, I need some booty. Not just any booty. Don't you haunt me, baby."

Caroline looked around the restaurant. Every pair of eyes, naturally, was locked on the two of them. People had given up all pretense that they were even there to eat. One guy was narrating the action on his cell phone: "The freak in the helmet says he lacks confidence. The blond hottie just took something out of her purse. What? Yeah, I think it might be that crappy Jets kicker." The celebrity quotient of the date was making it very, very hard for Caroline to resist one of her favorite pastimes: making a scene.

She looked down at the canvas toe of his enormous sneaker. "Is this your kicking foot?" she said.

Tim nodded, his eyes pleading.

Caroline planted a usefully sharp Louboutin heel into his toe, causing a noise like the snapping of a cracker. Tim shrieked, jerked backward, and grabbed his foot, which given how close he was to the table, kind of made it a given that he would both lose his balance and knock the table over on top of himself. The bowl of edamame bounced harmlessly off his helmet, but he did have some wasabi stuck in his chin strap.

Caroline stepped daintily out of the way of all this. "So I guess I won't be needing these," she said, quite loud enough for the entire restaurant to hear. And with that she littered his prone body with tiny square foil packets reading, "LEIGH'S X-TRA SMALL." Word got around the restaurant quickly. By the time Caroline reached the door the sound of laughter was ringing in her ears. The ringing she couldn't hear, of course, was even more satisfying: the sound of the phones on the desks of gossip columnists for the city tabloids.

As Caroline was telling Summer, even the kicker's name was unintentionally funny. "His last name is Kitsch, right? Tim Kitsch. Can you believe that? I was delicately trying to ask him what his name means back in his home country, just to be multicultural? It turns out that's not even his name. He changed it from something unpronounceable—something with seventeen syllables and umlauts coming in from every direction and a couple of clicking noises you make in the back of your throat— he changed his name from that to Kitsch. You know why? Because when he was at the city department of records to apply for a name change years ago, he hardly spoke a word of English, but he managed to ask some guy waiting in line what would be the closest American word that was an equivalent to his name. So the guy's obviously a joker and suggests Kitsch, and Tim goes with it. Now he's known by that name, I guess, so he's stuck with it. He would be cute if he weren't pathetic."

"So that brings us up to. . . ."

"Trot."

"No nickname for him?"

"Trot isn't a silly enough name?"

"Oh, right."

"I still, heavy sigh, miss him. I admit it. A little. I know, I know what you're thinking. I talk about him all the time."

Caroline had met Trot during one of her lengthier edgy phases, when her men had pretty much been required to display socially unacceptable qualities or at least have a tattoo and sulk a lot. This period had led to several exciting makeout sessions in grungy Delancey Street apartments with mismatched lighting schemes and bedrooms demarcated by hanging blankets. It had also led to more than one dismal expedition to readings in grim hipster bars where boys in silly hats tortured her and poetry simultaneously.

Still, Trot had more going for him than most of the aspiring and unwashed, the boys who slept by day and talked about forming bands by night. Trot's brain was like a can of soda you left in the freezer too long, busting out in every direction with his fame schemes. You could see him calculating every time you talked to him, sifting out the possibilities of every connection he'd made with producers, casting directors, agents, editors, photographers—anyone who worked the doors of Fame, Inc. was Trot's instant friend. Whether he wound up being the next John Lennon or hosting a TV game show involving pet videos didn't seem to matter: he was on a glory hunt, following the path wherever it might lead. He wore each mini-success— every promising meeting or scrap of praise—like a new coat of varnish. Long before he was anyone, as he was fumbling around trying to discover what statement he would make to the world besides, "Would you like to see our dessert menu?" he began to take on the bearing of a celebrity. But at the same time the real him was disappearing by layers. Not that Caroline had seen him lately, considering where he was now.

He had come recommended by the *Zagat Book of Guys*, commonly known as *Zaguy's*. Which wasn't actually a book but a Web site started by some Belle Connerie girls who realized that they could save a lot of time if all of their gossip about dating the handful of straight men left in Manhattan were posted in one place. The crimson homepage led to a site accessible only by password, which was slipped from friend to friend with the understanding that only the right sort of girl was allowed in. Every time you dated a guy, you would go to the site and fill out a questionnaire on him that would be fed into the guy's overall statistical average.

Years ago, before everything, Trot's *Zaguy's* entry looked like this:

L	EP	C/B	S
22	17	19	24

Trot Copperfield

348 West 101st Street, Apt. 4B, (212) 579-7324

"Some like it Trot" declare fans of this paralegal and actor who praise his "knack for imitating anyone he's ever met" even as others say "run, don't Trot away" from his habit of "hiding his personality behind his impersonations." Earning potential gets dinged thanks to Trot's apparently sincere wish to act full-time (though rumors fly that he is about to score spot on MTV reality show—any updates on this would be welcome), but Trot, who like all thesps had a difficult childhood he doesn't like to discuss (he hates his stepfather), does well with a 22 out of 30 in looks department and not bad in clothes/bearing. Many respondents note that Trot's mimicry conceals his essential blandness ("I mean, the guy claims he's only been drunk once in his life") but others argue that "he certainly seems to have talent" to aid dicey prospects among the footlights. Overall verdict: "a little bit of a cipher but at least he's not gay," which accounts for notably high score of 24 for sexuality.

There were some problems with *Zaguy's*. Guy ratings tended to rise when they were snapped up and became someone's boyfriend (at which point his new girlfriend would award him perfect thirties across the board to make rival girls jealous) but plummeted immediately after the breakup, when the girl would log on to a thousand different computers, if she had to, to bomb him with nasty reviews. But Caroline assumed that any time a desirable guy and a girl broke up, it was because the girl wasn't hot enough. This would never be a problem in her case. To Caroline this moment, a guy's return to availability, was like her old days haunting sample sales. You had to jump in there the minute they opened the doors, elbows flying, to get the goods.

All you needed was an introduction, but just about everyone in New York was connected through one of those friendship Web sites. It didn't take long to find a mutual friend and dash off a coquettish, intentionally stupid e-mail along the lines of, "Hi, I just noticed that you're friends with Emily, too. Isn't she great?" Of course, at that point the guy would drop everything, look up Caroline's profile and see her (impeccably styled) headshot. The let's-have-drinks-sometime e-mail would follow shortly.

"I should never have dumped him," Caroline was saying, not for the first time, when she noticed Summer was holding up a hand.

"Heard it before," Summer said. "Thanks."

There was just the faintest aroma of sarcasm in the air. *Sarcasm,* Caroline thought. I wonder who invented it? Whoever it was didn't get enough credit. It's not like we can get through our days without it. That made it a lot more important than the cotton gin or the telegraph.

Still, sarcasm didn't go with Summer's outfit.

"Sometimes the most important statement," Summer said, "is the thing no one will say."

Caroline was confused. "How do you mean?"

"I mean, when you were talking about last Saturday?"

"Right. . . ."

"Saturday on the Upper East Side. People with their hands full of shopping bags. Brightly colored packages. Stores with holiday displays. Awestruck children. A jingle in the air. Sidewalk Santas. It's Christmas, Caroline! And yet not once did you talk about any of this. Where's your spirit, Caroline?"

Caroline was caught off guard.

"Look, I don't do Christmas, okay?"

"You don't have to *do* Christmas, Caroline, it's in the air," said Summer. "Are you alive in this city—on this planet—in this month?"

"I'm sorry. I have Christmas—issues," Caroline said.

"Great. What are they? Tell me," Summer said. "I need to know."

"I—where'd you get that skirt, by the way? Who's it by?"

"Filene's Basement," she said, staring coldly. "The *basement* of Filene's Basement. Next to the plastic-jewelry rack."

Caroline didn't like Summer's new attitude.

"It kinda goes back a ways," Caroline said, chewing on her hair. Which she hadn't done since ninth grade.

"Oh, I see," said Summer. "It goes back? Like into the past? Where, like, your personality was formed? So it might be some kind of *psychological* problem, maybe? Then for God's sake don't discuss it here. Save it for your cab driver or your bikini waxer. Those are the people you should talk to about your deeply held neuroses and antisocial tendencies. And you and me, we'll just leaf through *US* magazine and dish about which celebrities have the worst face lifts."

"Did your shrink tell you to be more assertive with me?" Caroline said.

"What does it say on my shirt?" Summer said.

"What?" Caroline said.

"What does it say on my forehead?"

"Huh? Nothing," Caroline said. Was this some kind of shrink mind game?

Summer got up, turned completely around and started shaking her thing about two feet from Caroline's face. This was really exceptionally un–Summer-like behavior.

"What does it say on my butt?"

"Nothing, all right?" said Caroline. "What is your major *thesis,* already?"

Summer sat back down. "So we agree that it doesn't say WELCOME anywhere on me. Then how did I get to be your doormat?"

"Hold on, Miss Doctor Estherson," Caroline said. "You're paid. So what if you're a doormat? These boots are handmade, from Milan. It should be an honor to have them wiped on you."

"Caroline, I can't do this anymore," Summer said. "I know you think I'm a saint, but you're enough to make the pope roll his eyes and say, 'Whatever.'"

"Are you"—Caroline was aware that her voice was cracking—"dumping me?"

Summer looked sad not angry. "I'm so sorry about this."

"But you can't," Caroline said. "It's a violation of doctor-patient whatever."

"Caroline," Summer said, "don't make this harder than it is."

"But," Caroline said, "you're my friend."

Summer took off her glasses, threw her notebook in a drawer of her desk, and put her head in her hands. "I've never done this before."

"I want one more chance," Caroline said. "Please. I'll do anything." Caroline looked around wildly, seizing any prop that could help, her eyes finding twinkling lights in a window across the street. "And it's Christmas! Everybody deserves a little charity at Christmas."

Summer folded her hands under her chin, forming a little bridge of seriousness. She peered at Caroline as if she understood things.

"I'll give you one more chance," she said. "You can come back here on one condition."

"Anything," Caroline said.

"I want you to get a date for New Year's Eve. Not just any date. One with real potential, to a guy you can picture yourself marrying."

"Oh," said Caroline. "I meant anything that wasn't impossible."

"Caroline. . . ." said Summer, showing all signs of early-onset exasperation.

"Have you seen the men out there? There's gay guys, and there's sea monsters. Nothing in between."

"Did you ever think that the problem is not too little choice?" said Summer.

"How do you mean?"

"You're paralyzed by your options. You're the girl with three walk-in closets who has nothing to wear. I'm asking you—telling you—to start making some choices. Caroline, the alarm has gone off, you've taken your shower, and it's time to get dressed."

"Okay, I don't have three walk-in closets," said Caroline, in a huff. She had one. The room that used to be Carly's bedroom.

"Your hour is up," Summer said. "Come back next year with a wonderful, romantic New Year's Eve date to tell me about, or don't come back at all. Oh, and one more thing."

"Isn't that enough? Come on, Summer, if I wanted homework I'd still be in school."

"There's another guy issue you need to resolve."

"Who?" said Caroline.

"The guy you didn't mention at all today. The guy you never mention."

Caroline gave Summer a look. You could call it an unfriendly one.

"You know how just before you leave the house you should take off one thing?" Caroline said. "You just put on a big chunk of ugly costume jewelry that you bought from a guy with a folding table on Fourteenth Street."

"Caroline. You practically named him when you first came in."

"I did not. I strongly urge you to do some shopping at the clue store."

"Clues?" said Summer. "You want to talk about clues? A college sophomore would be able to read the symbolism behind your obsession with that new doughnut shop. Even a not-bright college sophomore. Even a *sociology major*."

"What is it," said Caroline, "with shrinks and reading into everything?"

"Now," said Summer, less than kindly, "your time is really up."

As Caroline got into her coat trying not to think of doughnuts, trying not to think of cigarettes, trying not to think of the guy who she most didn't want to think about, she said to herself never compromise. Never surrender. What would her mother say if she came home with just another guy? If he wasn't Jack Kennedy, Jack Nicholson, and Johnny Depp wrapped up into one extremely financially secure package, what use was he?

Caroline had never mentioned this to Summer because it was too weird, but she already had a specific image of what the ideal guy would look like, and no one in reality ever came close. On the front wall of her mother's shop there was a strangely timeless oil painting. The clothes were so classically cut that the picture looked as if it could have been painted within the last ten years, or a century ago. It was a portrait of an anonymous bride and groom looking quietly contented on their wedding day. The bride was lovely, blond, at peace. The groom was pleasingly handsome but the thing that stood out about him was this look of inner strength, of unshakable poise. Caroline had spent a lot of time in the shop growing up, and as a little girl she had frequently been struck by the sense that the groom in the painting was looking directly at her, only at her. Not in a creepy way. It was as if he was guarding her. Sometimes, when she had been very small, she would play a little trick on the painting. She'd be sitting on the floor with a coloring book or chatting with the customers who always fussed over her, when she would spin around without warning to see whether the groom was still watching. He always was. That made her, smile right back at him. The two of them had a secret.

The receptionist, Mrs. Bardell, looked dully up at Caroline as her jaw worked a wad of chewing gum.

"Are there any good single men left in this guy-forsaken town?" Caroline whined. New York was supposed to be a place for fairy tale romance, but no one told Caroline she would wind up dating so many of the brothers grim.

Mrs. Bardell looked like someone who had spent the last few decades with orchestra seats to the most neurotic show on earth.

"Sister," she said, "I didn't get married until I was forty-two. You know how I finally did it?"

"Patience?"

"Lowered standards."

Caroline gave her a hostile smile. "Thanks for not helping," she said, and turned to go.

"Listen to me," said Mrs. Bardell. "If he don't have a criminal record or a tan line where his wedding ring should be, don't rule him out."

Caroline was already letting the door snap shut with more force than was absolutely necessary. And when she got outside, what was the first thing she saw? An SUV pulling up in front of her. Out of it tumbled four people: Mommy, Daddy, and two adorably dressed mini-Moms, girls of about seven and nine who were decked out in blueberry-colored French capes and brilliant red cashmere scarves. They looked like a pair of Eloises. The girls dawdled giggling at some private joke on the sidewalk until their mother shooed them up the stairs.

"Come on Quebec. Come on Malta," she said, and the four of them disappeared into their brownstone townhouse. For a moment, Caroline could see the point of the whole thing: one man, two children, and a wife slash mother who enjoyed supreme executive control over them all. That happy woman got to preside over the choosing of four different outfits every morning. Nice. She got to pick out the weirdest, trendiest names for her daughters. Cool. But two kids meant being fat for eighteen months plus recovery time: no deal.

There was a voice that nagged Caroline from within, a ghost in the machine that spooked her. Maybe marriage wasn't for her. What man was reliable enough to sign up with forever? What man could make Caroline feel special every day? What man deserved her? Caroline's mother had always said: Darling, you and I will not stoop. The men will just have to grow.

Still, there was Trot. Handsome, successful, and by all accounts, not yet taken. It hadn't worked out between them the first time, but how cute would it be if they gave it one more chance?

Out on the avenue, she looked at her reflection in a store window. She couldn't even muster the energy to look at the shoes lovingly laid out inside. In the hour and a half since she had left her apartment, Caroline believed her face had visibly aged. Soon she would be forced to admit that she was no longer in the late part of her early twenties but in the middle part of her middle twenties, possibly even the early part of her late twenties. And it was all thanks to other people carving their problems into her face. Her mother had drilled a wrinkle across the breadth of her forehead. The man situation had sketched faint frown lines at the corners of her mouth, and the redheaded Thing at the office was practically a hard-hat construction worker who daily jackhammered those gruesome sneer lines that flared diagonally away from each of Caroline's nostrils.

To top it all, Carly. Her death had painted giant, tragic, flesh-sucking semicircles just under Caroline's eyes. Caroline peered intensely into her face, hatching plans. Botox? Caroline wasn't warm to the idea of giant needles, much less giant needles filled with, you know, botulism toxins. BOtulism plus TOXin? They weren't exactly chocolate and peanut butter, were they? More like, oh, deadly poison and deadly poison.

The solution, clearly, was for Caroline to keep her facial expression completely blank for the rest of her life. Starting today. Like this, she said to herself, practicing. No matter what happened, no disaster could cause her to frown. No joke could make her laugh. Placid. Calm. That was her. Like Grace Kelly. Maybe some elbow gloves would help. Long black silk ones. And a cigarette holder! Oops. Kill the little smile. Smile tracks all around her eyes! Disaster. She blanked her face out again. She looked like a newscaster. Ick. She thought of awful newswoman looks, dippy red blazers with contrasting white piping and of course hairspray. Now she was sneering. Blank out, woman!

That's when it happened. A mammoth white truck rumbled by. The eighteen-wheeler hurtled over the avenue, practically going airborne over the seams and bumps like a supersized urban Jet Ski. The truck was encrusted with layers of black dirt, and on the rear panel some roadside wit had written a message in the filth with a fingertip. Oddly, though, the message wasn't the usual "WASH ME." Instead, Caroline thought she saw two entirely different, chilling words.

Below the words was, Caroline could swear, this funny little drawing that looked very strangely like Carly's face. Like the dead roommate Caroline forced herself not to think about nearly every day.

As the truck with the two-word message stopped at a red light, Caroline was forced to remember the way Carly had died. Horrible. But Caroline wouldn't think about that. She'd think about nicer times.

Caroline and Carly. Carly and Caroline. They had shared a starter apartment together in Single Alley, learner's permit

Manhattan, that portion of the Upper East Side that was very Upper, and very East. In that building they had developed into one of the most-invited pairs of roommates in fashion's backyard. They had practically the same names. They were practically the same age. They shopped in exactly the same stores.

Carly and Caroline. Caroline and Carly. How many bushels of carrot sticks and celery had they nibbled together while squealing at the nighttime soaps? How many rice cakes had they crunched, reassuring each other that the number of calories in each of the tasteless air-discs was less than the number of calories burned while chewing them, making each one a negative calorie proposition? How many times had one or the other of them gotten up in the morning, gone to the bathroom, stripped naked, and wandered sleepily toward the scale, only to hear the other one yell out from bed: "Don't be an idiot, floss first, then weigh yourself!"

Now they'd been apart a year. One year, precisely, since the day when a cruel trick of fate had taken from Caroline all three of them: Carly, Carly's charmingly indolent boyfriend, James, and Caroline's classic super-vintage off-shoulder ice blue man-slaying Versace dress, which Carly had promised on a stack of fall fashion issues to return to Caroline the very next week.

Two weeks after the disaster, the bodies of Carly Jacobs and James Harthouse had been recovered by the Coast Guard. There was still no sign of the dress.

But now there was this truck, with its two ugly words traced onto its filthy rear door:

Heed Me

chapter three

WHO PUT THEM THERE? WHO COULD HAVE sketched Carly's face? Who could have known Caroline would be standing right here, looking in exactly this direction at exactly this moment?

The truck was pulling away. She ran along behind for a little while to catch up and get a better look, but her boots were philosophically and functionally opposed to running, so in this case "a little while" must be defined as approximately four seconds.

The big rig was snorting and belching its way down the avenue, its message fading to an unreadable jumble. Maybe it really just said "WASH ME" after all? And maybe the face beneath it was just a trick of the grime, a smudge, a nothing? She had once seen Coco Chanel's face in a cloud, after all. And that had happened on the very anniversary of the important day in fashion history when Coco had declared, "My friends, there are no friends."

My friends, there are no friends. What a perfectly on-trend remark. What an insight for the day before Christmas, when everyone Caroline knew had left town or was about to leave, and no one had invited her along to a ski house or a beach or even a rustic country cabin in the forest somewhere. Family time, each of them had pleaded in turn as Caroline tried to squeeze them for an invite. What use were friends if you couldn't use them?

Caroline opened the door of the cab that already stood parked next to her. She never had to hail a cab. Drivers who had grown up three continents away took one look at her footgear and guessed she wouldn't be going far unless she got a taxi or developed the ability to fly. Sometimes, on a lazy summer night when she was allowing some young Josh or Justin to romantically walk her home from a date, smiling at his little pleasantries with the front of her mouth while clenching her molars against the pain that started in her heels, inflamed the backs of her legs and ripped through her spinal cord, a tantalized cab would creep along behind her waiting for the signal to pounce, like a Secret Service detail or an FBI surveillance team. Stymied by the slo-mo cab, a long line of cars would settle into a crawling, seething mess behind it, making angry noises. It was kind of like a little parade, only instead of tubas and kettledrums the musical accompaniment was the sound of apoplectic drivers shouting elaborate curses at one another. Caroline enjoyed the idea that she could literally stop traffic.

Today Caroline directed the driver through the park. To get her mind off the strange message written on the truck, she tried to focus on the hack license posted on the thick plastic divider between the front and back seats. Taxi driver licenses always featured two things: an unhappy face and an unpronounceable name. Caroline looked at the picture trying to decide which the cabbie needed more: a seaweed wrap or an apricot peel? His beard was so dense it could conceal loose change and the mole between his eyebrows looked angry enough to run off and join a guerilla group in the mountains.

But as she was staring, just for one second, the beard began to melt away. The mole grew fuzzy, shrank, disappeared. A soiled turban became a pair of Armani sunglasses propped up on the forehead, the eyebrows seemed to wax themselves, and the whole face was moisturized and lightly Lancôme'd.

Mabouelezz Khalid became Carly Jacobs.

It couldn't be. Caroline covered her eyes with her hands. What day was this, anyway: Christmas Eve or Miss Creepy Face Day?

Carly's face. . . . In life, Carly had been fair-skinned, the type of girl who was sometimes hard to recognize on the beach because she was mummified under constantly reapplied layers of heavy-SPF antisun cream, the kind of professional-strength product that was not really needed by anyone except maybe a space traveler who is required to actually visit the surface of the sun. But when her face appeared on the hack license, Carly was looking a little pale even by Carly standards.

Caroline swallowed hard and rubbed her eyes with her fists, the way she had when she was a little girl. She counted to five, trying not to lose it.

When she opened her eyes, Carly's face was gone. Mabouelezz's was back.

"Yes!" she yelled.

"Yes, Miss?" said the driver.

"I am so happy to see your face!" Caroline said.

When the cab arrived at Forty-second and Seventh, Caroline was explaining to Mabouelezz for the fifteenth time that no, she couldn't give him her number, and no, she wasn't free that evening, especially not for falafel and a hookah.

"So sorry about your contagious disease," said the cabbie, idling on Forty-second after she stiffed him on the tip. "Maybe you will call me if you do not die as planned in the next sixty days?" The driver mimed a little phone by holding a fist to his ear with his hairy thumb and pinky extended.

"I am officially never making that gesture again," Caroline muttered as she slammed the door.

Now she was all alone in the dead center of Christmas Island. A few blocks from here there were giant toy soldiers lined up with their toy cannon on the roof of Radio City. A four-story illuminated bow wrapped the entire Cartier store. All down Sixth Avenue, each stodgy, ultra-establishment corporate headquarters had a theme: the eight-foot Christmas-tree ornaments in front of the Time-Life Building, the gigantic candy canes in front of Credit Suisse. The bushes on the median strip of Park Avenue were set with yellow lights that twinkled like snowflakes, and of course there was skating and an eight-story pine tree in Rockefeller Plaza. All of these horrors, and what did they symbolize? A day when everyone was entitled to get lots of presents. Caroline got presents every single workday, envelopes and boxes and bags and tubes stuffed with the most delightful goodies, and the best part of having her job was the knowledge that others did not. Christmas was therefore the worst day of the year.

The cab had let her off on the south side of Forty-second Street, so she waited for all the cabs and Lincoln Town Cars and buses to pass before she stepped into the street. As she did so, she was buzzed and almost toppled by one of those nearly invisible little mini-SUVs, the new must-haves that combined the cute bite-size scale of the VW Bug with the tanklike frame of the Hummer.

"Gah!" said Caroline, springing backward onto the curb. "HumBug."

Scurrying at last across Forty-second, she reached the overhang of the huge gray building where a hand emerged from a pile of stained laundry rattling change in a dingy cup, directly under the elegantly engraved marble name-slab

BELLE CONNERIE

"Sweet lady in the shades," said a reedy voice from somewhere in the rags.

Caroline ignored him.

"Next fall's Mantalinis, eh?" he said. "Cool."

Caroline halted right there. She turned around and removed the sunglasses.

"A little Clinique Precision Ionized Science Formula Super-balanced Hydrating Concealer would work wonders on your frown lines," said the voice.

Caroline tried to glare, but how do you glare at a heap?

"How did you know that?" she said.

His head still buried somewhere, he produced from within the rag pile a bottle of Koelner, the impossible-to-get new German bottled water that came in this cool retro-futuristic silver bottle. The guy tipped the bottle and poured it into a gap in the center of the pile where his mouth may have been. "Been sitting here a long time," he said.

"Thanks for your concern," she said. "Keep that sidewalk warm."

Just then he came out of the building: Trot. From his shabby hair to his I'm-a-pacifist military pants, everything seemed to be carefully chosen to give the effect of being put on without a thought. It was a look. And his shoes: tan workingman's boots. Not designer but still: the perfect brand for this sort of thing. The brand that said intentionally clumsy, in a manly way.

To Caroline's surprise, Trot's gaze seemed to be aimed everywhere but at her as he walked. They were heading straight for each other, and he showed every intention of just walking right by.

"Trot!" she said. "I can't believe it."

"Ah, Caroline," Trot said. He put on a self-consciously nervous look that suggested he was actually acting the part. He was like a talking mime.

"It's been a hundred million years," she said. "What are you doing here?"

"Here?" he said. Caroline thought she saw his Adam's apple jump. "Here in New York City, New York State, United States of America? The city where I live, in other words?"

"Here, coming out of this lobby," Caroline said. It was amazing how quickly Trot could turn you into his straight man.

"I'm not here. I was just cutting through here. From the Forty-third Street side. To, buy this, huh-huh, great! magazine."

Sheepishly he produced a thick, glossy book from his battered bike-messenger bag: a copy of the next issue of *Vogue,* featuring the English divinity Eddie Granger on the cover looking her haughty best. Granger was rumored to be dating Belle Connerie's reclusive zillionaire owner Paul Dombey, but—hottest new thing? Please. Not if she could only score the cover of the January issue, the one that was hardly thicker than a book of stamps. The September issue was so thick, by way of contrast, that a gossip blog had reported—in the few hours before it had mysteriously shut down—that potential new hires were told to stand in profile and measured against it. If your body was wider than that issue, you didn't get the job.

"This isn't a trial," Caroline said. "I believe you."

"What are you doing here?" he said.

"This," said Caroline, "is where I work."

Trot smiled in that disarming way of his. She admired the way everything about him fit together. He had a style. So many guys didn't bother to cultivate one, wouldn't play the here's-my-look game, weren't worth noticing. "Of course," he said. "You, huh-huh, *work* here."

"Come have a cup of coffee with me," she said. "Our office is closed today, I just need to pick up a couple of things at work."

"I don't actually *do* caffeine. But I'll come with."

Across the street at Captain Caffeine, Caroline ordered off the menu. She had achieved such a tolerance of her drug of choice that she could bolt a double espresso between yawns and then curl up for a nap.

"Molto Vesuvio Massimo," Caroline said to the pointy-side-burned counter guy, a studenty type in a name tag reading AUTHORIZED CAFFEINE DEALER who looked as though he considered himself above this job and probably all others. The counter guy turned to the manager/barista three feet away (name tag: JAVA JEFE) and raised the silver ring that pierced his eyebrow at her. Her left nostril, the one with the golden nose stud, twitched. An electrical signal seemed to pass between eyebrow jewelry and nasal ornament. An agreement was reached. The barista gave the nod and brought out the serious coffee. Soon it began to drip muddily from the espresso machine.

Trot watched all this with an excessively grateful smile. "And, huh, huh, some cold milk." The counter guy grudgingly gave him the cold milk, suspecting he was being mocked, but also gave him a look that said: Do not mess with us counter guys.

Fading demurely away from the register so Trot could have the opportunity to pay for her coffee, she struck up a strategic position near two seated finance dweebs. With her head half turned, she threw them a demure half smile through her hair, which was her most devastating pose. She allowed them to chat flirtatiously with her until they got the idea to stand up and give her their table. At which point she shut down all conversational operations and waved over Trot, who was picking up his cup of milk. She gave the two suits an "Are we done here?"

smile—lips tight together, face frozen above the mouth—and one of them asked for her phone number. She told him, "Five, five, five, one, two, one, two." Which he eagerly wrote down. Then he asked if it was 212, 646, 917, or 718.

Caroline gave one of her most eager smiles to Trot. "So I haven't talked to you since it all happened!" she said.

"Ah," said Trot. "Since I became this, uh, ginormous star." Trot's face had become a familiar sight in magazines and on handbills in the nine months since the debut of his one-man Off-Broadway show, *A Brief History of My Greatness, Vol. I.* Caroline hadn't been invited to opening night and wouldn't have gone anyway: She had hoped the show (billed as a "play slash performance art piece slash confessional slash diet cola") would flop. After it had succeeded, though—the first of many worshipful pieces on Trot in the *Times,* on the eve of its opening, had sold out a year's worth of performances—Caroline had been angling for a way to switch things back to suck-up mode.

And Caroline didn't suck up. But this was a special case, because the more elaborate steps Trot took to dodge fame, the famouser he grew. He had, famously, declined to move the show to "suburban, housewifey" Broadway; he had, famously, refused to have the show taped for HBO; and he had, famously, used his substantial share of the substantial profits to set up a nonprofit foundation (SLAM, for Stop LAnd Mines) that benefited children orphaned by war, urged politicians to steer more aid to impoverished parts of Africa, and also operated a store in Brooklyn that sold vintage 1970s lunch boxes and *Planet of the Apes* action figures. A weekly mock newspaper had printed a fake story titled, "Pope Asks Trot Copperfield to Be Less Sanctimonious."

The more Caroline read about him—and lately hip Web sites had been providing near daily updates of his publicity-shunning moves—the more convinced she became that she had made a little boo-boo in breaking up with him years ago, when they had been different people in a different city.

"What's it like?" said Caroline. "Everyone is raving about you."

"I, uh, find my name connected with a little praise," Trot said. He took off his coat, revealing a crappy brown T-shirt decorated with a brief ironic blurt

EDGY

Caroline studied the T-shirt. He *was* edgy, though, wasn't he? Except now you couldn't call him that, or accuse him of that, or say he was trying to be that, or whatever, because he beat you to the punch by mocking the very concept. Which was brilliant.

His restless silence made it clear that he either didn't want to talk about his incredibly successful show, or was playing the part of someone who didn't want to talk about his incredibly successful show. So they sat there for a moment and listened to the sound system, which was a little too proudly playing U2.

"Man," Trot said, "I *love* U2."

Caroline loved the way he spoke in italics. It came back to her what was so exciting about him, why he had never quite left her mind: The guy was cool. It was like he had access to deeper layers of sarcasm. Caroline used sarc as well as anyone, but the mistake she made was that she only unloaded it on the stupid stuff and the stupid people. Trot had it all dead-solid clear. He could make you understand, with his mock stupidity, how stupid *everything* was. So why let up on the irony, ever? Why give stupid a chance? The two of them were soul mates. Or at least "soul mates."

"They're so not the Beatles," Caroline said.

"The Beatles," Trot said. "They were, huh–huh, *geniuses.*"

Caroline laughed again, but nervously, as she poked around his words looking for the wit. Maybe this was a goof on the stupid people who liked the Beatles solely because the smart people said they were geniuses. Or possibly he was mocking people who threw around clichés like "genius" because they couldn't come up with a more insightful way to respond to genuine mastery of an art form. Or maybe he just thought the Beatles sucked.

But as of the time she had left the house this morning, it had still been okay to like the Beatles, Caroline thought. Trot gave her an uneasy feeling that she had to get on the Internet and check up on this. Except Trot was the kind of guy Internet buzz took orders from.

"You'll never guess what song my neighbor was playing this morning when I was leaving for work," Caroline said. 'Grandma Got Run Over by a Reindeer.' The horror, the horror."

Trot nodded, waiting. Caroline was uncomfortable. Normally guys struggled and sweated to entertain *her*. She felt like she was auditioning. She had to get the taste stuff carefully calibrated. Had to disdain the right things.

"I mean, is that the kind of song that goes with mass-produced 'holiday cheer' or what?" she said. "It's the ceramic Christmas tree of music."

Trot leaned back and stuck his thumbs in his ratty green Army surplus pants. "That song," he said, "is a major work. It's a piece of im*port*ance."

Caroline laughed, punched his arm. "You make me laugh."

"Me *too*," Trot said, opening his eyes wide, like a child's on Christmas morning.

"What do you mean?" said Caroline, hoping he would say that she also made him laugh, though he certainly hadn't laughed today. In fact, she was trying to remember what he looked like when he laughed, but she was blanking. She had known Trot for years. Had she seen him laugh?

Tenderly, ever so tenderly, Trot reached out and placed his hand over hers. "Sometimes, when I'm home, late at night? I tickle myself. There. I said it. It's out there. It's never coming back in here." He shook his head and pointed earnestly to his heart.

Caroline laughed some more. She could see how a philosophy started out as an attitude with this guy. She could also sense an invisible line of people forming behind him, begging to do whatever he did exactly as he did it. She wanted to be at the head of the line.

"So when are you going to get me tickets to see your show?"

"It's not a, uh, *show,*" Trot corrected. His voice was hard. "It's a piece."

Caroline chuckled, but a look from Trot made her stop.

"It's not juggling," he said sternly. "It's not *Oklahoma*." There was a tense moment. But he puffed out his cheeks and raised his eyebrows to signal all was well. Lightly humorous marks could be made again.

"No," said Caroline, teasing, "I've heard it's just this totally new art form, right? It's not just the old, 'I think I'll shamelessly exploit my crap childhood'? Because a lot of guys have done that."

Trot's face was like a door that had just been slammed and wouldn't be reopening any time soon.

If Caroline had been wearing a kitschy T-shirt at this moment, it would have read, "Oops." Or maybe, "Pardon Me for Speaking the Truth." There was backpedaling to be done.

"I'm kidding," Caroline said. "It's just that, I never heard you talk about your childhood before, so I just wondered if you were, in some way, kind of, I don't know, being creative? With the facts? But I could so totally be wrong!"

Trot munched on his lower lip and looked nowhere in particular, but definitely not at Caroline.

"When we were dating before, I never felt like I got to know the real you," Caroline said. "I really wish I could."

"The real me," said Trot, "isn't a commodity. That you can 'pick up' at the *store*."

"I didn't mean it like that," Caroline said. "I didn't imply it would be easy. I just, you know, you're kind of fascinating. I always thought that."

But Trot had the tired look of a man who has been told he's fascinating many times every day for the past year. He put on his coat. "I've gotta be somewhere," he said.

"Sorry! I didn't mean to hurt your feelings."

"You didn't hurt my, um, *feel*ings," Trot said, as though the idea were totally television, totally suburban. Caroline was left to wonder whether she had just hurt his feelings by implying that he had such a thing as feelings. Or if she had just indicated how totally uncool she was by using meaningless expressions of intimacy like, "Sorry I hurt your feelings."

Trot stood up, in an escape posture.

"Any New Year's plans, at all?" she said. She plucked the stirrer out of the coffee. A thick hunk of java stuck to the end of it. She licked it off with the tiniest, most delicate flicks of her tongue. A caffeine-addicted cat couldn't have done it any more prettily.

"Oh, just, I don't know. What about you?"

Her head tilted this way and that. "I'm just, you know, keeping my options open. A few offers have been made."

"That's, uh, *nice.*"

"But I haven't committed to a thing," said Caroline.

"Really."

Caroline heard the period. She didn't like the way it sounded.

She smiled and waited as if she was posing for a magazine ad for a product called Smiley and Waitey.

"So," Trot said, "great, um, *seeing you!*" And as Caroline walked him out, she slipped him her business card. The look on his face as she made this game effort suggested he would be calling when baggy sweaters that reached down past your butt came back into fashion, or when the sun burned out, whichever came last.

That didn't go as well as it could have, Caroline thought when she was back in the Belle Connerie building waiting for an elevator. She stood next to a woman with a narrow wisp of a body and a giant head. She was kind of built like a parking meter. But Parking Meter Woman, Caroline slowly realized, was the fabulous Eddie Granger. This month's *Vogue* cover. Should Caroline say something? No, of course not. Stay cool. Maybe Eddie would compliment Caroline's Mantalinis.

Caroline cocked her hip and removed her gloves in a theatrical way, but the weight of her non–Carly-related problems began to sink in. Like what to do for Christmas, now thirteen hours away. Like how to get back at her mother. Like what to do about the creepy-crawly, the creature, the . . . Thing that she hoped wouldn't be lurking anywhere near the building today.

The elevator arrived and made the sound all elevators made here in the Belle Connerie building: not a cheery, vulgar "Ding!" but more of a resigned tongue click. A front-of-the-mouth sound that was the aural equivalent of rolling your eyes. The doors yawned open insouciantly as if to say, Oh, all *right,* tread on me, I did all this for you but it's yours to walk all over just as you *please.* Its cheeky posteverything look sparkled with pristine emptiness. Its raffishly bare metal floor was spotless and yet hip to its own need to be noticed. It was the world's first openly gay elevator.

Position was key. Caroline, moving quickly, secured one of the rear corners, where she could observe (and make up insulting remarks about) everyone else's outfit from behind while no one else could see her. When you were at the very top of fashionworld, the idea was to be both glamorous and inaccessible, wreathed in mystery but dazzling in impact. With all inferiors, you played a game of hide and chic.

Caroline's eyes made a lighthouse sweep behind her Mantalinis. The sunglasses were hot beyond hot, a dazzling Death Star of trendiness that practically burned her face with their supernova of cool. On a visit to Milan two weeks ago, the superstar Mantalini himself had personally promised her that she would be the only person in America to have them.

"The only one, my little pink candy!" he had said in the kind of Italian accent you used to hear in pasta-sauce commercials. "The only one, my ripe succulent platter of chocolate-chocolate cake!"

"Stop," said Caroline, "You're making me hungry. Do you promise?"

"I promise on the pain of a thousand stabbing hot suns that will cook my eyeballs into soup if I give this to anyone but you, Signorina!"

"Grazie. And, ew," said Caroline, taking his hand in both of her hands. "That means a lot to me."

Caroline took off the sunglasses and scouted the elevator competition. Eddie, the English princess, looked spectacular. Even in profile you could see her transgalactically famous, carefully calculated tooth gap. Rumor had it that this flaw had been secretly added via years of orthodonture to remind you how perfect the rest of her was. All that London drizzle had grown her into a pale, frail Giacometti sculpture, the new state of the art in slender, the It girl who made Kate Moss look like a professional wrestler. Her cheekbones stuck out like fenders, but they were the only curved things on her body. She was definitely stopping by to receive worship or negotiate the details of her next photo shoot, Caroline decided. Or maybe to have a little rendezvous with her rumored boyfriend, the company's chief, Paul Dombey.

Girl Number Two's look was what happened when black met more black. Perfectly acceptable and therefore a perfect bore. If you took no chances, you got no style points, not in this building.

Number Three was a beaut: A gummy woman somewhere between 50 and 150 with a softly downturned gaze, shiny black hair, and long, long black eyelashes. Okay, the face wasn't bad. But consider the horrid bulky turquoise ski jacket she wore unzipped. Check the cranberry pantsuit. The pearls at her throat were completely the wrong kind. The big dangly earrings looked like they had been made by one of the younger designers—like, say, Number Three's kid, at Camp Hurliwanna. She had matched her belt, her handbag, and her eye shadow. She looked like a flight attendant who worked on an airline chartered by Talbots. Caroline scrolled down to the wedding ring—plain gold, didn't tell you much, Caroline hated wedding rings—and focused her laser vision on the engagement ring, which spoke volumes. Unfortunately for Number Three, those volumes seemed to have come straight out of the main reading room at the Passaic and Bergen County Branch. It was a tiny, round stone, a trifle, a speck of sparkle dust compared to the mammoth boyfriend-bankrupting ice cubes, the nuptial SUVs, that had been adorning the fingers of New York's cutest little fiancées and brides for many a year. A woman had one chance in a lifetime to slip her ultimate value on her finger for all the world to judge, and poor Number Three evidently was worth less than the sale rack in the bargain basement of the outlet store.

To top it all off, or rather to proclaim a new low in taste, there were these outrageously hairy boots. Caroline hadn't seen anything so furry since the last time she glimpsed a French girl's armpits. How many wookiees had given their lives to make them? The more Caroline looked at them, the more stunned she was by the system failure that had led to their being placed on human feet. In those fussy period movies, the ones in which everyone wore empire waists, Caroline had to laugh whenever someone referred to the dumpy unwanted sister as "plain." Unattractive people weren't plain, that was the *problem*. They were spectacular in their awfulness, they blazed as brightly as the giant crimson neon sign for the battered-fish-and-salad-bar restaurant across Seventh Avenue. Caroline wished for a gay man to share these thoughts with. Gay men *knew*. Their cruelty was such a precious gift in these confused times.

Passenger Number Two, the girl whose outfit had nothing to say, got off on seventeen and do you know what Mrs. Furry Boots said?

"Merry Christmas," she said.

Number Two stopped in her tracks, made a full turn. Protocol lapse. Elevator Silence had been broken! Her eyes lit up. Her *hair* lit up. You could tell she wasn't used to being talked to yet. Had probably only been with Belle Connerie a couple of years.

"And a Merry Christmas to you!" she said.

The elevator door closed while Caroline pondered this

betrayal of the unwritten rulebook. Elevators were for scoping, not chatting. The space was too intimate. There were too many sketchy ears listening in. What was Mrs. Furry Boots up to?

But what really bothered Caroline was the Merry Christmasness of it all. The first cases of it had broken out around November first, and by now it was an epidemic. Cab drivers Merry Christmased you. Guys on the sidewalk Merry Christmased you. (Guys on the sidewalk said lots of things, most of them vile. It was part of the burden of living in New York, and also part of the reason why Caroline couldn't imagine living anywhere else.) In Caroline's opinion, every nonentity who went around lobbing Merry Christmases this way and that should be beaten soundly with a canned ham.

On the next floor Eddie swiveled her perfect head on her perfect neck and—unbelievable—actually called out "Merry Christmas!" to Mrs. Furry Boots. The Christmas disease was catching. Its molecules were being transmitted right through the air, like the flu or one of those near miss cheek kisses you do when you see somebody you officially like but don't actually want to touch.

"Have a very merry Christmas," said Mrs. Furry Boots, just before the door closed.

The elevator started moving. "Where are you heading for the holiday?" The woman had turned completely around to address Caroline. Shame she had none.

"Oh, we'll be in Europe," Caroline said, though there was no *we* and the closest she was likely to get to Europe was the picture of the Alps on the package of Swiss Miss Sugar-Free Nonfat Cocoa.

"That sounds lovely," said the awful woman. "I just love this time of year. Don't you enjoy having a time set aside for family and giving and spirituality?"

Caroline looked at her as though she had just mentioned cholera, typhoid, and Wal-Mart.

"I don't actually have that much of a family," Caroline mumbled.

If Caroline hadn't been steaming over the holiday pleasantries, she might have noticed that Mrs. Furry Boots was getting off on the floor directly below Caroline's. If she had processed that information, she might have guessed what it meant, and that guess might have saved her one very unfortunate remark.

The elevator settled at twenty-three and the doors opened with a whisper. The woman took a step off, turned, and fired.

But she had evidently exhausted her supply of happy-holiday clichés. "Peace," she said, giving Caroline a kindly look directly in the eye.

"Likewise," Caroline said sarcastically, then, realizing that only one second remained until they parted, she scrambled around in her mental warehouse of brilliant fashion jibes and came up . . . empty. Nothing there! The place is stripped down to the dust bunnies! See the clerk about a rain check! Only half a second remained! The perpetrator was about to escape unchastised!

"Nice *boots!*" she blurted at last, just as the doors closed between the two women. Oh no. Not that. The woman was wearing a pair of muppets and the best Caroline could do was, "nice *boots?*" Muppets! She could have done so much more with that. "What do you call your boots, Elmo and Grover?" Or, "I didn't know Jim Henson had a fall line." All of this brilliant material, wasted, the way the best view of Manhattan was wasted on New Jersey dwellers. This was shaping up as the worst Christmas ever, Caroline thought.

But it was about to get much, much worse.

chapter four

WHEN CAROLINE GOT OUT ON TWENTY-FOUR, SHE felt her right heel land on something with a sickening crunch. She looked down hoping the damage was minimal, but the result was approximately what happens when graham cracker meets sledgehammer. Slowly she bent down to pick up the wreckage of a pair of Mantalini sunglasses. The newest thing. The only pair of them in the country, gone.

A tear escaped Caroline's eye and fell down her cheek, creating a possible makeup situation. Caroline opened her hand-sewn special edition Hermès bag and took out a compact—but what was this? Her Mantalinis. They were in there after all. Yet here was this other, identical, broken pair in her left hand. She felt dirty, cheated on. Mantalini: that sunglass slut. He had given a pair of glasses exactly like Caroline's to somebody else. Someone who had ridden this very elevator, this very morning. But who? Eddie? Maybe that wouldn't be so bad. She was, after all, a supermodel, the highest form of life. She might have been planning to wear them to a shoot, and photos shot today wouldn't show up in any magazine for months. But now the glasses wouldn't be appearing in that shoot at all, would they? Maybe this little mishap was taking on a different flavor entirely. Maybe it was Caroline's own little Christmas miracle.

Centered on the wall opposite the elevator was the giant gleaming corporate metal logo that said, in a highly stylized font

PRESENTS
Give to yourself

above a framed blow-up of the latest cover. Caroline paused to smirk at this reminder of triumph. Against a bright red background, the cover featured a close-up of a smiling, elfin nine-year-old girl who was paid more than any other actor in Hollywood, at least per pound. Behold the infant phenomenon herself, Nina Cru. The kid (real name: Ninetta Crummles) was so precocious that she had actually acquired an agent while still in the womb. She had signed her first modeling deal at the age of three days, for Newbies, the new silk disposable diapers (ad copy: "Nothing is too good for my baby") that had sold out from coast to coast. The child's sky blue eyes and unnervingly adult mannerisms turned out to be perfect for creepy roles in such Catholicism-and-cutlery horror films as *Broken Chalice* and *The Altar Girl,* and as the years wore on she'd maintained her trademark frozen stare through every flesh-perforating scene in *The Hurting, Rattle,* and *My Bloody Playdate.* She'd even gotten an Oscar nomination for best supporting actress for her latest effort, as an innocent budding ballerina inhabited by the spirit of a serial killer executed the very same day she was conceived, in *Splits*. At an age when most girls were still holding conversations with stuffed animals, Nina Cru had committed forty-six on-screen murders and played three different relatives of Satan. Her agent at William Morris couldn't wait for her to start getting adult-sized paychecks. To quicken the process he had put out word that Nina was available for grown-up magazine covers, but no one had bitten.

Meanwhile, research at *Presents* had shown that more and more parents were buying designer outfits and accessories for their children. But Caroline's boss, Sally, said at a cover meeting that the magazine didn't cover tot-sized clothes so going cover with Nina Cru was out of the question. That was when Caroline decided to stand up and be heard.

She gave an impassioned speech, one that afterward she would always think of as a spiritual moment, in which she argued that they could pair Nina Cru on the cover with a handbag; say, one from Fendi. The bag would sell the cover to adult readers, and maybe some little girls would buy the issue too, figuring that they had to know all about what Nina wore so they could pester their parents for the same. Coincidentally, Caroline had just that morning walked by the Fendi store, and had put herself in a near fever trying to think of an excuse to get them to send over their entire spring line without having to give a dreary promise that she would send it all back later. When she called Fendi and asked if they were interested in being on the cover, she had barely put down the phone when the messenger arrived with a large selection of complimentary goods. One went on the cover, but all went in Caroline's closet. The January issue was traditionally a slow seller but with Nina Cru on the cover under the line "Accessories to Kill for," this one went through. The. Roof.

Caroline owed Nina a lot. But still, as she walked by the framed poster, she had an icy feeling that the kid's eyes were following her every move. It was enough to make Caroline stop and turn around. She peered at the poster again. The same knowing smile was on the infant phenomenon's face. She was working that same devil-cherub look. It's not just me, Caroline thought. The kid freaked people out for a living. There was a rumor going around the magazine that at the photo shoot back in September, the photographer's Italian assistant had taken one look at Nina, crossed himself, and said a Hail Mary in Italian. Reports varied, though. Some who were present said he had simply scratched his eczema in three places and requested biscotti.

Through the glass doors, Caroline noticed the creepy little reception gnome, Mrs. Defarge, still knitting ferociously. Simpleton or evil genius? You make the call. Despite her theoretical job of greeting visitors, the old bag had consistently demonstrated the ability to never, under any circumstances, speak or even look up from her knitting. If you had one day told the crumbling fossil that from now on her job title was not receptionist but rather "incredibly hostile client-scaring, needle-loving creepy lady," she would not have needed to adjust her working habits in any way. No one in the building had heard her voice, nor could anyone figure out how such a hag managed to keep her job at Belle Connerie, year after year, decade after decade. Caroline didn't even have a clear idea what she looked like since she always wore a hooded sweatshirt. It was suspected around the building that she had some dirt on Paul Dombey, but nobody knew for sure. She might have had an affair with him when she was young. Then again, she might have had an affair with Benjamin Franklin. If, that is, she had ever been young. But as the twentysomethings flitted through Belle Connerie on their way to perfectly appointed marriages and country estates stocked with nannies and golden retrievers, Mrs. Defarge wordlessly stayed. All you heard from her was the clicking of her needles. All you noticed about her was the horrible fingers working, working.

Caroline tossed Mrs. Defarge a hopeful little buzz-me-in smile, but no luck. Mrs. Defarge just kept knitting something that never got any larger than the palm of one hand. The lady had been working here approximately 960 years, had without a doubt knitted enough material to make a doily big enough to cover the George Washington Bridge, yet she seemed stuck in time, always just beginning some little bootie or tea cozy with a cold metal clickety-clack. The horrible fingers still working, working.

Frustrated, Caroline waved her ID in front of the clear glass electronic seeing-eye panel to pop the door. Just as she heard the door unlock, another weird thing happened: she heard the faintest little scratchy noise. A rhythmic, gentle noise. Not an unpleasant sound. Not an animal sound. It wasn't coming from the wall. It sounded like it was being made by someone standing directly behind Caroline.

She whirled. Nothing. No one.

And still the sound went *scratchy, scratchy, scratchy.*

Caroline pushed open the door. "Did you hear that?" she said.

Mrs. Defarge, her face hidden by her hoodie as usual, continued knitting and nodded gravely in the manner that service personnel use to mean, "My responsibilities do not extend as far as providing any assistance to you."

Caroline quickly walked past the Thing's empty cubicle, went into her office, and shut the door. Taking a deep breath, she picked up the phone and hit speed dial 1: home.

Caroline's maid, Krystyna Krtzychzt, answered the phone. Miss Krtzychzt, a name it had taken Caroline weeks to learn how to pronounce correctly (it sounded vaguely like "Cratchit") had come five thousand miles from some desolate East European land plagued by a tragic shortage of economic opportunity and vowels. And here, at the end point of her journey, she had spent the past six weeks removing dirt from Caroline's somewhat undersized but impeccably located Upper East Side flat.

"Yes please" said Krystyna in the appropriately servile voice that Caroline loved. It was a myth that it was hard to find good help in New York these days. The place was positively swarming with clueless illegals. What was hard to find was really obsequious, unlimited help, the kind that never said, "I'm beezy that night" or "I would luff to, but who would peek up my keeds?" The kind that was smilingly, almost desperately, available to all offers of employment around the clock like your own personal dial-a-peasant. Caroline had had to conduct elaborate evasive maneuvers to make sure none of her friends found out about Krystyna and made competing bids for her incomparable services.

"How far have you gotten so, um, far?" Caroline asked.

"How far? From front door to the back of the living room and then back to the kitchen."

Why was Eastern Europe so literal? Was it decades of being governed by mean people? Was it that awful starchy diet? Krystyna had a problem picking up sarcasm, too, which meant a lot of conversational energy wasted. When addressing her servant, Caroline frequently found herself lapsing into a sort of prehistoric speech pattern in which she actually meant everything she said.

"I mean," Caroline said, "exactly what have you accomplished today?" Still too broad. "As in, what have you thrown away?"

"Oh," said Krystyna. "I find Snickers in a shoe."

"And what did you do with it?"

"I throwing it away!" said Krystyna.

"Good," said Caroline. "What else did you find?"

"I find a bag of Bugles where the part of the, how do you say it, where you make the coffee?"

"Yes, in the water tank of the espresso machine, good," said Caroline.

"And I find one box Raisinets in the pocket of raincoat," Krystyna said.

Caroline had forgotten about those. They were probably stale by now.

"And what did you do with all of these items?" Caroline said.

"I throw them all out!" said Krystyna.

"Good," Caroline said. "Did you find anything else that should be thrown out?"

There was an ominous pause.

"No?" said Krystyna.

"Krystyna . . . ," Caroline sighed. "I'm very disappointed in you."

"It's only three hours I've been being here," said Krystyna. "You making these things very hard to find."

"If they were easy to find, I wouldn't need someone as smart as you to hunt them down and kill them, would I?" said Caroline. "We've gone over this before."

"I know," Krystyna said, wild terror in her voice. "I throw away all the food, every day! But there is a lot of it. Remember that time there was basket of Kit Kats hanging out the window? It take me all day to find the string was holding it that was looking like part of that ball of yarn you used to be knitting from?"

Caroline remembered it very well, because she had scarfed uncontrollably from that very basket of sin for a long, lost weekend before Krystyna's daily search-and-destroy mission had successfully eliminated it. The knitting apparatus had been an embarrassing cover scheme that she was also glad to have been rid of. It had resulted in one lopsided pink sweater that she had given to Krystyna, who had smiled gratefully but never, apparently, worn it.

"Krystyna," Caroline said, "there's something you haven't found. You have until four o'clock today. I could hire somebody off the street who'd be better at this job than you."

"Miss Caroline, I will find!" Krystyna swore, loyal, terrified comrade that she was. Every bully needs a bullyee, Caroline thought with satisfaction, and the poor immigrant cowered so well. In truth, Caroline's threat had been idle: Krystyna was a genius at snack detection, a true prodigy with false-bottomed drawers, fiendishly unreachable spaces, and urban camouflage. It had occurred to Caroline that Krystyna might, if hired by the New York City Police Department, turn out to be some sort of Sherlock Holmes, but the homicide squad didn't need her as badly as Caroline did. Not eating at work, in this building, was one thing. Peer shame was like a press that kept you thin at the headquarters of Belle Connerie Publishing, home of more starved women per acre than anyplace on earth (except the places where there were actual shortages of food). The Belle Connerie cafeteria was the kind of place where a girl would take one look at the plate handed to her by one of the guys behind the counter and plead, "Um, Sir? Could I have a little less?" Home, though, home was where the bad things lurked, and if Caroline had only recently ordered her maid to conduct a thorough calorie-elimination search of her person and her bags when she returned home in the evenings, it had always been an essential part of Krystyna's job that she decontaminate the apartment daily so that Caroline could return to a no-cal zone. In between Krystyna's visits, somehow the apartment managed to restock itself with Twizzlers, Hostess Fruit Pies, and miniature chocolate-dipped Entenmann's Donuts. Caffeine, cigarettes, and neurosis still did amazing work, though, and as a result Caroline had never weighed much more than an eleven-year-old gymnast.

Caroline opened the door to her office and stood waiting for the Thing.

"Good morning!" said the Thing, popping up out of her colorless little cubicle, which as usual was decorated with a garishly large bouquet from some easily fooled guy or other. The Thing was small, really small, but she looked positively microscopic next to the giant pot of flowers. "Merry Christmas! My gosh, I thought you weren't coming in today! I think no one's here but me and the receptionist." She smiled and nodded and did a stagey bit of business with her eyes to achieve maximum effect, a vivacious sparkle that made men weep and babies laugh. Giving eye, Caroline called it. It even worked on women. Especially on women.

"Clinique Precision Ionized Science Formula Superbalanced Hydrating Concealer," Caroline said. "Instantly."

"Of course," said the Thing, bookish yet flirty in gray Ralph Lauren. "I'll call it in for you right away. Not that you need it. I'm sure you just want it as a gift for someone else. I don't even have to ask."

Caroline smiled, but not all the way. She wanted to do what she had to do today and escape without excessive fraternization with the peasantry.

"And how have you being doing on the assignment I gave you, *dear?*" She heated up the last word in a little saucepan of sarcasm. She never used the name Ursula. It was much more cruel to call her little terms of endearment: dear. Pet. Lamb. She wasn't even sure what the Thing's last name was. Something that sounded Asian. Neep? Jeep?

"Just about done!" said the Thing, in that ridiculous accent that sounded like it had been slow-cooked in molasses on a wood-burning barbecue in Virginia. That Southern-lite accent that Caroline had heard a guy at the Christmas party describe as "intoxicating." Not just any guy either: a guy who mattered, a senior vice president of Belle Connerie ad sales, Nic. A guy who had helped give Caroline those frown lines. Frown furrows, really. Frowns you could plant tomatoes in.

Caroline had *so* met Nic first. She had been accepting compliments from a circle of junior staff at the Christmas party when Kate Nickleby had broken in.

"Kate!" Caroline had screamed, genuinely pleased to see her, although not displeased to be seen socializing with someone as important as Kate, who, after all, had once apprenticed with Mantalini and just this year had dressed the president's party-crazed daughter.

"Caro!" Kate had fired back.

"Your spring line was amazing!" Immediately after making this remark, Caroline remembered that she had used the exact same words at the time the spring line had debuted in Bryant Park back in September. It was an awkward reminder that she hadn't seen Kate since.

"I am *so* sorry about the mix-up," Kate said. "It's just that we had an offer to do an exclusive spread with *Vogue,* and—I'm not saying that *Presents* isn't as cool as *Vogue,* not at all! But they got to us first."

"No biggie!" Caroline said, knowing that the *Vogue* offer came in three weeks after *Presents* had agreed to feature Kate's trendy line, and knowing that Kate knew that Caroline knew. You had to have a lot of imagination to work in fashion. An imagination that was sort of like a big tub of Clinique Precision Ionized Science Formula Superbalanced Hydrating Truth Concealer.

"How'd it work out with that athlete I e-mailed you about?"

"Ugh. Mr. Football? Neck Face? We had one date. Next question."

A tall figure in Ferragamo appeared at Kate's side. His eyes were the color of Moroccan suede, and he had shaggy cocoa brown hair, the kind that would fall softly over his eyes when he bent down to kiss you. His lips were such a rare shade of spring strawberry that she was just on the point of asking him what kind of lip gloss he used when she realized both of them were staring at her.

Kate and Nic were smiling. It seemed to be Caroline's turn to speak.

"Yes?" she guessed.

Kate and Nic laughed.

"I guess you did understand me," he said.

"What my brother—Nic—asked," Kate said, "was, are you always the most beautiful girl at the party?"

Nic smiled, and angels sang. But he was distracted by a cringing, limping, drooling troll who stutter-stepped up behind him and tapped him on the shoulder.

"Excuse me," Nic said, and turned around to talk to the hunched little guy. "What is it, Smike?"

Kate leaned in toward Caroline urgently. "Can I borrow you?" She steered her toward the heaving bar scene, where freshly coiffed women in maximum-impact outfits and professionally applied makeup were circling the few bewildered-but-delighted young straight men who had managed to gain entry to a fashion magazine party.

"College," Caroline said unhappily, shaking her head. "That's what it was like for *us,* in college. Man clusters hovering sweatily everywhere you turned. We lived in a man rain, a man deluge. What happened to all the men?"

"Um," said Kate, "we work in fashion? Maybe they aren't as interested in handbags. What did you think of Nic?"

Nobody played it cool like Caroline played it cool. It was her policy never to be guided by anyone else's questions. She had learned this idea on many a 7:50 AM slot promoting the magazine on morning TV, when ill-prepared hosts had asked her some completely off-the-wall question like, "So do you get lots of free stuff in your job?" And Caroline would be right there to instantly ignore the question and say something like, "Let me tell you about my job." (Pause. Question already forgotten.) "My job is to tell you that suede cowgirl hats are going to be absolutely mandatory this spring."

So. Nic? Caroline wasn't going there.

"Who is that weird guy with him? Is he retarded or something?"

"Oh, Smike?" said Kate. "No, he's just this big Yankees fan. Always talking sports."

"So I was right the first time."

"Listen, there's something I wanted to talk to you about," Kate said. "We've known each other a long time, right?"

Caroline nodded, recalling all the lovely chats they had had while sweeping up goodie bags at the exits to the impossible-to-get-into parties. "Almost a year."

"Right," said Kate. "And in that time I've noticed a change in you. Have you had any successful dates lately?"

This seemed to be putting things a bit bluntly, but Caroline wanted to be friends with Kate. "Not really," she said.

Kate nodded, bit her lip, ran an analytical glance up and down Caroline's figure. "I can see it in your body," she said. "You've become sexorexic."

Caroline gasped. Her hands flew to her waist and stealthily began to take measurements all the way back down. "Are you saying I'm fat?"

"Not fat. Just, you know, washed-out. Ground down. You haven't been getting your recommended servings of booty."

Caroline glanced at Nic, who was still deep in conversation with Smike. "Is sexorexia a thing?"

Kate nodded. "The hottest thing," she said, which made Caroline feel a little bit better.

"It's been *written up*," Kate said. "You've gone on an extreme sex diet, and you're starving your natural juices."

Her juices! Caroline's hands flew to her face. "But I moisturize!"

"I know, I know," Kate said, clasping her hand with sisterly affection. "But it's just not the same. You can do whatever to the skin, but you can't fake what's beneath the skin. That buck-wild glow. The shagging shade. Caroline, you're in a no-nooky spiral and you're heading for a crash into Spinster Mountain. The first step to treating sexorexia is admitting you have a problem."

"What's the second step?"

"Well, sex," said Kate. "Obviously."

"Oh," said Caroline. "I thought maybe there'd be eleven more steps."

"No, that's pretty much it," said Kate. "Get some. But preferably the really wild, demented, possibly illegal kind. It's best if you do it in public. Some place where you might get caught. It's a challenge in winter, I know. You just have to get creative."

Caroline looked through the ballroom's twelve-foot French windows at Fifth Avenue below. Normally the black horse-drawn carriages that clomped around Central Park were off-limits to the cool kids. They were strictly for tourists and movie shoots. But those carriages went through some shady corners of the park. And of course the driver couldn't see you. There were big thick blankets folded neatly on the backseat, and there was a little bit of privacy under the canopy . . . But how often did they wash those blankets anyway? Were dry cleaners open at 11:53 PM?

Kate was looking over Caroline's shoulder and smiling.

Caroline turned around. Nic was coming back over, getting cuter with every step. He looked so good, Caroline could barely take her eyes off his suit. What divine variety of wool was that? It looked like worsted cloud. She wanted to roll around in it.

"Your brother," Caroline said. "Remind me what he does again? You told me about him one time at Sundance, right? I mean—" she broke into a whisper— "was he in prison or something?"

"He taught public school in the Bronx," Kate said.

"Exactly," said Caroline, only partially relieved. "I knew it was something like that."

"It's a problem, these days, with our kind," said Kate. "Everyone wants to enlist for bleeding-heart boot camp. He didn't last long, I assure you. Quit after a ten-year-old attacked him with a croquet mallet Nic bought with his own money because he had read all these newspaper stories about the school lacking proper athletic equipment."

"So, is Nic, you know. . . ."

"Available?" said Kate. "Oh, yes. I'm going for more Pinot Grigio. Bye!"

Caroline turned around as Nic was coming into her touching radius. Caroline was planning to do a lot of touching. Emphasizing a point by touching his wrist. Putting a hand on his shoulder as if to keep herself from collapsing with amusement when he said something funny. Grabbing his forearm and saying, "No!" when he said something mildly surprising or alarming. All of this was bound to get the point across, plus she wanted to cop a few feels of his suit jacket.

"Hi," said Caroline.

"Hi," said Nic.

Caroline was just allowing a slow smile to develop on her lips when a red blur raced in front of her like a forest fire.

"Hi!" said her teeny assistant, Ursula. "But of course I'm interrupting. I shouldn't even be here, I'm so sorry! It's just that I'm a lowly little assistant and I don't know anyone." Caroline estimated her Southern drawl as approximately three times drawlier than it had been just yesterday, when Caroline and Ursula had both sat in on a meeting with Zoe from the London office. You didn't do the Southern act in front of Brits.

You might as well let long sticky strings of drool drain out of the corner of your mouth and onto your shirt.

Gorgeous New York men were another story.

"That's okay," said Nic. "Are you from the South?"

Ursula's eyes went wide. She covered her egregious cakehole with both hands. "Did muh big fat stupid mouth give me awaaayuh?"

As Caroline stood there for several humiliating silent minutes watching the two of them flirt, she examined Ursula for signs of sexorexia. There weren't any. Nope, she had that buckwild glow all over, from her do-me Manolos to her torch of red hair, and the Southern accent gave her an air of coming straight from one of those full-service sororities like Eta Bita Pi.

Eventually the two of them walked away together and left Caroline stranded, a conversational orphan. She stood in disbelief for a few moments, not even bothering to try to win adoption at another chat circle. Even Kate seemed to have disappeared.

Caroline lingered for an hour or so, but couldn't find anyone she wanted to supply her with the RX for her sexorexia. She wondered if there was some sort of herbal supplement she could be taking to alleviate the symptoms. Her juices were in danger. By the time she left the party an hour later she was in a deep funk, and while she was getting into a cab she saw a horse-drawn carriage go by. On the seat she swore she saw two figures moving rhythmically.

Seeing Ursula, now and forever to be known as the Thing, in the office on Christmas Eve, a day that the staff had off, did not cause a surge of holiday goodwill in Caroline. She had recently opened a dossier to keep track of the Thing's every misstep with an eye toward her eventual expulsion from the Belle Connerie paradise, though in truth the file remained somewhat sketchy, its contents limited to a yellow Post-it note on which Caroline had scribbled, "Dec. 3. Wore same belt twice this week." She wasn't exactly ready to go to trial just yet, but surveillance was under way.

Caroline wasn't sure what had gone on between Nic and the Thing, but her only remaining hope with respect to the fiasco was that Ursula, having cut in so rudely, wasn't aware that Caroline and Nic had even met. Presumably Ursula also didn't know Caroline was haunted by dreams in which she smeared the insides of Oreo Double Stuf cookies all over Nic's yummy body.

"You know you have the day off," said Caroline.

"So do you," said the Thing, smiling poisonously.

The two eyed each other warily, each looking for an opening.

"Well, when you're an *edi*tor," said Caroline, "you just have so much responsibility. Your stapling can probably wait until the New Year. But with *edi*tors, it's all boring budget meetings where you have to figure out how to spend the extra money coming in and lunches with other *edi*tors and hideous calls from designers begging you to feature them in packages you're *edi*ting."

"Of course!" said Ursula. "So right. I'm so dumb. But: on Christmas Eve?"

Caroline was getting well steamed. Silently she composed

more Post-it notes for the dossier: *Shows up for work even when not needed.* Also, *Asks too many questions.*

Then a darling little imp strolled into Caroline's mind, uninvited but terribly welcome.

"Not just today," said Caroline. "Tomorrow. In fact, would it be an awful bore for you to come in tomorrow? I need some help with a few things."

That worked. The Thing's face froze into a dismal stare.

"Nic and I were kind of planning on going skiing in Austria. Our plane leaves at eleven o'clock tonight."

Austria! Sweet chalets, cozy fires, the sexy smell of active men, the glamorous company of Euro-styled ski bunnies, the dizzying number of different ways you could burn calories. That should have been Caroline's trip to Austria. Those were her Alps.

"We did tell you the hours would be irregular," Caroline reminded her.

"Definitely!" said the Thing. "I'm so retarded. Only it's just that the office is closed until after New Year's, so I thought—"

"Ah," said Caroline. "See, thinking is what *ed*itors do. Is everything wrapped perfectly?"

"I've only got one more to do," said the Thing, looking morose.

"Let me see."

The Thing took her to the Closet. Caroline was holding the Closet Key, one of only five of the noncopyable instruments that gave senior personnel access to paradise.

Caroline opened the door, and they went in. Stuff! Everywhere you looked. A mountain of shoes, all in size nine, all neatly boxed and arranged by style and size. Racks of dresses, pants, shirts. Accessories to the left. Jewelry and perfume to the right. Leather jackets and outerwear standing at attention on a rack in the middle of the floor. The hat shelf. The miscellaneous shelf, bursting with a cornucopia of CDs and DVDs, miniature stereos, cute little cell phones.

There was a giant grubby charity billboard in Times Square that harangued New York in neon, "It's better to give than to receive." Every time she passed it, Caroline said to herself: Why not do both? Every week Caroline gave out her shoe size, her dress size, her ring size. And every week she received shoes, clothes, and jewelry.

The shelves of stuff set aside specifically for Caroline, instead of the models, were right near the front. They were packed to the ceiling with presents in sleek colored wrapping and intricate bows of silver, red, green, or gold. All month, the Thing had been in charge of taking in all the packages addressed to Caroline—all of those lovely items that arrived in daily heaps from Gucci and Prada and Armani and Marc Jacobs, every wonderful, tasteful, exclusive, pricey designer morsel—and wrapping them up like Christmas presents.

"I did wonder, though," the Thing was saying in her pitiable way.

"Yes?" said Caroline.

"I was just, you know, thinking, that if I wasn't putting cards on the outsides of the packages. . . ."

"What?" said Caroline, getting irritated.

"Just, how do you know what present goes to which person?"

Caroline's blood froze.

The Thing made a meek little noise. A smile crept across her lips. Her eyebrows floated a fraction of an inch toward her forehead.

"Of course, it's not really my place to ask, though, is it? I mean, why don't I just shut my little mouth?" The Thing put her hands over her mouth as though preparing to conceal evidence from Santa's police.

"Dear," said Caroline, thinking fast, "isn't it obvious?"

"Um," said the Thing, writhing in place. "How about, no?"

"I," said Caroline, who had an armload of luxury items, any one of which would have tested the credit card limit of the average pathetic mall shopper, "am going to give all these presents to charity. They're mystery presents, don't you see? For the, you know, people who aren't rich. Since everything goes to them, it doesn't really matter which one goes to which person. Does it?"

"Ah!" said the Thing, loading up with packages. "I completely get it. It's just that I was a little confused? Just at first? Because I thought you'd want to keep some of this stuff—at least one little old pair of shoes, maybe?—for yourself. You are so good! It's so kind of you to be so generous."

"It's really nothing," said Caroline, warming herself by the glow of the Thing's fawning. How many people at the office could the Thing be steered into telling about her boss's munificence?

"I only wish I'd known it before!" said the Thing. "That way, when you had me call in the stuff from the designers? I could have, you know, ordered it in all different sizes instead of only in your size."

Caroline nearly dropped a large red and blue package that had the exact heft and shape of that Vuitton suede carry-on she had been craving. "Lots of people are my size," she said stonily.

"Oh!" said the Thing. "Really! I didn't know that. I kinda, you know, just sorta thought that not so many poor people out there wore size zero. Aren't a lot of them kind of H-E-A-V-Y?" she whispered.

Caroline chuckled at the absurdity of the Thing's spelling out the word. As if an F-A-T person could get anywhere near hearing distance of the twenty-fourth floor of this building without being wrestled to the ground and advised that their kind wasn't welcome here.

"Darling," she said, "don't you see what a beautiful favor I'm doing them? I'm giving them designer clothes *and* I'm incenting them to lose weight!"

Even a very rude Thing could have no answer to such a brilliant application of Belle Connerie logic, so she and Caroline piled a luggage cart high with the gifts. As the Thing struggled prettily with the boxes, looking helplessly, beguilingly cute—save it for when a man's around, Caroline thought—Caroline wondered what size the Thing was. The woman was so thin she was barely human. She was more like . . . carpaccio. At times Caroline wondered if the Thing could even, possibly, be smaller than Caroline herself. But you couldn't go lower than zero.

"I'll send you back for the next trip later in the day," Caroline said, heading back to her office.

"Sounds great," said the Thing, back at her cubicle. "There shouldn't be more than, what, eight cartloads, maybe?"

Caroline's attempts to perform algebra had not been widely acclaimed in ninth grade, but she could instantly calculate the answer. "More like ten," she said. "Better call three cars to be safe."

The Thing had already speed-dialed the number. She covered the mouthpiece with one hand. "And what address are you heading to?" she asked.

"You know where I live, right?" said Caroline, opening the door to her office. "On Second Avenue?"

The Thing smiled a sickening smile.

"There's a Salvation Army right down the block."

Caroline could almost hear the Thing's smile pop. I always win, she thought as she disappeared behind her door.

On her chair was a curious item: a card. *The* card, presumably. The annual. The one she didn't want and couldn't figure out. The one she would miss if it ever failed to arrive.

chapter five

CAROLINE OPENED THE ENVELOPE WITH A THUMB-
nail and looked at the card. On the front, a snowman being built by some apple-cheeked children.
On the inside, the writing was sloppy and loose,
as though whoever had left it hadn't had time to finish:

Somebody is looking out for you—
Nemo

Another Nemo card. Caroline was puzzled without being interested. Nemo cards had been arriving every year since she started
at private school as a kid, and they never got any less stupid.

Still, how did it get here? Caroline went back out to the
Thing's cubicle. "That card on my chair," she said. "Did you
put it there?"

"Wasn't me!" said Ursula with her processed, Splenda
sweetness.

"Did you see who put it there?" said Caroline. "Think."

"I didn't see anyone go into your office, Caroline," said the Thing, sounding a little testy. "I wouldn't let anyone go in there. Who's it from?"

"Santa," said Caroline, turning on her heels. Back in her office, she dropped the anonymous card into a desk drawer and slammed it shut. It was a slow day, but even so Caroline had ten or twelve e-mails waiting for her. A press release from Pickwick Paperie, the fancy stationery shop on Spring Street, to announce a new luxury paper line. Caroline typed out a few words stating that of course she couldn't guarantee any kind of coverage in exchange for free product, but she did admire their monogrammed 80-pound linen deckle-edged stationery (in ivory please). An invite to the opening performance of Wackford's Queers, the sensational new gay ballet troupe. A somewhat sweaty notice from T&E, where an administrative figure Caroline had never heard of named R. Wilfer—a faceless wisp of humanity too deferential to even possess a first name, apparently—had noticed that her expenses were running about $3,500 behind last year. Could she possibly make up the difference by December 31 just to balance everything out?

"Can do!" chirped Caroline out loud. Then she called Krystyna again to give her some more calorie-destruction hints.

Voices approached outside Caroline's office.

"And this is our accessories director, Caroline."

Caroline whispered frantically into the phone, "Oreos in the bra drawer!" and looked up to see the last two people in the world she wanted to hear her sounding like some sort of snack-food pervert: her boss, Sally Brass, and a woman Caroline had seen once before. Caroline's heart fell into her boots. Neurons exploded in her brain. This was possibly the worst moment of Caroline's life since the notorious blind date with the accordion-playing Mormon butcher.

"Caroline," said Sally, "have you met the *inexorable* Arabella Allen?"

Arabella Allen! Caroline knew her only through the *Post*'s Media Ink column, which had just two weeks ago lavished several column inches on the rising new publishing executive who was riding into town trailing clouds of glory to goose sales of advertisements in *Presents,* which was already so stuffed with them that each issue had the heft of a dictionary.

"We're old friends by now, aren't we?" said Arabella, smiling down through her black lashes at Caroline.

Caroline hung up the phone and looked meekly up at the woman who in the past five seconds had gotten a promotion in Caroline's mind from Mrs. Furry Boots to president of Belle Connerie Publishing. As such, she could, and probably would, fire Caroline in the next five seconds.

"It's so *elating* to see you, Caroline," said Sally, who had risen to the top of the masthead via extreme displays of self-confidence and vocabulary. Every time she held a meeting the staff stuck around for a second, post-Sally conference dedicated to figuring out what the boss had just said. If anything subsequently went wrong, Sally would berate everyone for disobeying clear orders.

"Arabella," said Sally, who was stroking her new boss's back so vigorously between the shoulder blades that Caroline found the phrase "erotic massage" popping ickily into her head, "just closed this *histrionic* new deal with Circle Mart. They committed *egregiously* to buying twenty-eight ad pages in the second quarter! I'm *refulgent* with joy!"

"They're a key player in the midrange garment business, but they rarely advertise in BC titles," said Arabella. "This is the beginning of a stellar relationship."

"Irrevocably! Can you guess how she talked them into, et cetera?" Sally said, as breathless as a teen awaiting a pop star outside the MTV studios. "She showed up at the meeting dressed like this! Entirely in Circle Mart products! It was a *preternaturally* inspired gambit! She won them over *ontologically*. Of course she'd never normally wear these clothes."

Arabella chuckled modestly at her own wiles.

Caroline tried to assemble a few syllables, looking at Arabella's feet. "Circle still sells those b-b-b-b . . ."

"That's right! Those *aberrant* hairy boots!" said Sally. "The ones you and I wouldn't wear to our own autopsy! Arabella even wore those. She was willing to go a *voluptuous* distance to close a deal." The two of them laughed together. "That look!" said Sally. "That look was *inordinate!*"

The power of speech deserted Caroline. Her gaze remained fixed on Arabella's feet, which were now swathed in Mantalini's latest, most expensive creation, the shoes Caroline had begged him for just days ago, the shoes that he had sworn would not be available to anyone, even a supermodel, even as a sample, until late spring.

Arabella smiled down at Caroline. Her lip gloss was the color of sleet. "I'm really looking forward to sharing some ideas with you," she said. "There are so many ways we can fix *Presents,* aren't there!"

Caroline, who was unaware that anything about the magazine needed repair, gulped and forced out a few syllables of agreement.

"Of course," Sally said, "Arabella will be bringing in some of her own people. Won't you, Arabella?"

Arabella looked around Caroline's office with the eyes of a demolitionist. "It's a promise!" she said.

Just then the Thing was at the door, smiling and nodding and giving eye as though she had been ordered to demonstrate the operation of all muscles above her shoulders to qualify for her head inspection certificate.

"Can I get anyone anything?" she said.

Sally gave the confident smile of a flatteree. "Ursula! Arabella, I'd like you to meet Ursula Heep. One of our rising stars."

"Oh, not really," said the chuckling Thing, shaking hands with Arabella while her gaze roamed lustily around Caroline's office. "I'm just your ordinary humble little assistant editor. I've only got three years' experience and a useless degree. In French. From Dartmouth."

Arabella beamed. "That's so funny, because I majored in French at Dartmouth! And way back when, before I moved over to the business side, I was an assistant editor for three years at *Vogue* before they made me a senior editor." And the two of them, Arabella and her new Thing, stood side by side, glancing wonderingly all over Caroline's stylish, beautiful, pristine, tasteful, perfect office as though it were a basement bachelor pad with a neon beer sign and posters of hair metal bands stuck to the paneling with sticky blue putty. One of them, possibly both of them, made a disappointed little clicking noise that, in this building, was pretty much the equivalent of automatic weapons fire.

"Sally," said Arabella, "it seems you have a talented staff here. And so much *young* talent!"

"Crumbcake," Sally said to the Thing, "you must share with us *imminently* your holiday plans. Share, share, share."

The Thing didn't look at Caroline. "I was actually hoping to get some work done here."

"What an *archaic* non sequitur!" Sally said. "I forbid it *inimically*. You will not appear in this office on pain of death. That goes for your boss, too. Did you put her up to this, Caroline?"

"She, sort of, volunteered?" said Caroline. "There's always work to be done. Work, work." Caroline mimed the act of sweeping a broom, which even as she was doing it struck her as pretty lame.

And the three of them, Sally, Arabella, and the Thing, peered around Caroline's office again, searching for signs that anything besides Caroline's bottle of 90-percent alcohol hand sanitizer had been worked on today. Caroline's computer had been idle for so long that her screen saver had kicked in.

"Remember when I told you that some of our employees get too attached to their jobs?" Arabella said to Sally. "Sometimes it's so fun to just shake up the masthead."

"How does that suit you, Ursula?" said Sally. "Are you *ineluctably* ready to be thrust into the stately realms?"

"Oh, be an *ed*itor?" said the Thing, not looking at Caroline.

"I'm just a little workaholic, single, no kids, no life, really, but the magazine. You probably wouldn't even want me to be an *edi*tor who'd just drive up your light bills staying all night thinking up new ideas and even if I did they probably wouldn't be good enough for the *edi*tors' meeting. Like my dorky little idea of adding a pullout cardboard size wheel so the readers could figure out what all their sizes would be in Europe. And how I, you know, just blundering around as usual, found out through my friend at Dolce and Gabbana that they'd be totally interested in sponsoring the wheel. And that lots more European designers and even retailers might be interested in advertising with us if we gave the readers help with the size issue. I'm babbling. I have too many ideas! I'd be the worst *edi*tor."

"What an *extrinsically* amazing idea!" Sally said.

The three of them clustered around the Thing's cubicle for some minutes, talking in an excited whisper just loud enough for Caroline to detect but not loud enough for her to understand. Caroline caught a phrase that sounded vaguely like, "Dispose of her *systematically!*" but she couldn't be sure. Wondering if she should clean out her desk today or wait till after the holiday break, she was taking a sip of her hand sanitizer when Arabella stuck her head back in the door.

"Nice meeting you!" She hammered the "meeting" a little too hard, pounding it exactly the way Caroline had hit the "boots" part of "Nice boots."

"Thanks!" squeaked Caroline.

"And," added Arabella with a smile that was a distressingly close cousin to a smirk, "nice *office!*"

Caroline's spirit drooped a little more. But women's

magazine editors changed jobs all the time. Every time a new boss came in to shake things up, she was expected to reshuffle the masthead. It wasn't that much of a stigma in the industry to get the ax. It might be time to make some discreet inquiries over at Hearst or Hachette or Time Inc.

A little while later the Thing's head appeared in the doorway.

"Knock, knock!" she said. "Merry Christmas! See you in January. Oh, before I forget, Nic said to tell you he's really sorry if he hurt your feelings that night by talking to me instead of you. I asked him why he'd even want to glance at a hopeless little girl-wretch like me when he could have been talking to a really important, you know, *ed*itor, who's so much more wise and interesting and experienced because she's so much, um, older? And everything? But he just muttered something about your, um, lack of glow? Like, how he thought maybe you were sick or something? Which you're so super-not! Men, right? Bye-eye!"

With the departure of the Thing, the office was completely still. Caroline was rummaging through her handbag to make sure she had everything she needed. Stalling. Because there was nothing to do but face reality once she left her cozy little office for the weekend. She was about to turn the lights off when a form appeared in the doorway. And pretty much filled it.

"Afternoon, ma'am," said the UPS guy, in that brown handyman-style uniform that had that rugged, "Hi, I'm blue-collar and I won't hide it" feel. Some deliverymen actually looked sexy in it, but Mr. Barkis looked like a loaf of pudding. Though tall, he was also unbecomingly pudgy, a man whose bulk made the buttons of his shirt edge apart so that you could catch glimpses of the equally authentic white workingman's T-shirt underneath. He had a ridiculous bushy mustache, his face looked like he'd been wiping his hands on it, and his speech was not cowboy laconic but rather Queens jive, the wage-slave patois of that tiny throwback slice of the city workforce that was actually born somewhere out there in the B- and C-list boroughs, the ones separated from the main island by waterways that served as velvet ropes.

"Hi, Mr. Barkis," Caroline said.

"Can't ya gimmee a smile? Come on, it ain't that bad," Mr. Barkis said.

"That's where you're wrong. It is that bad. It's worse."

"Heah."

He handed her an exquisitely tiny little box wrapped in brown paper. Caroline loved tiny boxes.

"Sign heah."

Tired and cranky as she was, Caroline did indeed have, under these circumstances, exactly one smile left in the tank. Barkis was out of shape, uncouth, and an idiot, but he always brought presents. She took a pen, flipped it in her hand so that the dull end was facing down, and signed her name on his handheld electronic gizmo. Signing for packages just never got old.

"Thanks, Mr. Barkis," she said. But he stood there gazing at her, rooted to one spot like a mustachioed ficus. Did he want a tip? That would be unheard of. Caroline got hundreds of packages a week and wasn't about to start laying out cash rewards for each one of them.

But Barkis turned to leave, so Caroline tore off the wrapping and opened the little box: Clinique Precision Ionized Science Formula Superbalanced Hydrating Concealer. She completely needed this after the day she had just endured. But she was puzzled why it had arrived from UPS.

"But," she said, "I just called this in, like, two hours ago. I shouldn't have gotten this till after the holiday."

Mr. Barkis turned around again, his face lighting up. "I know, right? I was in the warehouse on Eleventh Ave, this comes in, so I tell Frankie, Hey, this here's for Caroline, I know her! It can't wait! And Frankie says, This ain't a messenger service, take it over Monday on your reg'lar run. And I says, what if she's goin' on vacation in Disneyland or somethin' glamorous like that? What if she's goin' to Branson for the New Year? What if this is stuff she can't live without, some kinda exotic personal cream she just gotta have to enjoy her holiday with? So Frankie says, I'm not payin' you any more overtime, and I says, Who's askin' for overtime ya so-and-so?—excuse my French, it wasn't language a lady should hear. I says, Frank, I'm goin' over there, are we crystal? And here's the big guy, from the looks of it just in time to catch ya before you leave. Compliments of the United Parcel Service. Ya excited?"

"Beside myself," she said. "News flash, the stuff I get in a week is worth more than you make in a month. Okay? Now if you'll excuse me?"

Barkis's big jolly smile slipped away. "Excuse me, ma'am," he said. "I thought I was doin' ya a favor."

"I hate favors," Caroline said. "Every time someone says they did you a favor, it means they want something from you. Well, I don't give out things, I take them in, are we crystal?"

Barkis's mouth opened and shut silently, like a goldfish's. Then he zipped up his coat, hung his head, and muttered, "Merry Christmas anyway" before he slipped away.

But Caroline would have to wait till Monday to get him fired. After she had gone down to the street to oversee the loading of her packages into the Town Cars outside, she came back upstairs to take a final look around, to see if she'd missed anything. As she closed her door and hiked her bag over her shoulder, the office was silent. Down the hall, the motion-sensitive lights in the corridors had turned themselves off. Caroline walked by the Thing's workstation. The Thing had left her cardigan casually draped over the back of her chair. Caroline did a slow reconnaissance lap around the area to make sure no one was around. She peeked into the aisle that ran between the cubicles to the ladies' room. Nothing. She poked her head over a partition to see if there was anyone at the copier. Nobody. Then she went back to the Thing's desk and hooked a single finger into the back of the sweater.

No. Impossible. Unheard of.

The tag read

-2

Negative two! A new size! The zero barrier broken! Staring at the label, gazing at this uncharted new world, Caroline felt like Christopher Columbus. Only with sweaters. The Thing had broken all tininess records, here in the land of incredible shrunken women! Caroline didn't know whether to call the newspapers or get sick to her stomach. She chose the second option.

She really, super, especially, extra didn't feel good. Which is why she needed a shot of the hand sanitizer from her desk. Which, on an empty stomach and combined with all the stresses of her being about to get fired and her mother and Summer and her friends all being away and her not having anything to do for Christmas and her need to find a date by New Year's, kind of gave her worse judgment than she would normally exercise. Which is why she playfully spilled some hand sanitizer on the sweater, and then decided it was so much fun that she went back into her office and got three more bottles of hand sanitizer and emptied them on the Thing's rag, until it was nicely soaked. And having all that alcohol in the air, and in her stomach, kind of made her feel like a ciggy, which is why she took out her matches and her Camel Lights and started to go downstairs. But because it was important to play a harmless little fun coworker's prank on Ursula, she kind of didn't exactly make it all the way downstairs but instead just—playfully—lit a match right there. Near the sweater. In fact, kind of right next to the sweater. Which turned out to be quite surprisingly not flame-retardant. It was a firetrap waiting to happen, really, so in a way Caroline may have saved Ursula's life by burning the teeny garment to ashes before the sweater actually spontaneously combusted sometime in the future. Which was what Caroline explained to the approximately forty-five firemen who seemed to appear instantly and were getting all finger-pointy and screamy and stuff, not flirty like they are on TV *at all*, while they were all scowling and fanning the smoke out of their eyes and stepping from island to island among the lakes of water that the stupid drama-queen sprinklers had flooded the place with. Which had been so totally unnecessary because after just a couple of admittedly dicey minutes of crying and looking for an empty steel wastebasket, Caroline had largely brought the fire under control all by herself, thank you very much, except for the singed black hulk that had once been Ursula's workstation.

The firemen let her off with a warning after she told them through her tears that her dad, whom she had never known, was dead and her mom had left her all alone in this great big mean city for the holidays and she was practically an orphan. All the senior management of Belle Connerie had long since left the building by that time anyway so there was no need for any of this to get back to anyone who might think arson reflected adversely on her skills as a manager.

Caroline slunk out of the elevator on the ground floor looking about as happy as a cat that fell in the bathtub. Her hair felt limp and slimy against her neck. Her boots squished as she walked. Her clothes were ruined. She wanted to be teleported home, to her down comforter and her hair dryer. Not that anything much was waiting for her there. She pulled her adorable woolly Coach bucket hat down over her face. At this hour of Christmas Eve, at least, there was no chance that she would be seen by anyone she knew.

"Nice *look*," said a voice by the reception desk.

It was her. Arabella Allen.

"Hi," said Caroline meekly. "I can ex—"

"Don't," said Arabella sweetly. "Leaving for the break?"

"Uh-huh," said Caroline.

"You've earned a long one," Arabella said. "May I have your building pass?"

Caroline swallowed once and handed it over. She was telling herself not to cry, but since she had just gotten drenched by the sprinklers, this was actually as good a time as any to cry.

"My Christmas present to you," said Arabella, "is a permanent vacation."

Caroline slunk, stunned, into the depressing joy of Times Square. She was fired; the city was practically bubbling over with holiday cheer. It was already getting dark outside and a chilly fog lay atop Manhattan like a fat gray tapioca. People got fired from fashion magazines all the time. Others had complained about the politicking, the housecleaning, the scapegoating, but not Caroline. She had absolutely no problem with this system, as long as she got to be the one doing the firing.

Times Square was an ant colony of excitable tourists and getting-off-early office workers scrambling in and out of the toy store and the CD store and the sneaker store clutching shopping bags, chattering about where they were going next, banging into one another as they thronged the sidewalks but instantly forgiving with a big smile or a slap on the shoulder and always, always, always, a cheery holiday wish. Normally New Yorkers had a different two-word greeting for one another, but today it was nothing but "Merry Christmas!" from Yankee Stadium to the Statue of Liberty. Even the urgent blat of the car horns was more subdued than usual. It was, Caroline noticed, like some other place entirely: Niceville. Politetown. Haveanicedayton.

The only plus was that across the street, on Forty-second

and Seventh, two ladies wobbling under their piles of shopping had hailed the same cab simultaneously. Better, both of them reached the cab's door at the exact same instant. Combat would ensue. Already they were exchanging words with each other. As Caroline approached the street, they were getting more and more animated. Caroline was just a few steps out of earshot, thinking, This will help my mood.

"No, you were here first."

"I insist you take it!"

"Please, I'll just wait here for the next one."

"I really wish you would take it."

Caroline rolled her eyes in disgust and brushed her wet hair out of her eyes. She thought about having the coolest job in the city yanked out of her hands, about Nic, about why Trot was acting so funny. She thought about losing Summer as a shrink and the impossibility of finding a date for New Year's. She thought about the [–2] tag and why her mother was deserting her for the holidays and most of all she thought about her father. A man who had died shortly after her birth. A man of whom she did not possess a single picture. Or a single memory.

Thinking all this, feeling slightly dizzy, she looked around for her Town Cars. But they weren't there. Where were they? Were they coming across Forty-second? Her hair slapped her on the cheeks. She wrung out a couple of fistfuls of it and stepped on a patch of ice between two idling cars and into the street. Where a honking black HumBug 3000 moving at demon speed darted out from behind a beer truck and sped directly at her. Caroline stepped back, onto the ice made doubly slick by the water she had wrung out of her hair. In an instant she was down, flat on her back, her legs sticking out into the path of the car. It actually seemed to be speeding up. She didn't have time to move, she decided. There was barely time enough to close her eyes. As she slipped into semi-consciousness she thought about getting hit by a four-thousand-pound car and decided she was okay with it.

Honking. Squealing. A few random screams. Tourists, Caroline thought dreamily. Haven't they ever seen a real New York accident before? She was aware of a bumping and jostling. Getting squashed by a motor vehicle wasn't actually so unpleasant, it turned out. It kind of felt like . . . felt like . . . being gently dragged. . . .

Caroline opened her eyes. She was aware that some time had passed, but she couldn't tell if it was seconds or hours. She wasn't in the street anymore. She was on the curb, safely out of traffic, watching the world come into view as though through a defrosting windshield. Her boots were beyond repair. Her makeup was streaked. Her hair was an upside-down bowl of dirty noodles. And she had barely avoided getting killed in a really embarrassingly lower-class way. Caroline was a celebrity of the New York fashion magazine scene, and how many celebrities are dumb enough to get run over by cars? Grace Kelly was *in* a car. That didn't count. Okay, there was that woman who married Paul McCartney. But she hadn't been a celeb at the time, so it didn't count.

Caroline had no memory of how she had gotten to the curb. She tried to stand but couldn't. A knot of sidewalk tourists had closed in around her to point and murmur. "Lucky that guy happened to be there to save her." "She looked depressed."

"That driver was a maniac." "Where do you think she got that scarf?"

Caroline looked up at a tightening circle of shoppers. Their faces blocked out the sky. Each of them was both pressing closer and yelling at the others to stand back. A guy who looked like a German tourist was videotaping her with a tiny silver camera.

With an effort, she opened her mouth.

"What happened?" she said.

A woman in a navy peacoat reached out to touch Caroline's cheek. "Are you all right?" she asked.

Caroline shrank back from the woman's loose-skinned claw. "No touching, please!" she said. "Not a petting zoo!" She rose, wobbling, to her feet and began to push her way through the crowd, which was getting thicker by the second. Every pedestrian passing on the sidewalk stopped to see what every other pedestrian had stopped to see. Caroline was a human rubbernecking delay, an haute couture take on the three-car pileup. Every time she squeezed between two people, six more blocked her path.

That's when her Town Cars pulled up. One, two, three. Dazed, she climbed in. The driver apologized, saying that the police wouldn't allow the cars to idle in front of the building, so the drivers had been going around the block until she appeared. Arranging herself in the backseat, she noticed the driver staring at her in the rearview.

"It's okay," she said.

The driver touched his cap.

"You know that charity thrift store on Second Avenue on

the Upper East Side? The one they call the Old Curiosity Shop?"

"Sure," said the driver.

"Okay," said Caroline. "We're going to my apartment right down the block."

By the time the cars pulled up to her apartment, Caroline felt a little better. She got out without wobbling much and told the chauffeurs to get some baggage carts from the lobby. The doorman looked at her, raised one eyebrow, and returned to his newspaper.

Caroline paused to get her mail out of her box. The label still gave the names of Caroline and Carly, just as it always had. Caroline had never gotten around to changing it.

That Christmas Eve plane crash. Only several days later had the black box been plucked out of the Pacific Ocean, and it was weeks before the transcript of the final minutes of the doomed Piper Seminole had been released. It was all imprinted on Caroline's brain exactly the way it had appeared in all the newspapers.

1:15 PM PST

PILOT (male voice): *Do you really think that's a good idea?*

PASSENGER (female voice): *What? My nail polish? I like it. To me it kinda says "Goth cheerleader."*

PILOT: *No, I mean that thing.*

PASSENGER: *This? Well, duh, the whole point of having your own plane is you get to make cappuccino. I'll just plug it into the cigarette lighter.*

PILOT: *Cigarette lighter? This isn't a Toyota Celica.*

PASSENGER: *It's right here, isn't it? I'll just unplug this—*

PILOT: *Don't touch that! Are you crazy?*

1:17 PM PST

PASSENGER: *So are you going to apologize to me, or not?*

PILOT: *For stopping you from getting us killed? Not.*

PASSENGER: *I am so getting a caffeine withdrawal headache.*

PILOT: *All right, fine, plug in your huge, bulky, espresso machine that interferes with proper operation of the controls of this aircraft. Because a really good cappuccino is worth risking your life for.*

PASSENGER: *Really? Yay!*

(muffled sounds)

PILOT: *You know, we'll be there soon. Can't you wait?*

PASSENGER: *Can't I wait? Could you wait for me to dump your best friend after he introduced you to me at the Kenneth Cole party?*

PILOT: *Uh, let's not bring Joss into this.*

PASSENGER: *You know, he called me last week.*

PILOT: *Okay, you plug it in right here.*

PASSENGER: *Yum! I can almost taste the cappys!*

PILOT: *Wow, this thing really is bulky.*

PASSENGER: *Maybe if I just jam it in next to this switch.*

1:20 PM PST

PASSENGER: *James! You forgot the skim milk!*

PILOT: *I didn't! It's in the cooler. Wait a minute, can you level off this espresso?*

PASSENGER: *Why?*

PILOT: *I'd kind of rather fly the plane.*

PASSENGER: *You never want to do anything for me! How about I fly the plane and you make the cappuccino?*

PILOT: *Because you have no flight training. Also, you had three mimosas for brunch.*

PASSENGER: *I've got my own steering thingy, though, don't I? Whee! Oops, I broke a nail.*

1:22 PM PST

PILOT: *Uh, honey? Don't touch that.*

PASSENGER: *This little—?*

PILOT: *For the love of God, no!*

(screaming sounds)

1:24 PM PST

PASSENGER: *Um, what was* that *all about?*

PILOT: *That? Oh, that. That was just something that in technical terms is called a DEATH SPIRAL, YOU IGNORANT FREAK!*

PASSENGER: *Well, you don't need to get all huffy about it.*

PILOT: *My nerves. Light me a cigarette, will you?*

PASSENGER: *I thought you said this piece of junk didn't even have a cigarette lighter?*

PILOT: *Here's my lighter. My smokes are in that cubbyhole.*

PASSENGER: *By the way, what does this button marked "oxygen" do?*

PILOT: *DON'T TOUCH THAT WHEN YOU HAVE A FLAME LIT!*

PASSENGER: *Okay, Mister can't-take-a-joke!*

PILOT: *I knew I should have brought about fifty nicotine patches.*

PASSENGER: *Hey, look, another plane! Let's dip our wings as a way of saying, "Hi guys!"*

PILOT: *Um, no.*

PASSENGER: *You just have to tilt that thingy like this, right?*

PILOT: *CARLY, FOR THE MILLIONTH TIME, DON'T TOUCH THE WHEEL!*

1:26 PM PST

PASSENGER: *Oh, goody, the cappy's ready. Want some?*

PILOT: *No thanks. We'll be landing soon.*

PASSENGER: *Yay! You can see Catalina! I love California. They should totally move New York out here. Wow, yum. Here, have a sip.*

PILOT: *Just a—ow!*

PASSENGER: *Oops, sorry!* (giggles)

PILOT: *Could I ask you to refrain from spilling red-hot beverages into my lap?*

PASSENGER: *Nag, nag, nag. Did I tell you about Joss's new Porsche?*

PILOT: *I thought you only talked to him on the phone.*

PASSENGER: *He e-mailed me some pictures. It's pretty hot.*

PILOT: *I'm tired. I look tired.*

PASSENGER: *You think so? I wasn't going to say anything, but . . .*

PILOT: *Hey, pass me some of that L'Occitane baume après rasage, will you?*

PASSENGER: *Ooh, I love how that smells on you, honey.*

PILOT: *Here, hold the stick for a minute.*

PASSENGER: *I love a man who wears aftershave.*

PILOT: *Yeah? Maybe just another dab.*

PASSENGER: *Oops!* (giggles)

PILOT: *Embarrassing.*

1:29 PM PST

PASSENGER: *It's okay, sweetie, it happens to every guy.*

PILOT: *Except Joss Bounderby?*

PASSENGER: (giggles) *Here, let me help you wipe that up.*

PILOT: *The air pressure must have made it explode or something.*

PASSENGER: *I think I've got a tissue.*

1:31 PM PST

PILOT: *How are you coming with those tissues?*

PASSENGER: *Lip gloss, Juicy Fruit, Tic Tacs, Altoids, Listerine strips, hairbrush, cell phone, other cell phone . . .*

PILOT: *You have two cell phones?*

PASSENGER: *Um, doesn't everyone?*

PILOT: *You never told me that.*

PASSENGER: *Well, one's unlisted. For, like, personal calls.*

PILOT: *You have a secret cell phone you've never told me about?*

(no response recorded)

1:33 PM PST

PILOT: *We have really lost altitude. I can't seem to get a grip on the wheel—oh my sweet Lord—CAN YOU FIND SOME TISSUES?*

PASSENGER: *I—darling—I can't believe you think I'm cheating on you with Joss.*

PILOT: *What? I didn't say that! Are you?*

PASSENGER: *Find your own tissues.*

PILOT: *This thing is so slippery—we're losing control—it's like trying to thread a needle with mittens on.*

(screams)

(more screams)

PASSENGER: *Um, would you stop screaming, please?*

PILOT: *Mayday, mayday! Losing altitude uncontrollably! I can't get a grip! I can't pull up!*

PASSENGER: *Um, is this what you call a "death spiral"?*

End of transmission

chapter six

WHEN SHE GOT TO HER FLOOR, CAROLINE MARCHED to her door, took one look at the silvery circular disk around the peephole, and immediately dropped her keys.

"Did you see that?" she said to her driver.

The driver, who couldn't see anything behind the stack of boxes he had piled on his brass cart, swore that he had not.

"Okay, pay attention!" Caroline said. "I was just putting my key in the lock when—"

"Yes, ma'am?"

"I—never mind." Caroline couldn't very well reveal to a chauffeur that she had seen the eye of her dead roommate in the peephole of her own apartment. Or that she was hearing the scratchy-scratchy sounds again. "Could you at least put the boxes down and go in first? Just to check things out?"

The two other drivers were coming down the hallway carrying packages.

"You guys?" Caroline called sweetly. "Can you all just go in and see if everything's all right?"

The three men brought in the packages while Caroline listened nervously outside. From behind her she heard faint scratchy sounds. From inside the apartment she heard walking. She heard murmuring. At last the three drivers came out. They stood in a little cluster nudging each other. Caroline was wide-eyed with dread.

"Ma'am?" said the first driver.

"What?" said Caroline, boiling over with terror.

"You've got—" said the second driver.

"What? What have I got?"

"You've got nothing left," said the first driver.

"They took it all," said the third driver.

"I've been robbed?" said Caroline.

"I'm afraid so," said the first driver. "There's nothing in there."

"Except a coffee table, a sofa and a cabinet," said the second driver.

"Not a single Christmas card hanging in the kitchen," said the third driver. "Not a sprig of holly in the place. No colored lights."

"No Christmas tree," said the first driver.

"No mistletoe," said the second driver.

"No eggnog in the fridge," said the third driver. "In fact, nothing in the fridge at all. Nothing in the kitchen cabinets, either. They cleaned you out. Place is bare."

Caroline rushed into her apartment and looked around. The entryway was nothing but scrubbed, utterly blank beige walls.

The sparse metallic kitchen contained not a scrap of food or a single cooking implement. The living room was as stripped down as a chic prison cell.

The three drivers followed her into the living room and hung their heads.

"You idiots," said Caroline. "This is the way it's supposed to look."

The three drivers looked at each other wondering which would be sadder: that a woman didn't want to admit that she'd been robbed, or that she lived like this.

"Come on," said Caroline. "Chop chop."

After an hour of unloading and arranging, Caroline and her three helpers had assembled a perfectly neat pyramid of swag in the corner where anyone else would have put a Christmas tree.

"It lacks something, still," Caroline said.

"Something holy," said the first driver.

"Something sacred," said the second driver.

"Something beautiful," said the third driver.

"Yes!" said Caroline, disappearing into her bedroom. In a moment she returned with a frame. "There," she told the first driver. "If you could just hang that for me? Exactly over the center of the pile."

When it was done the four of them stood and admired their work. A colossal pile of presents topped off by a framed picture of Caroline in a sundress and a darling floppy hat, looking like an advertisement for summer, at the Hôtel du Cap.

"So nice of you all to help," said Caroline, shooing them toward the door.

The three of them wouldn't go quietly, though. As she

opened the door, they lingered and shuffled and coughed and checked their watches and buttoned their coats in a tip-me dance.

"Ma'am," said the first driver. "Best holiday wishes. It's that season again!"

"You're absolutely right, guys," said Caroline, leading them into the hallway. "It's the season for giving."

The three drivers perked up.

"It's the time of year for thanks," Caroline added.

The drivers nodded and smiled.

"So, let's just say I'm giving you my thanks." And she shut the door on them.

When she had taken a shower and changed into dry clothes, Caroline decided it was time for the daily meal. Since today's lunch had been light (a Diet Coke and three aspirin), she could treat herself to dinner. As a reflex, she went through her cabinets one by one. First cabinet: empty. Good. Second cabinet: empty. Excellent. The third, fourth, fifth, and sixth cabinets were also bare. The point of bare cabinets was: How could you think about food if you didn't have pots and pans and ladles and spaghetti forks and spatulas and garlic presses around? Caroline only used one cabinet, which contained a cardboard box, a chipped blue ceramic plate, a mug that read UNLV RUNNIN' REBELS, a set of mismatched aluminum cutlery, and a random plastic spork. None of these items was attractive. Together, Caroline and Carly had hit on the awesome idea of getting rid of their fabulous designer dinnerware and replacing it with odd-lot junk to make mealtime even less appealing.

Caroline opened the flap on the cardboard box and removed

a packet labeled PowR PowDR, which contained all essential nutrients, vitamins, amino acids, and minerals necessary for human life, according to such internationally renowned nutritional experts as the sulky guy in a Jimi Hendrix T-shirt who worked the counter at the Vitamin Shoppe. She shook the powder into her mug, added water, and beat the grim colorless mixture vigorously with a fork until it started to liquefy into a sort of . . . well, gruel. Last night's misbehavior would not be repeated tonight. She was determined to lose four ounces by morning, and her digital scale stood prepared to render judgment down to the hundredth of an ounce.

As she stood by the counter eating her gruel, or rather stuffing spoonfuls of it in her mouth and wrestling it down her throat, it happened again: that noise she had first heard on her way into work. *Scratchity-scratchity.* The sound was so faint, so distant, that it could have been two molecules of sandpaper having sex, or someone sawing a log on the moon, or a Belle Connerie assistant grinding her teeth. As Caroline walked around the kitchen checking the backs of her cabinets and peering into enclosed spaces looking for roaches (unlikely: roaches fed on crumbs), she noticed that the sound remained the same wherever she went. It didn't seem to be coming from anyplace in particular. It was almost as if the annoyance was being broadcast from inside her head.

"*Stop* it," Caroline said aloud, trying to think of someone to blame for the noise. "Listen, whoever you are, whatever, instead of sneaking around trying to be all scary, why don't you just cut to the chase and walk in my front door?"

Just then there was a loud knock from the front door of her

apartment. Caroline dropped her mug of gruel. Her mug shattered. Watery gray goop washed all over the floor, possibly improving the taste.

It was here. Whatever it was, whatever was following her, had arrived to do its awful deed. It was almost a relief, knowing that at last the answers to the mysteries that had been swirling around her all day were at hand. "Who is it?" she said, fumbling for a weapon. Her grip closed around the nearest implement at hand.

There was no answer except another knock on the door.

"Who is it?" she called as she walked out of the kitchen and sidled stealthily to the door listening for evil. She moved the peephole-covering disc to the side and peeped. Nothing! Whatever it was, it was invisible.

"Who is it?" she called again, this time closer to a yell.

That's when yet another awful thing in a day full of awful things happened. First came the giggling. Then there was a single note on a pitch pipe, then it was someone singing about Dasher and Dancer and Prancer and whatever.

She unlatched the door and opened it. Standing in her doorway was a herd of urchins, a gang of pint-sized cheerbots flinging a Christmas carol at her. It was that sixty-toed miracle of modern science, the laboratory-assisted Swensen sextuplets from upstairs. All six of the smiling little girls wore adorable matching battery-operated red sweaters covered with a spastic array of randomly blinking Christmas lights, and all of them were singing perfectly, sweetly, and miraculously. Every year the newspapers came around to interview their adorable, hardworking, flannel-shirted miracle parents, Carl and Jo (or was it Joe and

Carol?), who had famously failed to conceive for a decade but made up for it and then some in one steaming hot night of Petri-dish passion. The parents, rustic farm-grade personnel from Iowa or Indiana or someplace, had subsequently made so much money from diaper commercials, reality TV shows, a *Hello!* magazine photo essay, and their own branded line of test tubes that they had moved to New York and signed with CAA. And not just any New York either, but Caroline's New York, the part that was designed to keep ugly people out.

The city had grown considerably safer and more prosperous lately, but one disadvantage was that people no longer lived with one finger on the panic button. Everyone felt free to presume that their fellow tenants were chatty and welcoming instead of armed and dangerous. Children padded up and down the halls without fear of kidnapping, and single women went to sleep without double-checking to see if their Mace was within reach. Last Halloween, when the Swensen six had showed up at Caroline's door hissing and meowing in matching kitten costumes, Caroline had had to scramble to find something to put in each of their bags. By the time she was finished the brats had totally cleaned her out of rice cakes.

"Rudolph the red-nosed reindeer," they sang brightly. "Had a very shiny nose! And if you ever saw it—"

"You could even say it blows," said Caroline, and slammed the door on six little smiles.

Walking back to her kitchen, she muttered, "Children should be seen, not a herd." She wiped up the mess on the floor as the scratching grew a little more audible, but she ignored it. She opened a floor-to-ceiling refrigerator that was concealed in the wall with ruthless cunning. Ah. Her treasure trove. From above her head to the floor, in neat shelves as wide as her arm, stood nothing but neat rows of Diet Cokes. To an untrained eye, they would all look much the same. But how different they were. Top row, left-hand side: the few remaining bottles of the legendary '03, bottled in Barcelona and kissed by lusty Mediterranean sunshine. Last year's Tokyo collection, a new discovery, had a chewy, solemn texture and a powerfully insistent aftertaste for that mysterious flair of the Orient. And here was the genuine classic, the Atlanta stash straight from Coke headquarters, as straightforward and zippy as a fifteen-year-old cheerleader. The Atlanta stuff didn't age well, so Caroline had twelve-packs flown up weekly and discarded any leftovers. She reached down to select a bottle of the rare Rocky Mountain vintage that connoisseurs believed contained an extra pop of fizz thanks to the delicious wintry air's effect on its carbonation.

Still the faint scratching sound continued to grow louder.

"Precious, precious elixir," said Caroline, twisting off the cap and listening for that telltale burst of fizz. She could tell a Rocky Mountain Diet Coke from an Atlanta bottle blindfolded. But the scratching sound continued.

"Heal me, aspartame," said Caroline, who had a tendency to glug the beverage at moments of high need. "Citric acid [glug] and caramel [glug] color, make me whole. Phosphoric acid and potassium benzoate [glug, glug], git on down my throat!"

"Yum!" said a voice behind her. "I'm dying for a sip!"

Caroline dropped her Diet Coke and whirled. She looked, closed her eyes, rubbed them hard, and looked again.

"Get it?"

It couldn't be. Caroline gaped at the blurry vision. Carly. Only this was not cute Carly, shopping Carly, gossiping Carly. It was Ghost Carly, floating in the air, emery-boarding her nails. *Scratchy, scratchy, scratch.*

Caroline swore she could practically see right through her, but then that had also kinda been true while Carly was alive. Around her neck Carly wore some kind of weird accessory that draped down her front and around her waist and wrapped around her legs and then back up to her shoulders and arms. It wasn't like a belt. It was more like bondage gear or something. A chain! A ginormous chain, that's what it was. Except the links appeared to be forged out of twisted stalks of celery and carrot sticks. Every few links were bonded to flat horrible round things. Could they be . . . rice cakes?

"Carly!" Caroline said. "You scared me!"

"News flash, I'm a ghost," said the apparition. "It's part of my skill set."

"I am so totally calling nine-one-one," said Caroline.

"Call nine-one-one," said the spirit. "Call six-six-six. Call Ghostbusters. I'll wait. Listen, do you have any of that new Honeythunder moisturizer? I've got—"

"Dead skin?" said Caroline.

"Bingo."

"I can't believe this. What's going on here? I totally don't have time for this today. You are from hell!"

"Close," said Carly's ghost. "Purgatory."

"This is a joke, right? Some sort of video projection?" Caroline went around the room examining the apparition from every angle, looking for electronic devices. "You're not here. I'm imagining you. You're some sort of Mallomar-induced hallucination. A piece of Oreo that went down the wrong tube. A Pepperidge Farm Milano."

"Stop! You're making me hungry!"

"Oh. Do you want something? Can you eat?"

"Not in front of people," said Carly's ghost.

"Oh, just like when you were alive?" said Caroline.

"Sort of," said Carly's ghost. "Only now it's because I'm kind of, um, sheer? So like everyone can see my food slowly being digested. It's kind of rank to watch."

"Got it," said Caroline, who felt her own stomach dropping.

"Plus I'm going for more of a scary look than a gross-out thing," said Carly's ghost. "Fine line, I know."

Caroline shook her head in disbelief. But it was true. This was Carly's ghost, and she must have come with an important message from the great beyond. Either that or she was finally going to return that ice blue Versace dress.

"You must learn to trust me," said Carly's ghost. "Why are you being so hostile?"

"Hostile? What makes you think that? I'm not being hostile."

"Then put that spork down."

Caroline looked at the white plastic utensil, which she was sort of clenching in her left fist in what might be termed a ready-to-stab pose. It probably had limited value as a defense system against the paranormal. She put it down.

"Let me look at you," she said, her eyes running up and down the hovering vision. "You're so thin."

"I know," said Carly's ghost.

"You're so pale," said Caroline.

"I know," said the ghost.

"You look fabulous!" said Caroline.

"I know, right?" said Carly's ghost. She raised her arms over her head and did a little spin. As she did so her chains of carrot sticks and celery bumped against the rice cakes with a flat, dietetic sound.

"Death really agrees with you," said Caroline.

"Please," said Carly's ghost. "You look just as good as I do."

"Um, thanks," said Caroline, wondering if solemn emissaries from the Other Side were allowed to be sarcastic. A thought came to her that she was being rude to what was, after all, in some way her old friend. "Do you want to—can the, you know—bodily challenged?—sit?"

"Sure. We can sit. We can stand. We can waft. We do a lot of wafting. I find it very aerobic, actually. And we don't mind being called ghosts, either. Makes us sound scary, doesn't it?"

"Please, then, sit. We have so much to talk about. Like, I can't believe what you're wearing!"

"You're telling me," said Carly's ghost, following her into the living room and taking a seat next to her on the sofa. "I wouldn't be caught dead in this! Except I am."

"So what's it like in the, um, postalive space?"

"No rest," said Carly's ghost sadly. "No peace. No shopping. I spend my days wafting here and wafting there. They lay out every flavor of human misery for us like some big salad bar of sorrow. Today it's get a load of the hideous diseases, tomorrow it's a big scoop of crushing poverty. They send me to the most unbelievably out-of-the-way places, just so they can clobber me with an Indonesian famine or a Sumatran earthquake."

"Uch, you actually have to watch all those losers?" said Caroline. "You can't just change the channel?"

"Uh-uh. And of course I can't do anything to help. It's all supposed to be ironic punishment? Because I supposedly never did anything to help anyone when I was alive? I call it Cosmic Sarcasm. You wouldn't believe how sarcastic these people are. And I totally got no credit for going to that Donna Karan Save the Butterflies benefit. Remember that night we all dressed up like butterflies? Super fun!"

An uh-oh crept into Caroline's mind. "You didn't get any spiritual credit for that?" said Caroline. "Because I sort of never even paid the donation for that event."

"You didn't? It was five hundred dollars a ticket," said Carly. "How did you work that? Wow, I guess I'm a beat ahead of you. Although it didn't impress them, anyway."

"Who's 'them'?" said Caroline, her eyes narrowing conspiratorially. "Who's really in charge?"

"They won't tell me!" Carly's ghost wailed. "They don't tell me anything. They just throw me in randomly with the other agonized lost spirits, send us all off hurtling through time and space, and along the way they make with the flaming-hot torture of our immortal souls. I haven't been treated this badly since the last time I flew coach."

"Quel bore," said Caroline.

"Which brings me to you. I'm supposed to save you from all of this, show you a better way than the one we both chose. Like,

I'm getting you off Carly Street and back on, I don't know, Righteous Road."

"Me?" said Caroline. "Whoa, whoa, whoa. Back off, ghoulie. Don't bring me into this. I liked being your roommate and all, but we mainly just shared accessories, not a path of life."

"See, that's the thing," said Carly's ghost, leaning forward and pointing her emery board at Caroline. "They think you and I are a lot alike."

The two former roommates gazed into each other's eyes for a long, solemn moment. Then they shook their hair.

"It's so stupid!" they said, pretty much in unison.

"So, big segue to spiel time," said Carly's ghost. She pointed a bony finger at the far wall. Doors silently parted to reveal Caroline's expensive home-entertainment system. The TV came on.

"I could have just done that with my remote, you know," Caroline said.

"I am but the first spirit that will haunt you tonight. There's three more coming at ya. Expect the first when Daniel Metaman makes his first self-hating remark."

Caroline looked at her watch. Carly's ghost had totally messed with her sense of time. *The Humorous Hour of Daniel Metaman* began in three minutes, or rather in eight minutes: Caroline always set her watch five minutes fast. If the show started in eight minutes, the host's first self-hating comment was due in approximately nine. Caroline shuddered. The guy was supposedly a comic talk show host, but he always had a dark side to him. In fact, he was kinda mostly dark side. She wondered if he was part of the whole purgatory industry.

"Expect the second when a crowd of worshippers experience the Rapture."

"Second Coming?"

"No. Food processor infomercial on channel one twenty-seven. Some of them really are miraculous."

Caroline gulped. "Will I have time to change outfits in between?"

Carly's ghost made a let's-wrap-this-up gesture. "Expect the third when channel eleven starts broadcasting a three-hour program consisting of a close-up of a log burning in a fireplace."

"They're still doing Yule Log?" said Caroline.

Carly's ghost shrugged. "It was rated fourth in its time slot last year. Tied with the papal Mass."

"I'm *so* impressed," Caroline said. "The Other Side has complete knowledge of all aspects of humanity. Either that or you guys can afford a copy of *USA Today*."

Carly's ghost fell silent. She held an index finger to her lips and wafted over to the windows, her chains of carrot sticks and celery bumping against the rice cakes. She raised a finger and the windows flew open. Then she turned to Caroline. Silently, she beckoned, imposing her will on Caroline, making her move. Then the outlines of Carly's ghost became blurred. What color she had faded. She was starting to look like a ghost that had been sent through the copier too many times.

Without being quite sure whether she had moved there or been pulled, Caroline found herself right up against the open window and sticking her head out into the biting cold. Floating in the air fifty feet above Second Avenue was a parade of sad spirits and moaning phantoms. Some of them looked a lot like

Carly, imprisoned in chains made of low-calorie, low-flavor foods. There was Carly's boyfriend, James Harthouse, lugging an espresso machine around eternity and cursing his fate. There was an old, orange-haired Park Avenue matron twisting and turning in the wind as she battled to tear herself free of a strangling mass of liposuction tubes. Then there was the subcategory of punitive accessories. A fashionable forty-something woman was bound head to foot in Gucci belts so tight that the stylized G's pressed purple welts into her flesh like tattoos. Another professional-looking woman was so overloaded with Fendi and Marc Jacobs and Louis Vuitton handbags, all of them looped through her arms and shoulders or dangling around her neck, that she kept losing her balance, haplessly turning over and over in space. The apparition of a pretty young blond with perfect hair and makeup had feet bound up in hideously tight shoes that gripped her bare calves with wire bindings and heels that weren't heels at all, but long sharp daggers.

I get it, Caroline thought. Stiletto heels.

"But, Carly, or spirit, or whatever you want to be called," Caroline said, "what is the point of all this painfully ironic punishment?"

There was no answer. Caroline turned around. She was alone.

chapter seven

CAROLINE CRAWLED INTO BED WITH A DIET COKE (Bangkok-bottled; assertive, kinky, with hints of blackberry and vice). She put it on her night table and brooded. How did you explain an uninvited reappearance by your dead roommate on Christmas Eve? Option one: Carly had never died in the first place. So her accident and funeral and crying mother and all that stuff had been staged. Which didn't seem likely, especially since Carly's ghost really did look pretty much dead. Second possibility: Someone was playing an elaborately staged prank, with projectors and piped-in sound effects and stuff. Complicated and expensive, and to what purpose? For that to be true, Caroline would have to have a fiercely dedicated enemy committed to driving her crazy. But who didn't like Caroline?

Most likely, of course, was that she had simply been under a lot of stress. I mean, in one day, she had gotten fired, been threatened with dumping by her shrink, gotten a horrendous phone call from her mother, and been forced to listen to "Grandma Got Run Over by a Reindeer." Who wouldn't freak out and imagine weird stuff after all that? In college Caroline had once known a girl who, under no pressure whatsoever, liked to cut little marks in her own forearm with a steak knife because she said it was one of the things she had to do to prepare herself for life as the future Mrs. Brad Pitt. Put Ghost Carly on the crazy scale established by the girls she knew in this city? Please. This little episode didn't even move the needle.

So she burrowed under the covers with the caffeine rocking through her veins to beat out a gentle lullaby. She started to feel sleepy. What if she just hid under the duvet for a while? How would that be? She giggled softly. She could make a fort here. She yawned. She hoped she would have a really . . . nice . . .

Dream. Caroline awoke in some sort of fabric cave. She couldn't breathe. No. She could breathe, she had just forgotten how. She gasped. It was okay. Her head was under the covers, at the wrong end of the bed. How long had she been asleep? She didn't know. She wasn't wearing a watch. Wait, what about Carly's ghost? Well, Caroline was just at this moment waking up. So obviously she had been asleep while she was talking to Carly. The whole thing had been a dream. Right? Except why did she remember talking to her before she fell asleep? Did she have a dream about Carly and then have a dream about falling asleep? It could happen. Nervously she pulled a Milky Way out of one of the squares of her comforter and chawed on it like a rabid raccoon.

She poked her head out of the covers and looked around, but it was too dark to see anything. She turned on the light.

Nobody there. She listened for a few moments. Nothing. Time to plot her next move. The TV. She flicked it on and pushed the button on her remote marked "info." Daniel Metaman normally was on Channel 2. But what was this? As she scrolled through Channel 2's entire Christmas Eve and Christmas Day schedule, she saw no mention of Metaman. None. He wasn't on at his regular time, or before that, or after that. He was pre-empted! By the pope saying Mass from Rome. I can't believe it, Caroline thought to herself. Who would have ever guessed that on this one night of the year only, the pope would outrank Daniel Metaman? I'm in luck. There is no Daniel Metaman tonight, thus there will be no ghost visit. So tomorrow morning I get to open my presents!

And on that thought she sank into a deep, happy sleep.

Which lasted about forty-five seconds.

The light came on in Caroline's room, an overpowering, retina-frying star blast that could not possibly be created with the mood lamps she possessed. The shock of it made her sit up straight in bed, but she yelped and turned away, shielding her eyes with her hand as she felt her pupils pop. The light was so intense that there was only one possible explanation.

"Who installed track lighting in my bedroom?" she yelled out blindly to no one.

"It's just me," a young female voice said lightly, evenly. "Don't be afraid. Here, put these on." A small black object came flying at Caroline and landed softly on the pillow next to her. Caroline picked it up: Mantalinis.

"Oh great," Caroline wailed. "Does *every*one have a pair of these? Am I not special *at all*?" She put them on and looked at her visitor. She still had to shield her eyes, the light was so dazzling. It took a moment for her vision to adjust, but when it did, Caroline saw a familiar face. It was young yet old. Unlined yet mature. Innocent yet all-knowing. It was. . . .

"No!" said Caroline. "No! It can't be!"

"Oh yes," said the voice, quietly.

"Go away, terror munchkin!" It's that Milky Way bar, she thought. It's making me see a ghost that looks just like Nina Cru.

"News flash," said the spirit. "I am the Ghost of Christmas Past."

"How past?" Caroline said or, rather, shrieked. "Way past? Like, back to acid-wash jeans?"

"No, your past."

Caroline squinted at the phantom. She wore calf-high suede boots for winter, yet a clingy, almost ethereal summer dress. A cashmere scarf was draped loosely around her neck, yet her arms were bare. She was girl-woman, she was summer-winter, but she was most of all creepy-creepy.

"You're blinding me!" Caroline cried. The sunglasses made her vision a little better but she still had to shield her eyes with her hand.

"It's the glow of celebrity," said the Ghost of Christmas Past. "It blinds everyone in my path. This will help." She put on her own pair of sunglasses and a nondescript baseball cap. Just like that, her recognizability plummeted. The light in the room faded to a normal wattage. Caroline took off her sunglasses.

"Look, Nina—"

"Spirit."

"Okay, Spirit, maybe your publicist put you up to this. You know, the Ghost of Conniptions Present? The Specter of High Blood Pressure? I know she's excitable. I know I didn't return her phone call yesterday, or the last fifty or so before that. But I had nothing to do with that cover line about accessories to kill for. Okay? I did not mean to imply that you would butcher another human being for a handbag. Now go back where you came from and save your terrorizing for the multiplex."

"Rise!" said the Ghost of Christmas Past. "And walk with me!"

The duvet and the blanket and the sheets rolled back one by one. And Caroline, clinging to the bed with all of her strength, found herself floating over it. As she floated gently toward her uncanny visitor she said, "You totally cheated. Metaman wasn't even on tonight."

The Ghost of Christmas Past shrugged her slender little shoulders. "You didn't check the other channels. There was a rerun on cable."

"Oh, ha ha, I get it, should have read the fine print. Like, under the 'cheesy loophole' section."

"Probably not the last one you'll be seeing tonight," said the Ghost of Christmas Past with her million-dollar wink.

"Oh, you're so wonderful! Great big massive child star, huh?" said Caroline. "I have two words for you: Macaulay Culkin."

The Ghost of Christmas Past shrugged. "Good thing I'm immortal," she said. " 'Cause it'll take eternity for me to spend just what I earned by third grade. Do you know, the year I signed an eight-figure contract was the very same year I learned to count to eight?"

"Please," Caroline said, "enough. But just between you and me, I've heard good things about wafting. Is it like swimming? Does it burn calories? And, like, since this is all kind of a dream, do the calories I burn now count in real life?"

"Touch my dress," said the wee nuisance.

Caroline did so. "Nice," she said, rubbing the fabric between a thumb and forefinger. "Love the bias cut. Are you allowed to say who designed it? Just give me a hint. Are her initials V.W.?"

And the two of them rose into the air, wafted toward the window, and passed right through it. The spirit and Caroline floated over East Ninety-first Street and into the past.

They floated through a gray space and found themselves in a dreary little ward where two rows of cribs faced each other across a linoleum floor. Overhead were two flickering fluorescent light sticks and three more that had long since stopped flickering. In the cribs the babies howled, sending up a chorus of misery that went unheard by any adult. Except one.

In the last crib on the right, one adorable little baby in a white onesie was trying to make good her escape. With rubbery effort, she rose to a standing position holding the metal bars in her tiny fists. Grunting quietly, she managed to hike one leg over the edge and dangled it there. Next she placed her neck atop the bars and looked down. She could make it. She was indestructible. As she lifted her other leg out of the crib, her head was pointing straight to the floor.

❧   ❧   ❧

THERE WAS A SOUND of a stick clacking to the floor. A man in a gray jumpsuit whose name patch read EARL walked up quickly to the crib, placed his hands under the baby's armpits, and lifted her as she was about to fall. Detangling her limbs from the bars, he gently laid her in the crib on her back, pulled her purple blanket up under her chin, and sang her a lullaby that was almost completely drowned out by the screams of the other infants. The baby seethed at first, but then stopped fussing and seemed to relax, or perhaps begin planning her next breakout attempt. Earl went back to his mop. As he pushed the dirty water around the floor, his glance kept darting anxiously back to the baby's crib.

A door swung open at the other end, and the sound of thickly padded white shoes began to approach. Earl wrung out his mop and slipped away, unnoticed by the entering nurse.

She was a creased woman no longer young who had clamped over her ears a fuzzy set of headphones that seemed to be attached to her for the purpose of drilling the chorus of a Christmas tune directly into her brain. She sang along to every word of "Holly Jolly Christmas."

The nurse wore a black cardigan, a scuffed name tag that said only GAMP, and a face the texture of a spoiled pear as she clomped down the middle of the room with a clipboard and a cigarette. She was worried about only one of the darlings under her care: her cat, Mrs. Harris, who just that morning had seemed peevish and distant, and had hardly touched her tuna.

At each crib she stopped, satisfied herself that the wailing infant inside was indeed alive, pinched the few who were asleep until they too began to cry, and made a mark on her sheet. When she got to the last crib on the right, she lingered. Inside was a beautiful baby, wide-eyed with fear but silent. Such love-liness.

Hovering overhead with the spirit, Caroline did not attempt to conceal her surprise.

"Wait a minute," she said. "Who's that? You're not say-ing—"

"I'm not saying anything," said the spirit. "I'm showing."

"But—" said Caroline.

"Just listen," said the ghost.

"Ooh, you're a fancy one, aren't you?" said Nurse Gamp, shutting off her music and pulling the earphones down around her neck like a stethoscope. All around her babies continued to wail like police sirens. She took the pen out of her mouth and poked the perfect blond girl-child in the tummy. "Most of the babies that come through have something wrong with them, you know. Factory defects, only there's no warranty from the manufacturer." She laughed at her own wit. "You're perfection itself. I'm tempted to take you home. Ooh, what's this?"

Nurse Gamp reached into the crib and ran her fingers over a square of bright purple that had practically fitted itself to the contours of the baby's little body. Blue was for boys, pink was for girls, but industrial gray was for orphans. Purple amounted to baby treason. Whimsy was not smiled upon in this baby dungeon.

"Nice," said the nurse. "Precious stuff." She ran her thumb and forefinger over the cloth until she found a label in the cor-ner, which was under the baby's left foot. "Cashmere, very spe-cial," she cooed as she began separating, one by one, the baby's fingers from the blanket. "You won't mind loaning it out for a time, will you? Mrs. Harris needs this more than you do. And where you're going there won't be much of a need for fancy blankies."

As the last pinky on the baby's left hand gave way the baby began to make a frustrated sound.

"Come now, just think of it as like a little Christmas present for Sarah and Mrs. Harris!" said Nurse Gamp. "Giving is supposed to hurt a little. It's only natural, you know."

As Sarah Gamp tried to pull the blanket from underneath the little girl's body, though, it seemed to be stuck on something. The baby shrieked in pain, as though Sarah were ripping the skin off the thing.

"What's all this, darling?" said Sarah. "How about a little show of appreciation for the quality of nursing around here? I gave you a nice big Christmas Eve bottle not three hours ago. And what did you give me in return? Not even the smallest tip."

With that, the girl reached up with both hands, dug them into the blanket with the force of a mountain climber thrusting forged steel crampons into a wall of ice, and began rotating her body furiously in reverse. Nurse Gamp was so surprised at this advanced display of motor control that she momentarily lost her grip. She crossed her arms over her formidable bosom and chuckled as the baby wrapped herself as tight as an egg roll. The baby was now squawking at a volume normally associated with heavy-metal guitar solos. In a distinguished career of robbing babies of whatever valuables they arrived at the orphanage with, Sarah Gamp had rarely encountered determined resistance.

"Selfishness isn't becoming at Christmas, darling," the nurse said, carefully placing the earphones back over her ears and hitting play on the next song, "Grandma Got Run Over by a Reindeer." Since the song had become her special favorite, Nurse Gamp had added, like a scat singer, improvised filigrees of her own to the classic—little tossed-in "hey!"'s and "ho"s! to extend its holiday cheer.

As she sang every word of the demented carol, Nurse Gamp tried to extricate the little fighter from Mrs. Harris's blanket.

"Grandma got run over by a—hey!" Sarah sang.

The kid was as flexible as a little stick of mozzarella, though, and whether it was due to lack of muscle tone or coordination, Sarah found she needed both hands to remove a single limb from the blanket.

"You can say there's no such thing as Santa-ho!"

When Sarah lifted a leg, the baby wrapped her other one around the blanket like a red stripe on a candy cane. When she successfully tore an arm away the baby flipped her entire body on top of the blanket. Frustrated, Sarah sighed and bowed to the inevitable: she would obviously have to cover the baby's mouth with one hand and pinch her nose shut with the other until all the fight drained out of the little brat. She was reaching for the baby's face as the song reached its final chorus.

"Grandma got run over by a—hey!"

It was at this moment that she became aware of two women standing on either side of her.

Sarah switched off her holiday tune.

Hovering above with her ghost, Caroline cheered. "Yay!" she said to the spirit. "Look who's here!"

"Yes, Mrs. Corney?" Nurse Gamp said to her boss. With a nod to the seething infant, she added, "The poor child was about to, er, asphyxiate." There would be plenty of time for blanket-snatching later. The child's career as an orphan had barely begun.

"Yes, I guessed that," said Mrs. Corney, the director of the institution. Mrs. Corney's faith in Nurse Gamp was limited but this was, after all, an orphanage. You didn't find the best sort of people hanging around them. "This is Mrs.—"

"La," said La, "will be fine."

"Pleased to meet you. Welcome to Akron," said Nurse Gamp, who wondered exactly how much La had witnessed. It was at times like these that Sarah was especially proud to be a paid-up member of a union. The last nurse in Local 657 to permanently lose her job hadn't really even missed it that much, since by that time she had already been fifteen months into her prison sentence.

"It seems—I know this is odd, but it seems Mrs., um, La, has changed her mind," said Mrs. Corney. "She will not be placing the child after all."

"But she can't—I mean, it just isn't—"

"Of course," added Mrs. Corney, with a slight bow to her client, "La will have to pay all customary and routine adoption fees. Including the fee for the customary and routine background check. I trust all the arrangements will be satisfactory for all parties? There will be no need for anyone else to know about this, Mrs. Gamp."

"To get her back I need a background check?" said La. "I didn't need a background check to have her."

"Regulations," said Mrs. Corney and Nurse Gamp in unison. This word, both had found, generally ended all arguments. What could anyone do about regulations?

"Come on, Caroline," said La, hoisting the baby into her arms.

Sarah Gamp eyed the five-pointed white star centered above the top horizontal seam of Mrs. Harris's blanket.

"We're going home," said La. "Daddy won't be there to hurt you anymore."

Sarah decided to make one more try. "Pretty blanket," she said. "I have a little one at home who would just love—"

"It arrived with her," said La. "And it's leaving with her." She kissed the baby uncertainly on top of her head. "Even if it was her father's present. Cashmere, after all."

"Is it?" said Mrs. Gamp.

Several feet overhead, Caroline looked at the spirit. "I was given up for adoption? What does this tell me about my father? I don't know anything about him. Mother would never tell me. Apparently he did something horrible when I was little, and they never spoke again."

The spirit shrugged.

"Thanks, really helpful," Caroline said. "How did you get this job anyway? I've had a nicer time dealing with the IRS."

"Tight deadline. Work to do," said the spirit, and instantly the scene changed.

It was a charming country town, the kind with immaculate gravel roads, quiet little B and Bs and trees that can't wait for the fall shows. A boy on a bicycle pedaled past. A bunch of wild daisies grew under an oak.

As Caroline and the Ghost of Christmas Past watched, time passed. The immaculate green campus lawns grew a coat of snow. The maples shed their leaves and deferred to the pine trees, who stood proud and ready to emcee the winter. The administration building, a white clapboard cube that had once housed a forgotten patriot, began puffing a friendly stream of fireplace smoke out a chimney or two. By a split-rail fence that surrounded the main quad, a pair of horses was actually being harnessed to a sleigh. It was as if this was the very spot where Currier turned to Ives and said, "Buddy, I have an idea."

"Do you remember this place?" asked the spirit.

"Remember it?" said Caroline. "Who can forget argyle knee socks? When I was in eighth grade I started up a petition about that. I sent it straight to the U.N. Human Rights Commission."

"Come," said the ghost, and smiled. The two of them floated over the two main facing dorms and on to a neighboring row of smaller clapboard buildings.

"We are here to discover the secrets of your past," said the spirit. And suddenly they were in a little classroom. The clock read 7:59. A cluster of excited sixth graders giggled and whispered by the door. One of them stood on tiptoes and peeked through the tiny square window of the door. The air fairly murmured, "Here she comes." Silence followed, broken by occasional giggles and shushy sounds. The girls scattered as Caroline, aged ten, approached. Young Caroline didn't enter rooms. She Made Entrances.

Even in a roomful of uniformed girls still in the probationary period of adolescence, Caroline stood out. Her blond hair was the blondest. Her blue eyes were the bluest. Her white headband was the headbandiest. Her school uniform, all argyle and navy, looked like the definition of basic-classic. At her most perfect, Alice in Wonderland would have taken one look at Caroline and asked, "Why am I such a slob?" Caroline's eyes were narrow and knowing. She seemed to look at nothing yet see everything. The other girls stood around in small groups nudging each other, whispering, awaiting acknowledgment. A nod from Caroline and the day was made. A cutting comment from her within hearing range of the others, and you lunched alone.

"Fear can be so cute," said Caroline, smiling at the smaller version of herself. "Isn't it sweet, the way I ruled with an iron fist in a cashmere mitten?"

In the scramble to withdraw from the door before Caroline came in, a recent transfer to the school was left alone. She was a slightly too-tall girl with unruly curly hair who stood in limbo by a wall display. The girl had a tight grip on both armpits. If there had been a closet nearby, she would already have been in it.

Young Caroline walked up to within a foot of the girl, gave her a confidence-shattering glare and issued a two-word summary: "Yeah, right."

Fits of whispers. News on the march. The curly-haired girl's argyle socks were obviously much less cool than Caroline's argyle socks. The curly-haired girl's navy pinafore was a hopeless, dowdy imitation of all the others in the room. Plus, she was all . . . curly-haired. The verdict was in. A social career was given lethal injection. Lepers wouldn't talk to the poor girl now.

By the time the bell rang Caroline was leaning back in her chair in the last row, going to work with her lipstick. Spread out inside her three-hundred-page Social Studies book was a five-hundred-page magazine.

"You didn't talk to any of the girls in your class?" the Ghost of Christmas Past said to the grown-up Caroline.

"Look, here's a Flintstones multivitamin for you to chew on, kid. I was trying to remain wreathed in mystery. If they can't talk to you, they talk about you. Anyone can be talked *to*. But only stars are talked *about*. I was creating my own cult of personality. It's like Coco said: 'How many cares one loses when one decides not to be something but to be someone.' "

The teacher, Ms. Peecher, came in.

"I've got a surprise for you today, girls," she said.

In the back of the class, gum snapped like a burst of anti-applause.

"Social Studies is canceled!" said the teacher.

A general cheer arose.

"That's right," said Ms. Peecher, nodding with satisfaction, "today, instead of finishing our lesson about how to discipline domestics and social inferiors, we're going outside. Who wants to build a snowhuman?"

Every girl but one raised her hand. As a stampede of argyle headed for the mud room, Ms. Peecher came over and sat on the desk in front of Caroline. The girl kept her head tilted toward her magazine.

Hovering above the classroom, the Ghost of Christmas Past looked at adult Caroline. "You didn't even look up," she said.

"Hello, she was interrupting me at the exact moment when I discovered why you should never wear horizontal stripes," said Caroline.

Ten-year-old Caroline, though, looked a little nervous. She didn't even look like she was concentrating on the page. You could tell by the way she had stopped chewing her gum.

"Caroline," said Ms. Peecher, "don't you want to go outside and play with the other girls?"

Caroline put her hands in her lap and looked at them. "I sort of can't."

Ms. Peecher laughed. "Anyone can build a snowhuman. Look outside: six beautiful inches of fresh snow!"

"I'm not, I'm not. . . ." Caroline's voice trailed off helplessly. She looked up.

"What?" said Ms. Peecher.

"Dressed for it?" Caroline whispered.

Ms. Peecher pursed her lips. "Come on, now," she said. "I saw you wearing a coat this morning. Chinchilla isn't really made for playing in, but it'll do. And weren't you wearing boots?"

Caroline breathed in sharply and curled her feet under her seat in shame. "That's just it." Her voice faded into a whisper. "I'm wearing the wrong boots."

Ms. Peecher bent over to look at Caroline's feet, which at

the moment were a showcase for whimsical white calfskin elf boots with a delicate heel.

"These boots are more for being looked at," said Caroline, miserably. "They're not authorized for actual frolicking. I have to stay on sidewalks, and only ones that have been thoroughly shoveled and salted."

"Who told you that?"

Caroline swallowed. "My mother."

"Yes, I do believe she has a point there. You're heading for a nasty fall if you take those babies off-road."

Caroline hung her head.

"But," said Ms. Peecher, "this is winter in Connecticut. Didn't your mother give you anything practical to wear on snowy days?"

Caroline bit her lower lip and finally looked up. "She said practical is the enemy of fashion."

"I see," said Ms. Peecher. "And when did she tell you that?"

"The first time? Well, probably in the womb. She used to put these little headphones on her belly, and. . . ."

"Is she coming to pick you up today for the holidays?"

Caroline looked at the door to make sure no one was peeking. She looked out the window, where girls were already leaping and laughing and stuffing snow into one another's hoods. She flipped through her magazine and took out a postcard stashed between the Calvin Klein and Pucci ads.

Ms. Peecher looked at the picture of the beach at sunset and turned the card over. She read it aloud. "'Greetings from sunny Río, exclamation point. Super fun times, underlined, and so many thrillingly dangerous men, exclamation point. Pussycat, you won't meow too loudly if I tell you I'm unavoidably detained through the New Year, question mark. Work is too boring, all sorts of dreary photo shoots to finish up, unhappy face, period. It's much more Christmassy back in wintry Connecticut, anyway, exclamation point exclamation point exclamation point. Take a sleigh ride for me, go caroling, decorate trees, be kind to beggars, do all that wonderful Yuletide stuff pour deux, darling, underline, exclamation point exclamation point exclamation point exclamation point. Love and kisses.' Well." She handed back the card to Caroline.

"I know the school is closed but I was sorta hoping I could stay here through the holidays," said Caroline.

Ms. Peecher patted her hand. "I'll see what I can arrange."

"Oh, and Ms. Peecher?" said Caroline. "I don't want to do any caroling or Christmas tree decorating or sleigh rides or anything. If that's all right by you."

Ms. Peecher went to the closet and rummaged around in the bottom. "I think I have an old pair of L.L. Bean duck boots that might just fit you," she said.

"Um, Ms. Peecher?" said Caroline. "My mother said she'd be upset if she ever caught me in that kind of clothing."

"Well, this is kind of an emergency, so I'm sure she wouldn't be too upset."

"I can kind of guarantee she would be, actually."

"What were her exact words?"

"She said, 'I will put out my own eyes with a red-hot poker if I ever hear of you wearing mail-order rags.'"

"I see," said Ms. Peecher. Involuntarily, she took a step back from the strange child.

Hovering overhead, adult Caroline nudged the cherubic little spirit. "Can I borrow your handkerchief?" she said, sniffling.

"Allergies?" asked the Ghost of Christmas Past with a gentle smile.

"Yeah," said Caroline, blowing her nose. "I'm totally allergic to blatantly manipulative ghost-driven appeals to sentimentality. Especially on Christmas."

As Caroline's nose ran and her eyes watered, she and the Ghost of Christmas Past rose and wafted silently away. Fog came and went, and the scene below changed to a different school, on a different Christmas.

Caroline and the small ghost were sitting in a snowy tree overlooking the horseshoe-shaped driveway in front of Sageberry Hall, where a line of tiny women sat ensconced in boxcar-sized automobiles. As the women waited, even smaller versions of themselves rushed chattering toward them from every direction. Bags were thrown into backs of cars, doors were slammed, hugs were hugged. One by one, each girl parted from her friends and drove off with her family.

Then the door of the squat neocolonial opened and one last little girl trudged forth, slouching as if to hide a body that, while not at all overweight, could not fairly be described as underweight either.

At this point in Caroline's adolescence embarrassment was not so much a mood or a habit as a full-time job. In an effort to compensate for her recently developed embarrassment over her childish princess look, which had lasted from birth until about six months earlier, she now wore an asymmetrical go-to-hell haircut bleached white with a shock-tuft of bright pink. She wore one bright blue argyle knee sock pushed all the way down, the other pulled all the way up. Underneath her short navy peacoat, one tail of her white shirt hung out, and under it she wore a ripped CBGB T-shirt. Her skirt was pulled up so high the hem was barely visible under her coat. The only flaw in her look was her Prada bag, which she told everyone was a cheap knockoff purchased on one of her many imaginary trips to the dirty chaos of Manhattan's Lower East Side. In fact it was a genuine article that had come from an embarrassingly clean and reputable shopping mall in Stamford.

Behind her, bent almost double with exertion, an eager boy in a blue blazer and a rep tie with a loosened knot sweatily dragged a massive Harvey Nichols of London trunk whose logo had been covered by a Sex Pistols sticker. A single untamed lock of his chestnut hair sprang up defiantly from the crown of his head. Acne was pushing up through his face like a range of ant-hills. His weight was of the kind that made relatives say the words, "big-boned," though really his bones were just well-padded. He smelled like cookies.

The two of them were each individually awkward, but together they were a working illustration of the difference between looking bad on purpose and just looking bad.

As the boy who smelled like cookies bumped the trunk down the polished marble steps of the entryway, the girl provided him with a running stream of comments describing the various errors he was committing in the effort. The boy remained silent except for his grunts of exertion.

"Oh, God," said the young Caroline, aching with embarrassment at his pathetic noises, "will you just keep it down?"

"There's no one left, is there?" said the boy, who was in the same grade as Caroline but studied at the Hall's brother school across the quad. "Isn't that why you wanted to wait until everyone was gone?"

Caroline lit a cigarette and held it in the most pretentious way her fourteen-year-old fingers could devise. "You *so* don't get it, Philly," she said.

The remark hit hard. You could see by his expression that in his exploratory investigations into the nature of girlness, he had failed to get a vast number of its. According to oft-repeated opinion, not getting it was his sole social achievement. He didn't ask what it was, knowing that merely to ask about it was to prove that he had not gotten it.

"And what is that smell, anyway?"

"Who me?" said the boy, getting really extremely nervous.

"You smell like . . . calories," said the girl. She looked at him suspiciously, as though accusing him of smuggling unsightly pounds in his bodily aroma.

"It's just, uh, cookies," said Philly. "I think. I mean, I made a couple dozen cinnamon raisin in the dining hall this morning. Plus some gingerbread cookies, some oatmeal, a few chocolate–chocolate chip. . . ."

"Stop," she said, lighting another cigarette with her hands while she crushed out the first one with her foot. "You're making me hungry."

"Okay," he said, worried that he was not getting it again.

"Who were you making all this stuff for?"

"The dining hall workers."

"Ugh, the townies in the little paper hats?"

"The grown-ups. Who work there for real. I'm on the breakfast shift three times a week anyway, so I'm up at four-thirty whether I like it or not. I thought it would be a nice little present for them, and also that maybe they'd stop cutting the fingers off my gloves when my back is turned." He held up a hapless mitten, wiggling his cold and naked thumb through the opening.

"It's *so* unfortunate, isn't it?" said Caroline. "It's really too bad that you have to be such a dork. Working right in the dining hall where everyone can see you? You're *so* embarrassing."

"I don't care if everyone knows I'm scholarship," said the boy. "Keeps me feisty. Plus I'm not just learning the dumb stuff they teach you in class. I have a trade. I can bake."

"Philly," said Caroline, "you are just too, too. Who else would go to prep school to learn how to be a prole?"

"You think the algebra is going to suddenly become useful someday? Do you hear adults talking about Venn diagrams and the quadratic equation?"

"No," Caroline said. "But we need to do all that stuff for, um. . . ."

"For what?"

It was not until this moment that Caroline realized what the purpose of school was.

"To prove we're different," she said, definitively.

"From who?"

"The working class, you dullard."

"I'm working-class. I'm going to be rich someday, but I'll always be working-class." Here Philly began, embarrassingly, to shout.

"I'M WORKING-CLASS! I'M WORKING-CLASS!" He went up to a fir tree and shook it until its pine needles began to rain on his head. "I'M WORKING-CLASS!" A pine cone plopped squarely on his skull.

"Cease! Philly, just go stand over there, will you? God! Do you have to exist?"

Philly hung his head. "You don't have to be so hard on me, you know," he said.

Caroline didn't answer.

"Don't you think there's enough negativity in the world?" he said.

"No," said Caroline. "Be elsewhere."

So Philly walked. He walked and walked. He stopped. He gave Caroline a whimpery, doggy look.

"No, farther," said Caroline. "No, farther." As the boy re-treated to the horizon, Caroline sat down on her trunk and began listlessly swinging her feet against it. Minutes passed, but Caroline was too aware of the boy's gaze from where he lurked under the building's overhang.

Without looking up, Caroline yelled, "And stop staring at me!"

Hovering overhead, the bite-sized ghost turned to adult Caroline. "You weren't very nice to him, were you?"

"He got on my nerves," Caroline explained. "He went to our brother school, but he signed up for all these classes in our school, every year. It was like he became one of the girls. He always seemed to wind up in my electives. I mean, come on, what kind of guy takes History of the Hemline? He was following me. Plus he sent me all these stupid cards. How dorky can you get? Did James Dean ever send anyone a card?"

"Maybe he liked you," said the ghost. "Do you feel bad, considering what happened with him later on?"

"Ugh," said Caroline. "You're worse than my shrink. We are not discussing that."

The boy who smelled like cookies disappeared behind the building. Free from his gaze, young Caroline felt she was on a brief, rare embarrassment vacation.

Swinging her feet on the trunk, pounding her heels into the side, she opened her handbag to look for another cigarette and came up with a fistful of the morning's mail. Catalogs, cards from people she didn't like, official school blah-blah. And one card with no return address.

Like the other cards, its postmark said it had been mailed nearby, from the same post office that served the school. Caroline opened it: as usual, it was a picture of a jolly Christmas scene—this time it was a Victorian painting of a hearth decorated with holly and a father smoking a pipe as he ladled out eggnog to his doting wife and children. As always, the signature caught her eye first:

Nemo

Above it were a few handwritten words that appeared to have been scrawled by a child. "You look pretty today, though you seem to be trying to hide it. Anyway, someone is looking out for you. Merry Christmas." Then the single, strange word of the signature.

Caroline had gotten a similar Nemo card every Christmastime since her first year at this school. Which had also been Philly's first year. As she did every year, Caroline would make an especially hurtful point of not mentioning the card to Philly. It was best to ignore the whole thing. Let the twerp do what twerps did best: squirm.

Caroline walked over to a trash container disguised as a rustic wooden barrel and deposited two of the cards. She kept the one from loverboy, from "Nemo," which she planned to throw in a box with the rest of the Nemo file: all the other similar cards she'd gotten from the same loony over the years. There was comedy value in them, at least. Some day she'd rub Philly's oily little face in them.

As Caroline went back to her trunk and sat on it, Philly reappeared from around the corner of the building carrying a small brown paper bag. Caroline studied him with exquisite indifference, tossed her hair, resolved to disdain whatever pathetic little present he had brought her to go with his card. A plastic ring perhaps? A chunky bracelet he had made in wood shop?

Caroline was gazing obliviously into the middle distance when Philly appeared in front of her.

"Hi," he said. "I thought you could use this. I don't expect any thanks."

With that, he dropped the bag in her lap and beat a retreat. Caroline resisted opening the bag for a few painful minutes, but since Philly was well away and partially obscured by a copy of *Forbes* he was reading, she supposed it would do no harm to take a peek. Caroline could not now and never would be able to resist a present.

Pinching the brown paper awkwardly between the fingers of her gloves, Caroline opened the bag and prepared to sneer. Inside was a lump of heaven: a perfect jewel of a chocolate–chocolate chip cookie. She could not reveal to Philly that a cookie was exactly what she'd been craving all morning.

Quietly, with a burglar's stealth, Caroline popped the cookie out of the bag and took a bite. It was to other cookies what Christian Dior was to the guy who designed the "I'm with Stupid" T-shirt. Never before had she come so close to believing in a divine entity of baked goods. She ate it in four nondainty bites, each of them better than the last. She popped a compact out of her bag to check for crumbs and quickly refolded the bag to cover all traces of what had just transpired. Her gaze shifted to the rotunda where boy and magazine were sitting. Perfect. She had been so smooth, so delicate, so noiseless that Philly hadn't even noticed she'd opened the bag, so no thanks were necessary. Caroline sat on her trunk in a perfect pose of indifference.

"Did you enjoy it?" Philly called out, not looking up from his *Forbes*.

Caroline fumed for a moment. "I thought no thanks were necessary?" she yelled. "Were you expecting a Nobel Prize?" A guy who could bake like that was worth something, but too bad he was so obvious, so open, so completely nonmysterious. Plus the kid had a soft, disgusting pot belly. What she wanted was an angry young man, not a hungry young man.

In the distance, Philly put down his magazine. "I just want to know how you think it tasted," he yelled. "I worked in some changes to the recipe just this morning. If it doesn't work, I'll go back and tinker with it some more."

"You made this?" Caroline yelled.

"Yes!" Philly yelled.

"Okay, don't yell!" Caroline yelled. "You might as well come sit by me."

Philly approached the way a Labrador approaches a frisbee, all panting and waggy. He explained that he didn't really like the dining hall's cookie recipes, and he had spent the last few days fooling with the formula, though while he was putting in long unpaid hours sinister reactionary forces had issued him a stern warning not to tamper with the way things were done around here, a message that was delivered in the form of maple syrup, which he discovered filling the pockets of his coat when he left the dining hall. Anyway, this was what he came up with. He thought it was pretty good but he needed an unbiased opinion.

"Do you think it's pretty good?" Philly said hopefully.

Caroline looked at him coldly, determined to allow no hint that he had just delivered to her the highlight of term. "No," Caroline said. "I do not honestly think that cookie was pretty good."

Philly looked beaten. He ran his fingers through his hair. "You're right," he said. "It's not good enough. I'm going to have to make it better somehow."

Just then a car pulled up and made its slow way along the gravel driveway to the two students. It was a prehistoric automobile, something called a station wagon, with real fake wood panels.

"There's my uncle," Philly said. "You need a lift?"

Caroline stood up and slouched as if to say, I didn't create this punk harlot persona to be seen getting into station wagons. She was working a go-to-hell look, not a go-to-Applebee's look.

"Me?" she called. "In that?"

She felt a little pang of shame at the way the boy who smelled of cookies shrugged and opened the door to the car. There was nothing wrong with him, Caroline thought for a moment. Nothing much, anyway. Perhaps she should do him the favor of telling him everything he was doing wrong.

"Look," she said, "let me give you some advice. Don't send mushy cards to pretty girls. Don't do favors for pretty girls in the hopes that they'll notice you. Be Mr. Above It All. Be Mr. Cool. Be Mr. Oblivious. Don't be Mr. Obvious."

"Mr. Obvious," he said, chewing the word like an oversized chocolate chip cookie.

"There has to be a little mystery, you know? Here's something my mother always taught me: Elegance is refusal."

Philly opened the car door. "Here's something Bruce Springsteen always taught me: it goes, 'Refusal, and then surrender.'"

"Ugh," said Caroline. "Beyond obvious."

"At least I'm not a phony," Philly said, as a humming black Mercedes convertible pulled hastily into the far end of the semicircular driveway. With an exciting spray of gravel, it jolted to a halt just behind Philly's uncle's crapmobile. A woman in a snow white turban with a diamond stickpin and an ankle-length sable got out of the car.

Philly stood there with the passenger door open, gawping. The man driving the station wagon, a middle-aged man in a sheepskin-lined denim jacket, opened his door and got out. Scrunching a flat cap in his big meaty worker's hands, he addressed himself to the woman in the snow white turban. "You must be Mrs.—"

"Uh-uh," said the woman, wagging some fingers. "Stick to Ms., please."

La looked at her daughter. "Darling!" she said. "You look three pounds heavier." She turned to Philly's uncle. "What are they feeding these children? Is this a school or a goose-fattening farm?"

Philly's uncle looked puzzled. "I don't—"

"No need, really," said La, waving at the air as though shooing an insect, or clearing away fumes. "Rhetorical question."

"Mother," said Caroline with a look of squirming doom. "I'd like you to meet—"

But La was ahead of her. She had already done an assessment of Philly, from the ground up.

"Nice *boots*," she said.

Oh. My. God. It was true. Caroline hadn't even noticed before. What had gotten into her? He was wearing the most horrible stained mint green Kmart Klondike plastic boots trimmed with mangy fake fur along the top. It wasn't even fake mink. It was more like fake gerbil.

"Philly," said Caroline, smirking at his boots, "thanks for your help. Were you waiting for a tip?"

Philly looked stunned. "I just thought you might need help with your trunk."

"*Friends* of yours?" said La, glancing back and forth from Caroline to the two strange males with an expression that said, "*Scientific experiments* of yours?"

"I think the answer to that is, um, obvious," said Caroline, looking at Philly and crushing another cigarette underfoot. Philly looked a lot like the cigarette.

Philly's uncle placed a reassuring hand on the kid's shoulder. "Best be going," he said. He reached out a hand to La. "I'm Joe," he said. "Nice to have met you."

La looked at the hand as though it were a bear trap. "Well, technically, of course, we didn't. But farewell anyway."

Philly and Joe had gotten in the car and started to move forward when Philly rolled down his window. He stared at Caroline. "You know, it's not fair," he said.

"What isn't?" said Caroline.

"What you do to people," he said. He was winding himself up into some sort of tiny tantrum as his eyeballs shot back and forth from La to Caroline. "It's not fair, it's not fair, it's not fair."

"Nature isn't fair," La said, waving him away. "It creates people of taste and style and beauty. And it also comes up with you."

Philly rolled up his window. He, Joe, and the car all looked equally humiliated as they crunched down the gravel path.

La turned her attention to Caroline. "Exactly how much did you gain? I need it in pounds and ounces."

"Well, I'm still growing, so."

"Is it that bad? I mean, so bad that you have to use the growing child thing as an excuse?"

Caroline didn't answer.

"Are you horribly excited to be going home?" asked La. "And did you pack that ice blue off-shoulder Versace dress? Good. I want it back. If you haven't wrinkled it beyond repair."

"Nice to see you, Mom," said Caroline, though the statement came out sounding like a question neither of them could answer.

"Well, let's have a hug! If I can get my arms around you," said La. The two embraced as if each had a flesh-eating virus. Then La held Caroline at, or pushed her to, arm's length and appraised her one more time with a cruel, cruel stare. "Good news. We're having a wonderful holiday meal. Your daddy just bought a turkey. So I guess we're having two butterballs for Christmas."

"Which 'daddy' are we talking about?"

"You know, Daddy Will."

"Oh?" said Caroline. "The one from Pasadena?"

"Such sass!" said La. "Darling, need I remind? He's an important man. He's going to make a wonderful father to you."

"So you got married? Congratulations. I didn't know."

"Not married, exactly," said La. "But we're going to use psychology. You call him Daddy. He'll get the picture. Consider this an audition. Don't screw up."

"So he's definitely going to marry you?" said Caroline.

"Because I thought maybe you didn't want to get married after what happened with Daddy Chadwick, Daddy Paul, and Daddy Troy."

"Of course I want to get married," snapped La.

"And Daddy Vance, Daddy Simon, and Daddy Jasper—" said Caroline.

"Cease," said La, lowering her voice to an urgent whisper. "You think I've been a single mother all your life by choice? If ever someone was made for marriage, it's me."

"I hope it happens for you someday, Mother," said Caroline.

"Oh, shut up, cookie breath," said La.

"I wasn't being sarcastic. I was trying to—" said Caroline.

"Get your box," La said. "It'll have to go in the front seat. It's too big for the trunk of the car."

It was true: the trunk of the car would have had difficulty accommodating a hatbox.

Caroline picked up her trunk, staggered two steps, and dropped it on the front seat.

"It's a two-seater," said Caroline. "Where am I going to sit?"

"Well," said La, "I guess I don't have room for you this time. I'll come back and get you. Actually, it's a European car. I'm not sure you'll fit. While I'm gone, try jogging around the campus a couple of times. Try not to jog by any bakeries." She was already in the driver's seat, belting herself in.

"Wait," said Caroline, cursing Philly under her breath for giving her the cookie.

In an instant, the scene changed, and the ghost and the adult Caroline were hovering over a massive colonial brick house in Greenwich. When the Mercedes pulled into the driveway, La was driving and talking on her cell phone, the trunk was standing up on one end in the passenger seat and Caroline was sitting under the trunk, looking less than comfortable.

Caro and her trunk staggered out of the Mercedes, up the carefully laid stone steps, and into the kitchen, whose door suddenly opened. Behind it a smiling geezer in sweater vest and tie opened the door, jammed a hand in his pocket, and started rummaging.

Exhausted, Caroline watched as the trunk fell out of her hands and hit the floor with a satisfying, emphatic thud.

"Oh dear," said the gentleman in a lightly pleasing English accent. He stopped playing with whatever was in his pocket and came out with a five-dollar bill. Which he handed to Caroline. "I wasn't expecting a delivery," he said mildly.

Using the last four or five calories she had left over from the cookie, Caroline kicked the trunk. "I'm Caroline," she said, or growled.

"William Dorrit," said the man. "What store are you from? I'm afraid it may take a moment to find my checkbook."

Caroline arranged her mouth into a screaming position.

"MothER!"

William Dorrit was backing away and curling into a protective crouch by the time Caroline reached maximum volume. La was leaning against her Mercedes tossing her head back and laughing at something her cell phone was telling her. As Caroline's yells became increasingly impossible to ignore, La nodded and placed a single index finger in the air. She appeared to be registering the wind power of Caroline's vocal cords.

A moment later La strolled up the steps and closed the kitchen door behind her. "Introductions all done?" she said brightly, snapping shut her cell phone.

"You didn't tell your *boy*friend you have a daughter?" Caroline screamed. Mr. Dorrit was aimlessly wandering around the other side of the kitchen, opening doors. When he found a broom closet, he lingered fondly and gazed into it as though considering whether to climb in.

"Darling," La said, shedding her camel-hair coat, "it's early in our relationship. We haven't discussed all the important matters in the world, you know. I don't even know what pets Mr. Dorrit may or may not have. William, do stop trickling so."

Mr. Dorrit, who was indeed at the doorway at the far end of the kitchen removing himself from the room molecule by molecule, halted in his tracks and awaited further instructions.

"Tra-la," said La, ringing for a servant on her cell phone. "Who's for tea? You'll take yours sans sugar, of course, Caro darling? Remember what Coco said: Elegance is refusal."

In the living room, Caroline, William, and La were talking, though not to one another. La spent twenty minutes on her cell phone making complex arrangements to buy something that seemed to involve Saturday delivery, the color loden, and a waiver from the Human Rights Division of the State Department.

Caroline ignored the petits fours arranged on a mammoth, disgusting silver platter and concentrated on her tea. It seemed to restore her, though she felt a little weak.

"So what do you do, Mr. Dorrit?" Caroline asked, determined to be far more polite to William than she would ever be to her mother. Sometimes niceness could be a weapon.

"I'm in debt."

"Pardon?" Caroline had met many deadbeats, most of them sitting side by side with her mother, but not a one who would admit it.

"I'm heavily into bonds, you know."

Floating above the scene, it all came back to adult Caroline. The previous week several disgusting kinky magazines with titles like *Bond for Glory* and *Bondage Illustrated* and *U.S. Bonds* had made the rounds from room to room in Sageberry Hall amid much giggling, which explained why at this moment the teen Caroline was attacked by an image of her mother trussed up in black leather straps with silver buckles chomping on a bit between her teeth and writhing with anticipation from her patent-leather knee-highs to her Goth eye makeup. Once you have pictured your mother in bondage gear, the image becomes exceedingly difficult to shake. But Caroline was the picture of politesse, as long as La was in hearing range.

"So do you, uh, dominate?" Caroline asked Mr. Dorrit.

"Pardon? Oh, yes, I suppose you could say I do."

Caroline nodded, gulped her tea, nodded again. She felt slightly woozy. "Popular, isn't it? Lots of clients."

"Hundreds," said Mr. Dorrit. "All over the world."

"Where do they come from mainly?"

"I can tell you," he said, leaning forward with a conspiratorial twinkle in his eye, "there are a *lot* of Germans, of course."

"Well, obviously," Caroline said, and the two of them laughed.

"I don't know how to put this, but—" Caroline was about to ask him if he personally enjoyed being beaten with a whip or perhaps having objects inserted into his person when her mother's phone made a see-ya-later noise.

"William is a *colossally* successful bond salesman, did he tell you that? He's the founding father of Marshalsea Investments," La said, putting the phone on the coffee table. "Oh dear, don't you look flushed. Doesn't she look flushed, William? Are we having our monthly guests in from Tampa, my darling?"

"Mother!" said Caroline, who blushed again. Her near translucent skin appeared to be suffering the ravages of an advanced case of scarlet fever.

Caroline tried to think of the blandest image she could possibly muster. Khaki chinos, she said to herself, again and again. Khaki chinos. Khaki chinos. But the spiked black leather dog collar and the patent leather knee-highs and the bit, oh my God, the bit. . . .

When Caroline awoke a strange man in a worn-looking pin-striped navy suit and a tie decorated with polka dots and ketchup stains was standing over her sticking his fingers in her eyes. Several long hairs were stretching out like weeds from his crazy black eyebrows. He looked like one of the consulting physicians listed at 1-800-QUACKERY.

La popped up on the other side of the sofa. "She was suffering caffeine-based delusions, I think," she said. "Before she hit the floor, the last word that crossed her lips was 'cappucci-nos.' "

"Look up," said the doctor, who was now blinding Caroline with a miniature flashlight while groping her neck with his fingertips. "I've seen this all before," he said. "You'll have to monitor her. Here." He scribbled something official-looking on a tiny white notepad, tore it off, and handed it to La. Vicodin? Valium? Heavy sedation appeared to be Caroline's best bet for getting through the holiday weekend.

Caroline sat up woozily and blinked as her mother was ushering the man and his eyebrows out the door. "Thank you, Doctor," La was saying. Caroline's vision fixated on the tiny piece of folded white paper. "So few physicians make house calls these days."

"Please? You can just call me Technician Nahteev," said the man. "I'm not an actual licensed doctor yet. Except in Yemen."

"Well," said La, closing the door behind him and zeroing in on an easy chair. "It's been a trying day, hasn't it, William?"

William looked up from the sports page. "Indeed."

"How long have I been out of it?" Caroline said.

"Fashionwise? I'd say years," said La. "Are you hungry? Pork roast for dinner in a minute."

Caroline's well-established lifelong hatred of giant brown slabs of greasy baked oinking meat was irrelevant at the moment. All that mattered was the prescription. "Can I see that?" she said, reaching for the white folded miracle.

"Oh. Certainly, dear," La said, and rose to start work on her next gin fizz.

Caroline unfolded the piece of paper:

No caffeine one week.

"Beautiful handwriting some of these minorities have, isn't it?" La said, giving her sterling silver swizzle stick a workout.

❧   ❧   ❧

THE GHOST OF CHRISTMAS PAST waved her little hand over the scene and turned to the adult Caroline. "I couldn't help feeling sorry for you," said the little spirit, handing her another handkerchief.

"Nobody feels sorry for me," Caroline said. "My contacts are irritating my eyes. And I wish you'd told me we'd be doing so much outdoor wafting. I'd have brought lip balm."

As they floated through the clouds, the scenery gradually changed again. The grass and trees turned into concrete and street lamps. Highways emerged, full of rows of cars jostling for the exit ramps. As Caroline and her ghost passed from the highways into a network of streets, she grew confused. The pavement didn't have that sun-bleached look of L.A., and New York didn't have all these diagonal streets. What other cities were there?

"Oh no," said Caroline. "We're not going here. Take me back now, you wee monster. I already lived this once. I'm not going through it again. If I have any say in the matter, can I put in a request to roast in hell instead?"

"You didn't learn your lesson the first time around," said the spirit. "So you have to do it again. Think of it as like summer school."

"Look, can't you cut to the moral?" Caroline pleaded. "Just give me whatever fortune cookie saying you want me to absorb—'Be nice,' 'Buy more cheesy Christmas decorations,' 'Join Amnesty International,' whatever—but spare me from this."

But the spirit just smiled and shook her head as the two of them descended into the worst place Caroline had ever known to get an up-close look at the crappiest chapter of her life.

chapter eight

 Two portly women were walking along a lonely wide avenue whose grave white buildings looked like museums, set a forbidding distance back from the street. One of the women was wearing a raspberry-colored skirt and matching jacket with giant black fluffy pom-poms for buttons, a ruffled white shirt underneath, and white panty hose. The other was wearing a blinding noonday-sun yellow pantsuit over a black T-shirt being stretched beyond the call of duty to barely cover each of her many upper-body contours. Each was wearing white sneakers and a laminated ID card on a lanyard around her neck. The one in the golden pantsuit had carefully decorated her lanyard by gluing a multicolored series of beads to it at regular intervals.

"I know where we are," said Caroline to the spirit. "With the dullest people, with the dullest jobs, in Dullest City. The first time I flew down here I thought the travel agent told me I was going to Dullest Airport. Anyway, she was right."

Across Independence from one of those monumental neo-classical buildings that said, "Um, hi? Did you know we're important people in here?" was Le Bon Café, where twenty-one-year-old Caroline sat partially hidden by a giant no-fat cappuccino.

"See anyone you recognize?" said the ghost.

"Trot, when he was twenty-five," said Caroline. "He was so different then. He had just moved back to New York after striking out in all the hipster capitals: San Francisco, Seattle, Austin. Unless Milwaukee or St. Louis suddenly developed an underground arts scene, New York looked like his last chance to prove that 'multitalented' meant something other than 'unskilled.' When he came down to visit me in D.C., I was expecting a huge Christmas present."

Instead, he said, "It's not going very well, is it?"

"Uchh, I'm *so* glad you said that," said the twenty-one-year-old Caroline as she rummaged in her bag. Outside, a policeman strolled slowly by, turned around, and came back again as though he could think of no better way to occupy his time.

"I feel for you, Trot, I really do. But, come on, after you did that speed metal band thing? The one where all the songs were made up of lines from Dr. Seuss? Way too cute. And then to try out for that stupid MTV reality show by doing this Hipster-Intellectual-Guy-with-Secret-Romantic-Side act? And then doing that Web site where you posted all those precious pictures of people's favorite objects from when they were little? You know what my mother said about you? She said, 'How much of a career can he make out of wounded whimsy?' It's like you're trying to be oh so tortured and deep, yet playful, wise beyond your years but only if you're still twelve, all that Holden Caulfield kind of crap. Maybe you should just be yourself for once. Whoever that is."

Trot stiffened. "I'm not talking about that. I have some ideas about what to do next. It's a sort of one-man stage show."

"Yeah, that'll really work," Caroline said, taking out a short, shiny silver cylinder. She glossed up.

"Look," said Trot, "that isn't why I asked you here. I wanted to tell you, I think we're at different places, okay?"

"What do you mean?" she said.

"I just think," he continued, "that there are three of us in this relationship. You, me, and your lip gloss."

Caroline rolled her eyes with exquisite disdain. "Well, I'm not giving up my lip gloss."

"Maybe we're not compatible," Trot said.

Caroline felt herself bracing a little. But something clicked on within. She was remembering something her mother had often told her: Why defend when you can attack?

"You know," Caroline said, "we've always thought there was something funny about you."

"We?"

"Mother and I. We've often discussed the acting thing. Frankly, we find it kind of weird. It's like you don't have a personality of your own."

Trot looked defensive. "Acting is, it's what I want. I've decided. What do you want?"

"Not to act. To be," said Caroline.

"Be what?"

"The star of my life. It beats what you're doing. You're not experiencing this conversation. You're just taking notes on my mannerisms so you can use them if you ever play a woman, aren't you?"

Trot was silent.

Caroline attempted to snap her bag shut, but unfortunately it was a zippered nylon Hervé Chapelier number. The zip sound wasn't as dramatic as she'd hoped.

"Mother was right about you," she said.

❧ ❧ ❧

CAROLINE LEFT TROT with the tab, checked her watch, and stormed out, thinking: Mother always said the preemptive breakup is the most satisfying one. And she hurried back across Independence Avenue to "work."

As she waited for the light to change, she wiped a drop of moisture off her cheek: an anger tear, not a sadness one. She was pretty sure of that. A sketchy guy with a grocery-store shopping cart piled six feet high with junk wheeled up to her. He was hunched, withered, and slow. He rattled a coffee cup at her like a Styrofoam maraca.

"Spare some change?" he said.

Caroline looked at the light. Still red. It wasn't this specific dumping that bothered her so much. It was the idea, the label, the *brand* that now attached to her: dumpable. The word was practically stamped all over her. Looking at this guy with his proud cart of refuse, she felt stung. She wanted it to end. For things to be nice. She actually felt like giving this pathetic human being a little something. A little something would prove a little something. It would be a way of nudging the world, reminding it: Caroline didn't deserve this kind of treatment.

"Okay, fine," she said, opening her purse. She unfastened one of the little silver buckles on her pea green Marc Jacobs wallet and shook out a few coins. "Here," she said, handing over the coins. She was about to drop them in the cup when she noticed it was full of pebbles.

"Um," she said, distracted, and in that moment she saw the flash of the knife. Involuntarily, she drew in her breath. She felt like she was sinking through the sidewalk. The knife sliced her shoulder strap, and the bag hit the ground. The filthy man picked up her purse and sprinted away. Caroline's vision turned fuzzy as she watched him run. Stupidly, she thought: Why would he leave behind his shopping cart full of treasures? He only had Caroline's wallet. Caroline, on the other hand, had his smelly carriage full of rags, empty milk cartons, twisted coat hangers, and soggy magazines.

Ding. Her mind cleared. Incensed, Caroline took off after him. But the District had other ideas. Almost immediately, her right heel found the exact matching sidewalk fissure, got stuck, and snapped. She thought about breaking off the other heel and continuing in hot pursuit. But as she limped in frustration a cop stepped out of a flower shop off to the right and ran after the purse snatcher. The sight was, to say the least, unusual. D.C. cops did not give chase or stop crimes in progress. You'd normally consider yourself lucky if one of them succeeded in giving you correct directions to the Kennedy Center.

The thief, looking over his left shoulder at Caroline, didn't even see what was coming up on his right. The cop was younger, fitter, and faster. Within a block he had sped up alongside, resnatched the purse, and tripped the thief, who crashed to the sidewalk and stayed there, panting on his hands and knees, as the cop's hand rested on the butt of his service pistol.

"Yay!" said Caroline, hopping in place. But then the cop did a strange thing. Instead of handcuffing the perp, he stood over him, just talking.

"Why don't you cuff him?" yelled Caroline, though the cop was barely within earshot.

The cop actually turned his back to the thief and set the bag down on top of a metal box full of Washington City Papers. The sketchy guy took this opportunity to tear off down the avenue. The cop bolted after him. This was reassuring, exactly the kind of incompetence Caroline expected from the District. She walked over and retrieved her bag as bad guy and bad cop receded into the distance.

"Look at this mess," said the older Caroline to the ghost, as the two of them followed the younger Caroline into the office building. "Outside, the building says Greco-Roman splendor. Inside it's all about looking like the back room of the post office."

"What were you doing here in the first place?" said the spirit.

"My mother got me this stupid job working for Senator Casby," Caroline said, as she watched herself hang up her coat. "Look how terrible I look. Dumped and mugged in five minutes."

The younger Caroline was still flustered. But she considered that at least her mother would be pleased. She was always nicer to Caroline when a relationship didn't work out, always quick to swoop in offering a weekend spa trip and a running pep talk on the ridiculous, unfixable flaws of guyness.

When Caroline the intern turned around, a large woman loomed in front of her in a terrifying red paisley garment that put the *moo* in *muumuu*. Once in her life, Caroline had seen a larger piece of cloth than the woman's caftan, but it had "Barnum & Bailey" written on it. It was the senator's gargantuan chief of staff, Victoria. Caroline secretly called her Volumnia.

People like Volumnia put in long hours for low pay in a dull gray government-issue working environment, but in exchange for all that they got to train the next generation in bitterness. Volumnia tortured and abused the pretty young things who paused briefly to nab internships here before moving on to far more useful lives. The Volumnias of the District were attics of knowledge, full of details about how things did—or more often did not—work. Like every D.C. rookie, Volumnia had arrived wanting to change the world. Now she spent the days explaining to everyone she worked with why they couldn't change a twenty without a Constitutional amendment.

"Caroline, did you take care of those files?" said Volumnia, not sweetly.

A little voice inside Caroline told her to be respectful to Volumnia because people like her had powerful positions as well as appetites.

Caroline ignored the little voice.

"Did I take care of the files?" said Caroline. "Absolutely. I petted them, and I gave them a snack, and I told them they were a lovely shade of manila."

The words were no sooner spoken than Caroline's thin arms were being loaded with important government folders that were, however, not so important that you couldn't give them to a young intern who plainly had no interest in doing anything except killing a semester's worth of suspension time before returning to college.

"The senator," said Victoria, "wants these taken directly to the Circumlocution Office."

"Circumlocution Office, got it," said Caroline.

"Do you know where the Circumlocution Office is?" asked Volumnia.

"Sort of," said Caroline. "I mean, I assume it's in Washington, isn't it?"

Volumnia sucked in a deep breath and let loose a large, angry sigh.

"Straight down the hallway and hurry up!" she said. "You don't want to be late for the party."

Caroline took off her broken shoe, changed into sensible low Prada heels, and headed down the east corridor scanning nameplates. Meagles. Doyce. Clennam. Everyone was identified as either an assistant deputy or a deputy assistant. There was a really important difference between them, but Caroline had forgotten what it was.

When she reached the end of the east corridor, Caroline hadn't seen any Circumlocution Office.

A red-faced man she passed in the hallway told her the Circumlocution Office was actually down the south corridor. Whimpering slightly, Caroline trudged along reading the names by the doors: nothing close to Circumlocution. When a woman popped out of a rest room, Caroline buttonholed her.

"Excuse me," Caroline said. "Circumlocution Office?"

"Ah," said the woman, who poked around in her ear as though trying to unearth the answer. "Circumlocution, Circumlocution. I was just there the other day. I believe it was that way," she said, pointing down the west corridor with a bit of ear wax.

"It can't be," said Caroline.

"I'm sure it is," said the woman. "Last door on the right."

So Caroline dragged herself on. At the end of the hallway she crossed paths with a fairly cute boy. Well. A very cute boy, actually, with cool black-framed square glasses and just the right amount of gel to make his hair look intentionally messy, which was the one kind of messy you didn't find in D.C. One lock of hair stuck straight up from the crown of his head. His clothes were drab but presentable: well-cut gray flat-front wool slacks, a pressed blue shirt with a subtle herringbone weave, and— bonus!—there were no, repeat no, cuff links. So the head was good, the clothes not wildly objectionable. The deciding vote would be the footwear. Caroline glanced. And shuddered. Chunky, cheap, weather-beaten Timberlands.

But she still had to find the damn office. So she raised her game a notch and pitched a maximum girly crying fit, the kind that discombobulated men and fired up their chivalry juices.

Caroline put her head down and blubbered, "Circum, circum—"

"Circumlocution Office?" said the cute guy.

Caroline perked up. She stopped crying, which was easy because no tears had actually escaped her eyeballs. "Do you know it?" she said. "And do I know you?"

"I don't think—" said the guy, and in his look of uncertainty Caroline spotted the twelve-year-old in him. That lock of unruly hair hadn't changed.

"Philly?" Caroline said. "What are you doing here? Let me guess. You're in charge of the national cookie baking initiative?"

Philly laughed. "It's Philip now, actually, and—wow, it's so cool to run into you," he said excitedly. "But I'm working on taxes. On small businesses. Senator Cuttle is big on helping out on entrepreneurship. In fact, I have an idea for—"

"No time for speeches," Caroline said, flicking her hair like an angry pony. "Circumlocution Office, pronto. Know where it is?" She snapped her fingers.

"Caroline, I. . . . Forget that. How are you? I mean, I haven't seen you for years," Philip said.

"During most of which time I've been looking for the Circumlocution Office. Do you know where it is or what?"

Philip's features froze into a cold smile. "Down that way," he said, pointing at an anonymous door in the distance. "Can't you see it? I mean, it's *right there*. Obviously."

"It is?" said Caroline. "Thanks, li'l Philly. See ya around, kid."

"Right at the end," he said as she marched away. She didn't turn around. Philly shook his head and disappeared into an office marked Sen. Cuttle.

Caroline took a deep breath and straightened her stack of

folders. Her semi-phony tears forgotten, her posture straight, she remembered who she was. She approached the last door in the hall regally.

As she put her hand on the doorknob she saw a tiny plate next to the door: Sen. Casby. She was back where she started.

She began to cry for real, first quietly, then not. One by one, each of the folders slid out of her hands and landed on the floor. She bent over to pick some up and slipped on a pile of slick manila. She was splayed on the floor, one leg tucked under, the other sticking out, when the door opened. It was the senator, that gray multimillionaire and conscience of his time, the Honorable Christopher Casby.

"What on earth are you doing, Caroline?" he said.

"Nothing's going right, everyone gives me conflicting directions, I'm tired, I'm hungry, there isn't anyplace to shop around here and I just feel so stupid because I haven't been able to find the Circumlocution Office," she said, tears streaking her face.

Sen. Casby opened the door wider and turned around. Inside the office people were busily pushing desks to the sides of the room and piling chairs on top of them. Except Volumnia, who stood by the door with her arms folded across her chest.

"Hey everybody," said the old man. "Caroline wants to know where the Circumlocution Office is!"

The entire room burst into laughter. Volumnia's plus-sized body went into laugh spasms. She rocked back and forth and made a series of feral little yelps, like a coyote receiving shock therapy.

"I'd say you found it, young lady!" said the senator. "Come on in."

"But these folders—" Caroline said.

"Victoria?" said the senator, raising one white eyebrow over his handsome steel blue eyes.

"Worthless!" said Volumnia, still choking with giggles. "Another series of reports about government waste. All that stuff can be tossed."

Caroline glared around at the faces of her colleagues, legislative aides and liaisons to his various committees. Except for the senator, who had been movie-star handsome when young, the faces were not pretty. They were not well dressed. All of them had come here to take charge of the country as revenge for not being able to get a date in high school. And now they were all having a great big nerdy D.C. laugh like some kind of national chess club.

"You see, Caroline," said the senator, "Victoria played a naughty trick. Sending newbies to look for the Circumlocution Office is sort of a Washington ritual. It's our little form of hazing. We try it on everybody when they first get here. Hell, it even happened to Ted Kennedy. He was handsome and fit like his brothers when he arrived, a hundred and seventy pounds and dashing, did you know that? His first week on the job, he does three laps around the building looking for the Circumlocution Office. When it's all over he bursts into tears, shuts himself inside his office for days, and leaves orders that no one can see him except for the pizza guy. He was never right after that, poor man, never right."

"How could you do this to me?" pleaded Caroline. "I thought you were a serious politician. You're supposed to help people, not abuse them. I'm telling Mom."

The senator's big, square, smiling face turned serious. "Now Caroline," he said, putting his massive arm around her bony shoulders and walking her toward his inner office, away from the giggling crowd. "Let's be reasonable here. Maybe I can do something to make it up to you. Do you want another military base in your state?"

"I just want to get away from, from—" Caroline stammered.

"Away from who?" said the senator.

"The ugly people!" Caroline wailed.

Sen. Casby stopped and turned around to look at everyone in the suite, which was not so large that you couldn't hear a screaming woman from the other side of it. At least a dozen staffers stood glaring at Caroline's back. *No manners,* they murmured, and *Who does she think she is?* Three or four were so upset that they scratched their hairy brown warts.

Sen. Casby took her into his inner sanctum and shut the door. "Caroline," he said in the honest, carefully modulated baritone that had won over so many people, starting in his early career as a radio voiceover man and continuing throughout his long career as a judge. No one said obvious things quite so magnificently. "It's been such a pleasure to see you grow as a person in the short time I've known you. I shouldn't be saying this, but I'm going to be absolutely frank with you. I consider you a close personal friend of mine. Someone I need on my team. A lot of people around here have smarts—and, ah, you do, too—but you know what's rarer?"

He paused and waited for Caroline to do the audience participation part.

"What?" she said.

"Good old-fashioned gut instinct," he said. "I've sensed it in you. You know why? Because I have the gut. And my gut tells me you've got the gut."

"Stop," said Caroline. "You're making me hungry."

"When your mother told me you'd run into a little trouble at school," the senator continued, in rounded, authoritative tones, "I said to her, 'Caroline sounds like the kind of girl I need in my office, right now.'"

"Because you so needed the kind of girl who skipped finals to attend the Cannes Film Festival?" Caroline said.

"Because I needed a self-starter," said the senator. "Because I needed initiative and creativity. Because I needed someone who could see the big picture. I know you're not cut out for a life on the Hill. But I'll tell you a secret, Caroline. I am personal, close personal, friends with the CFO of one of our leading names in American fashion."

"Calvin Klein?"

"Close! Lane Bryant."

Caroline felt like she was going to be sick. But there was nothing in her stomach except a skinny cappuccino and dissolved Altoids.

"Your mother's a very special lady, Caroline," said the senator. "I treasure our friendship. And I treasure her daughter."

Caroline sniffled. "Enough to help me out with a job issue?"

"Anything," said the senator. "Anything within my power."

"Good," said Caroline. "Then fire Victoria."

The senator's smile froze awkwardly on his face. He looked like a stroke victim.

"Huh-HA!" said the senator. "Victoria has been working for me for twenty-two years!" he said. "Do you know what she's been doing all that time?"

"Counting her chins?" said Caroline. "Combing her mustache?"

"She's practically been my brain," said Sen. Casby. "If I want to remember my anniversary, or know whether I should vote yes or no on the education bill, I go straight to her. She's a fixture in this town. She's like the Jefferson Memorial."

"We're talking size, right?"

"Huh-HA!" the Senator said again, in some sort of weird compromise laugh that had been carefully constructed to appeal to several different constituencies. He opened the door and clapped her on the back. "Enjoy the party, Caroline."

As the first guests trickled in, Caroline began composing a resignation letter in her head. What was keeping her in Dork Central even one moment longer? It certainly wasn't her coworkers, people like the bucktoothed woman with the red beady eyes who had come to Washington to save the rats she defended as "urban wildlife," possibly because they were her relatives, or the suckup who on Caroline's first day had taken her aside to whisper, "Senator Casby's going to be president some day. Have you experienced his handshake? It's a handshake of hope. It's a handshake to the future." Or people like Philly—sorry, Philip, who was coming through the door right now. He nodded in her direction, stopped at the bar, and headed over with two red plastic cups.

"Sorry I played that little trick on you," said Philip, handing her a gin and tonic. "I'll hate myself in the morning."

"You have my permission to start right now," said Caroline.

Now that she wasn't distracted by her fool's errand, it was hard not to notice his yummy fudge brown eyes, his artfully tousled hair, the V-ish shape of his torso in a land where most men tried to be larger than life but wound up larger than sumo wrestlers. Philly had lost the cookie fat of their private school days. And then some.

On the other hand, he was a total jerk.

"I know it's stupid," continued Philip. "But that old Circumlocution Office gag is sort of part of the code around here. Along with the Constitution and practical footwear."

Caroline smiled gradually.

"How is your holiday season going?" he asked.

"It bites," said Caroline.

"Oh," said Philip. "Is Christmas especially hard without . . . him?"

"No," she said. "Christmas is not especially hard without a father. The Thursday after Labor Day is not especially hard without a father. April twenty-sixth is not especially hard without a father. No day is especially hard because every day is hard without a father, especially a father you never even met. It's this ever-present dull pain. He's always on my mind. Or rather, missing from my mind. He shows up in my dreams. Always. Whether I'm awake or asleep, he's always there. Except, not."

"What do you think he, um, was like?"

Caroline was too ready to answer. "Large hands. Smells like leather. Honest and tough. Maybe a little distant, chooses his words carefully but funny when he has something to say. Quirky. Hard to get to know, if you aren't in his inner circle. The kind of dad who makes fun of your prom dress but he's a rock in an emergency. And tall. He has to be someone who could protect me from anything. Had to be."

They looked at each other. Philip gave an embarrassed little subject-changing smile.

"So what are you doing here? You look so New York."

"I got suspended from school for a semester. My mom is dating Senator Casby, so she got me a gig. I thought, maybe I'll meet someone cool. Just one cool person and it would have been worthwhile. Instead. . . ." She made a gesture that indicted the room. "This. The Land That Cool Forgot."

Philip set his cup down, walked over to the bar, and turned around. He slouched a little, shot his cuffs, gave the world an accusatory glance. Then he spotted Caroline out of nowhere, glanced away shyly, looked right back at her. He smiled. She smiled. Then he sauntered back.

"Hi," he said. "I'm cool."

Caroline giggled. "Nice to meet you, Mr. Cool."

"And you are—?"

"Leaving."

"Allow me to buy you another drink."

"Sorry, no time. But if you give me the cash I promise to buy myself a drink later and think of you."

"Why don't I come along and provide a visual reminder?"

"No need. Isn't cool a state of mind?"

"More like a state of ecstasy."

"Personally, I'm more interested in the state of Alabama."

"That's just where I was heading! Let's share a cab."

"I have a few errands to do. You go first, I'll catch up later."

"Okay, let's skip the drinks and get married instead."

"I hardly ever marry strange men at office parties."

"I told you, I'm not strange. I'm cool."

"This evening is over."

"Perhaps. But the night has just begun."

"Maybe for you. Not for us."

"Maybe you don't trust us?"

"Maybe you're smarter than you look."

"True, if I look like Einstein."

"You think you're so cool."

"That's *Joe* Cool. With a *J*."

"Joe. Philip."

"What?"

"Get me a drink."

Philip smiled. "That was the last of the tonic. Gin and ginger ale okay?"

"Yes," said Caroline. "But I'll have the ginger ale on the side."

Hovering above, the ghost smiled at the older Caroline.

"Oh, shut up," Caroline said.

"I didn't say anything."

"You're worse than my shrink," said Caroline.

As the last word came out of Caroline's mouth, a hush

plopped onto the room. It was as though federal mirth funding had been repealed at exactly 8:18 PM.

Everyone was gawping at a hulking futuristic motorcycle cop who was clomping slowly through the crowd in calf-high leather boots, a big scary helmet, the kind of aviator shades that said, "Hi, I'm available to guard Southern chain gangs," and a starched black uniform that struggled not to tear itself to shreds as it stretched across the plain of his massive chest. He hooked his thumbs in his gun belt as though hoping someone would save him the trouble of speaking by requesting that he open fire.

"Evenin' folks," the cop said in a drawl that sounded like it had been cut in sheets and laid out to cure under the South Carolina sun for the month of August.

No one said anything.

"Officer," said the senator everyone knew was gay, "if there's something—"

"SHADDAP!" said the cop, circling the room. His handcuffs jangled softly against his belt as he snarled at eighteen-year-old interns drinking blackberry schnapps. He glared at their supervisors, the twenty-five-year-old law-school grads who worked as L.A.'s, and the supervisors' supervisors, the forty-five-year-old human clots. When he finally got around to the three duly elected senators, his look suggested extreme irritation of the bowels.

All of them—the senators, the ambitious young staffers, and the time-serving old ones—held their breath thinking: maybe if I remain perfectly still, my headshot won't turn up on CNN tomorrow.

"I'll git something straight with you ladies and fellas," he continued. "We've had reports of unnecessary noise makin' and dancin' and carryin' on. We've had reports of underage drinkin'. We've had dis-gust-in' reports of liberties taken with young females. Now whut I wanna know is—"

The room gulped.

The cop popped off his helmet, flicked off his sunglasses between his thumb and forefinger, and beamed. "Where can I get me some a that?"

The room exhaled, burst into laughs, silently evaluated the dryness of its underwear. Two words bounced around the room: Captain Cuttle.

The man in the cop getup was Capitol Hill's number one prankster, America's most famously tortured veteran and incorruptible truth teller, and very possibly the next president of the United States, Sen. Kingman Cuttle himself.

Cuttle was an ex-Navy captain, and for years he'd been the most popular surviving symbol of an unpopular Asian war. So he was kinda like the coolest pants at JC Penney, Caroline had always thought. This particular pair of pants, however, had been shot, severely burned, and finally hung on wooden pegs and beaten with bamboo rods for four years in a rotting 110 degree dungeon. The senator had later published a best-selling memoir about the experience, jocularly titled *The Spa*. (He swore to interviewers that he wasn't joking when he told them that prolonged imprisonment had cured his acne.)

In the three weeks that she had worked in Sen. Casby's office in the same building, Caroline had sometimes passed Sen. Cuttle in the lobby, where he'd often be found fetching a tray of lattes to surprise his interns or talking Redskins football with the probably illegal immigrant (and therefore nonvoter) who worked at the newsstand. Always, Sen. Cuttle had given Caroline a broad smile and a "How ya doin'."

As Philip and the other guests started to form a bottleneck of sycophancy around the man who encouraged people to call him Capt. Cuttle or Sen. Kingman, Caroline almost unconsciously stepped around behind Philip so that the senator would be sure to get a good look at her from her better side.

"Hey, hey, hey," the senator was saying as he slapped the men's shoulders. The women he gave big hugs to, and the women he knew he grabbed around the waist and tango-dipped as they shrieked with delight. It was brilliant shtick. Caroline watched it all without looking.

"Who's this?" Cuttle was saying to Philip. "Your date? I always thought you were gay."

Half a dozen staffers around Cuttle guffawed and nodded to one another. Another zinger. With any other senator, half the people in the room would have been on the line to tell a reporter about this outrageous breach of good conduct, but being a former POW put Cuttle above ordinary rules. How could you possibly make a claim of hurt feelings against a guy who had stainless steel shins and a plate in his head? The man's body contained so much metal he was affectionately known to the popular press not as Capt. Cuttle or Sen. Kingman but as Sen. Tin Man.

"I'm Caroline," she said. "You may have met my mother La. Lately she has been, escorting, Senator Casby."

"Escorting?" said the Tin Man. "Is that what you call it?

Undertaking is what I call it. When Casby goes out for a drink, he orders a formaldehyde martini. I mean, you and I learned about the Civil War in school. He read about it in the newspapers."

Everyone laughed again, especially Sen. Casby, who was standing six inches away from the Tin Man trying to look like a bronze statue called *Youthful Vigor*. His posture, however, suggested *Melting Snowman*.

"No hard feelings, old-timer," said Sen. Tin Man, laughing. "Let's you and me pose for a picture. All right? You?" He pointed to a young male staffer who had been wandering around the room with a digital camera.

Sen. Casby perked up. A picture with Sen. Tin Man? It wouldn't take long to leak it to the press. Together with a little anonymous item about how Sen. Casby was in the running to be Secretary of the Treasury in the future Cuttle administration.

"Come on Chris, boy, try and look alive. I know it's a stretch," said Sen. Tin Man. "Stick your paw out, that's right, ready to snap the photo there, son?"

"Yes, sir," said the young staffer. Sen. Casby put out his right paw as instructed and left it there, suspended in space for a moment.

"And, bam!" said Sen. Tin Man. He extended his hand to Sen. Casby. And left it there.

Sen. Casby looked at the disembodied beige lump of hand he was holding. His next spoken word wasn't so much a word as a string of Anglo-Saxon speech fragments. And it wasn't so much spoken as screamed.

The room hesitated, drew its breath, and laughed, louder and longer than last time. As he hollered and blanched, Sen. Casby dropped a heavy life-sized latex model of the human hand on the floor. He looked like he was about to join it there. The room got out its cell phones, pressed two-thirds of 911, and awaited developments. No one actually went so far as to rush to Casby's side and ask him whether he was aware that he looked like he had just been pulled out of a morgue drawer.

"You want a piece of me?" said Sen. Tin Man, waving the stump where he ordinarily plugged in his right hand. "Huh? You want a piece of me? Boy, you got it, pappy!"

The hovering Caroline spoke to the ghost in a very small voice. "Please," she said, "it was sweet to see Philly again. Can't we just leave it there? As a nice little memory morsel? Afterward, things started getting weird. I'll admit I have regrets about a lot of stuff, okay? If we can just end the scene right now."

"Sorry," said the spirit. "No à la carte ordering."

The room was whistling and applauding. And that applause provided the perfect entrance for the extremely, perhaps excessively, fashionable woman who happened to choose that moment to open the door and walk in. She kissed and smiled her way over to the younger Caroline, whose stomach was flinching.

"I know her," said Philip.

"You met years ago," Caroline said.

"I mean, I know her from billboards, or TV commercials or something," Philip said.

"Do you want to get out of here?" Caroline whispered, tugging on his sleeve.

Philip looked at her. "Don't walk away."

"Not walking, sprinting," she said, but too late.

"Caro!" said La.

"Merry Christmas, Mother," said Caroline uncertainly.

"Chris tells me the grandest things about you. It was a foregone conclusion that you'd be the brightest new star in Washington," La said, beaming.

"Mother, this is—"

"The waiter?" said La. "Double vodka, rocks, that would be lovely."

Philip shifted his weight in his Timberlands and looked at Caroline.

"Mother, he's not—"

"Very well dressed for a waiter, I know dear. It's Washington, not New York. All the waiters here dress as if they were janitors or senatorial aides or something."

Philip cleared his throat. "I am, actually, an aide to Senator Cuttle," he said, extending his hand. "Philip."

La looked at the outstretched hand, shivered, and then threw her stole around her bare collarbone as if an Arctic breeze had whistled through the room, which, of course, it had.

"Double vodka rocks, was it?" he said. "Always glad to serve the constituents."

And Philip made an exit that, Caroline noted, was rather graceful. The bar was only ten feet away, but it was far enough to discreetly cede the social repair job to Caroline.

"Mother," Caroline stage-whispered, "you were being rude to Philip. He was at our brother school when I was prepping, remember? He's a very important L.A. to Senator Cuttle, who's a lot more important than Senator Casby, don't you think?"

"Darling," said La, "Senator Casby has the most viselike crush on me, didn't you know? You might have to treat him with a little more respect someday."

Caroline's nostrils flared a little with disbelief. "You think he's going to—are you two going to be—?"

"It's been discussed," said La. "All the signs are there. Dear, I've been proposed to thousands of times, I have a very scientific eye for these things. But of course I've turned them all down. Do you know why?" she said, looking over her shoulder at Philip, who was taking baby steps back to Caroline, carefully holding a large red plastic cup in each hand and pressing a third between them.

"Yes," said Caroline.

"Good, then you won't be surprised when I tell you. It's because of you. None of them were ever good enough to be your stepfather."

Philip was back. "Double vodka rocks," he said, thrusting the middle cup in La's general direction.

"You're a dear," La said, although the tone of voice she employed was more commonly associated with statements like, "You're standing on my big toe."

Caroline took her drink. "Mother," she said, "Philip is working on some important new tax legislation for small businesses. Isn't that right, Philip?"

La cut off Philip's response before it started, merely by raising her chin. It was a devastating chin. Few would dare to contradict it. And the chin's capacity to sow confusion and terror was nothing compared to what the eyebrows could do. Caroline had once seen a two-millimeter repositioning of La's left eyebrow cause Diane Von Furstenberg to get so rattled that she touched up her lips with nail polish during a Ralph Lauren show in Bryant Park.

Now La's chin was aimed squarely at Philip's throat, and her right eyebrow was preparing to strike. Caroline saw it, and stepped in to try to save him. With—

"He's like the Stella McCartney of Capitol Hill."

Immediately after saying these words, Caroline had the sensation that she had walked up to the cobra and sharpened its fangs.

"Oh!" said La. "Then you must have a very glamorous family."

"Not really," said Philip.

"And you have an exciting business of your own?" said La, nodding enthusiastically as if Philip had just said it was only a matter of time until he inherited the throne of Paramount Pictures.

"Really, I'm just helping out the senator with a few things."

"What sorts of things?" said La, her hands clasped eagerly.

"We're working on various initiatives that we hope to bring up in the next term. Also, there's, um, helping with the queries that come in. From constituents. And answering them, of course."

"I see," said La. "So you're a kind of . . . file clerk?"

Philip bit his lower lip.

"Then that would explain why you dress like one!" La said. "Tell me, where did you get those shoes?" She motioned at his chunky nut brown Timberlands. "Home Depot? No, silly of me, you made them yourself? In the introductory leatherworking class at summer camp? When you were thirteen? And since you make your own shoes, then, in a way, you're *just like Stella McCartney*." This was the point where La actually reached out and grabbed a not-small portion of Philip's left cheek between her thumb and index finger.

"Caro," she added, "I had no idea you dated office boys!"

"I don't," said Caroline. She glared at Philip, her eyes ordering him to say something, to fight back. Instead, his gaze just shifted uneasily between La and a fixed point in the middle distance.

"What other radical ideas have they been teaching you up at college?" said La. "Never mind, I don't want to know. There's no class in this country, is there, anymore? People can just go off and marry whomever they please. Coal miners, construction workers, civil servants."

"Mother," said Caroline, forcing the sound out through clenched teeth using some sort of ventriloquist's trick, "you're dating a government employee."

"Darling," said La, "calling Senator Casby a government employee is like calling Coco Chanel a sales clerk at Ann Taylor. I can see the bottom of my cup, Philip, there's a good lad."

As La shook her ice cubes at Philip and he unhesitatingly fetched her another drink, the older Caroline tapped her spirit on the shoulder. Or tried to.

"Are we done here?" she said. "If you're trying to remind me of why Philip was completely inappropriate for me, you've succeeded."

"You'll learn," said the tiny sprite. "Everyone does."

"From you?" said Caroline. "Listen, Tinkerbell, next time ask them to assign you a class in something you know by heart, like scenery chewing."

"Any thoughts on what we've just witnessed?" said the spirit. "Could you have handled that better?"

"I haven't thought of little Philly in years," Caroline lied.

"We can tell when you're lying," said the ghost.

"Um, really?" said Caroline, twirling her hair around her index finger.

"Psych!" said the ghost. "I *so* got you. You're into him."

"Oh stop it."

"Touch my dress."

"What if I don't?" said Caroline.

"Fine, I'll just leave you dangling in limbo above an eerie netherworld of things that once were. Okay? Does that float your boat?"

Caroline sulked, looked at her fingernails, and decided to rummage through her bag for a stick of gum. But there was no gum. Also, no bag. To be completely technical, Caroline didn't, at this moment, have an actual body that could be used for gum chewing. A lifetime of accumulating the correct accessories had come to this. She had nothing when she needed everything. It was like showing up at the Oscars in a Gap turtleneck, the way Sharon Stone once had.

The little ghost folded her arms across her chest. "I'm waiting. I have all eternity."

"I hope your puberty is torture," said Caroline, reaching out to touch the ghost brat's garment.

The office party turned blurry, shivered, and folded in on itself, leaving a blank space that grew gray and, finally, black.

Caroline didn't remember closing her eyes, but now she opened them. She was in a big soft fluffy bed, an altar of cotton. Her sheets, graced by the most elegantly contrasting stripes of ivory and eggshell, were 900-thread count. Home again. No more spunky/demonic child stars. No more heavy irony. No more dealing with her mother from a position of inexperience.

She rolled over on her side, propped herself on her elbow, and looked at her exquisite Movado bedside timepiece. Right now the clock said 12:15 AM. Which meant it was really 12:10, as she always set her clocks five minutes ahead. But while she stared at it she realized in horror the second hand had stopped its majestic sweep. One of two completely inexcusable things was happening: either time had come to a standstill or Movado had gifted her with a bum clock.

Of course, Caroline had been dreaming. That was the simple explanation. She got out of bed, reached for her slippers, and removed a Kit Kat bar from each of them. As she devoured them, she hatched a plan.

Going to the kitchen, she chose a Japanese Diet Coke from

the Yokohama bottler. This variety supposedly contained so much caffeine that it had inspired among true connoisseurs a legend that it was actually used by ER nurses to treat cases of cardiac arrest. Caroline bolted down the first bottle and then opened another. No sleep, no more weird-you-out dreams.

At least that was the plan.

chapter nine

WHILE CAROLINE GUZZLED IN THE KITCHEN, THE living room lit up as if the sun had risen behind her couch. Caroline almost ran in. All around the room were hung thick velvety green and red curtains. The room was stacked floor to ceiling with the most amazing treats. Boxes of Twinkies, Ho Hos, Devil Dogs, and Ding Dongs. The entire family of Little Debbie. On the mantelpiece, a tantalizing row of red boxes containing steamy hot McDonald's fries. Pints of Häagen-Dazs and Ben & Jerry's, every flavor, arranged in an eight-foot pyramid. Cans of whipped cream and tubs of Cool Whip. Hot fudge sauce and jars of chopped peanuts and almonds. Box after box of Snickers bars, Reese's Peanut Butter Cups, M&M's, plain old irresistible Hershey Bars. Gallons of full-fat milk to wash them down with. My God, there were at least a dozen gallon tubs of Skippy peanut butter. Not a rice cake or carrot stick in sight. There was so much to eat that Caroline didn't at first notice the fat guy sitting on her couch.

Relaxing with his feet up, as though waiting for the M5 bus to make its next stop between the lamp and the armoire, was Mr. Barkis, with his brown uniform shirt completely unbuttoned and his white T-shirt fully on display as if to say Yes, this is what a blue-collar yokel looks like, and do you have a problem with that?

"Oh my God, you scared me," said Caroline. "Do you have a package for me? You could have just left it with the doorman."

"That ain't why I'm here," said Mr. Barkis. "I moonlight as a ghost. Major, major OT, I'm tellin' ya, ya should try it."

"You're kidding."

"Yeah, right? But not really," said Mr. Barkis, trying hard to look grave. "I am the Ghost of Christmas Present. So, like, check me out."

Caroline was checking out everything in the room except Barkis. "Does that mean we're still operating under ghostly-netherworld rules?" she said. "I just need to know if calories consumed now will count in real life."

"Knock yaself out," said Barkis.

Caroline opened a pint of Ben & Jerry's Karamel Sutra and took a whiff. "Wait, does that mean you're sure these calories don't count? Or you just don't care?"

"I like a girl's gotta little meat on her bones, know what I'm sayin'?"

Caroline closed the ice cream and turned her back in a snit. "I am not a steak."

"Yeah, you're definitely not a rump roast, if you catch what I'm sayin'. So you wanna take a little ride wit me?"

"It's optional?"

"Not really," Barkis said. "I was jus' makin' conversation."

"Color me unshocked. So what am I supposed to do?" she said, examining his wrinkled, unbuttoned uniform shirt. "Touch your garment? Is it okay if I wrap some cellophane around my hand first? No offense."

"Garmint?" he said. "I was thinkin' we'd take my truck."

In the elevator on the way down, Caroline buttoned up her suede car coat, tied her scarf cutely around her neck, and evaluated her new ghost. He didn't seem to be exhibiting much ghostly behavior. He wasn't translucent or floaty or anything. Was the Afterlife's dress code come as you are? Caroline had an unnerving suspicion that there must be a more exclusive heaven, and she had to do something to get on the list.

To be polite, it was necessary to speak.

"Interesting pair of white sneakers you're wearing, Mr. Barkis. So fun! How the heel lights up when you step on it. It's a . . . statement," she said, though the only statement he was successfully making was, "I need help."

"Yeah?" said Mr. Barkis. "My nephew has a pair a these. I figured, why not? I'm a little kid at heart, I know. But I figyah if ya can't be a kid at Christmas, when can ya?"

Rudy the doorman was snoring in his chair as Barkis led Caroline out to his brown UPS truck, which was parked in front of a hydrant. There was a sheaf of parking tickets on the windshield. Barkis grabbed them, hopped into the driver's seat, and stuffed them into the glove compartment, which was bursting with hundreds more parking tickets.

As Caroline climbed up, Barkis settled in and started up

the truck. Caroline stood on the bare metal floor in front of her seat, crouching under the roof, hesitating. Strewn all over the worn vinyl passenger seat were empty soft drink cans, french fry wrappers, leaky pens, mysterious stains of several colors.

"So, you gonna sit?" said Barkis, as he pulled into the street.

"I'm fine standing," said Caroline.

Barkis seemed to doubt this.

"Really. I'm not a princess, I'm just not used to proletarian transportation systems, you know? I prefer wafting, actually. Can't we waft? It's so environmentally friendly. Zero emissions."

"That's okay, you don't need ta sit," said Barkis, as he hit the clutch. "Suit yaself." And with that he shifted gears and stepped on the gas. Caroline was flung back into the seat, her butt on top of several crumpling, crumbling, moist, possibly moving things. She did not hesitate to scream, "Ewww!" But the word was inadequate.

"It's okay, it's okay," said Barkis. "Just sweep all that stuff on the floor, don't worry about breakin' any ah it. You break it, you bought it, all right? Just kiddin'. And if you see my pet ferret undah there, don't touch him, he bites, all right? Again, kiddin', just pullin' ya leg. My ferret don't bite, lately. Not blondes, at any rate. I mean, not *natural* blondes. Kiddin'!"

As the truck rolled through sparse traffic on Second Avenue and Caroline struck a prim ferret-avoidance perch, day began to break. The sun seemed to be zooming up into the sky. Barkis kept up a steady stream of exhausting chatter in which he referred to himself in the third person, usually as "Homeboy" or "the Kid." His speech was sprinkled with fifteen-year-old hip-hop phrases that he often misused. He seemed to believe that "pimpin'" meant "in a good mood," and he kept referring to women as "the ladies." The sky was bright now.

"Where are you taking me?" Caroline said.

"No chance, no chance," said Barkis. "You'll see when you see."

The area north of Times Square was in full throng. Trucks and cabs bore down on the occasional out-of-state car, complete with children's noses pressed to the backseat windows. The sun was already going down.

"Heh, heh, wouldja lookit that?" Barkis said. "Every time I think about Christmas, I see it through the kids' eyes. It's all so new to them, ya know? The sparkle, the lights, the wondah. It's like everythin's coated with magic dust. And all the giant decorations, alla that holly and wreaths and candy canes hangin' from the buildins. I wondah what alla that stuff means? It's gotta have a deepah meanin'. And Yuletide. What's Yule? Don't ya wondah?"

"Not at the present time, no. Try me in fifty years."

"It's gotta mean somethin'," said Barkis.

"But nothing should mean anything, that's the point," said Caroline. "The minute something becomes symbolic it stops being cool and starts being homework. That's what I can't stand about Christmas and Hanukkah and Kwanzaa and whatever they come up with next. Well, one of the things I can't stand about them. They're so retro, so hopelessly stuck in their stupid symbols. It's the same old look, year after year."

"So," said Barkis, "Christmas is, what—"

"Tired, that's right. It's been over two thousand years. Time to get some work done. I mean, eggnog? That's not a cocktail, it's an omelet in a glass. And mistletoe? What is that, a license for sexual harassment? Don't even get me started on the red-and-green Christmas card with the adorable photos of gap-toothed toddlers. Am I supposed to congratulate people because they *reproduced?* How much skill does that take? People should send out photos of themselves hooking up their digital cable. Then I'd be impressed."

Barkis was quiet.

"Listen," said Caroline, "are we really going to ride around in a UPS truck all day? I mean, where's the magic in that? Are you even a ghost in the first place? Or are you just a truck driver who tipped my doorman a few bucks to get into my apartment?"

"Hmm, yeah, good point," Barkis said. "I'll be sure and take up alla ya ideas wit the magic department. I'm pals wit the head fairy." He slammed on the gas as he swerved around a corner onto West Forty-second. But traffic had come to a halt going west so he peeled out of his lane and started barreling down the eastbound side of the street, into oncoming traffic.

"Okay, okay, okay," said Caroline. "I'm sorry! Cut it out! We're going to die."

"Nah, we got too many places ta go ta taday," said Barkis, shifting heavily. Caroline noticed that he was shifting into what appeared to be seventh gear.

Barkis slammed on the accelerator again as a HumBug picked

up steam coming the other way. Caroline hid her face with her hands and braced, screaming.

Caroline had read (in a magazine) that these last seconds before an accident take on the feel of eternity. But by the time she counted to ten, first in English and then again in French, she felt like uncovering her face, just to get a read on the situation and figure out how much longer it would be until she'd have to start picking tiny HumBug parts out of her teeth.

But the HumBug was below, stuck in traffic. The truck was floating through the air, zipping across Forty-second above the street, above the other cars, even above the buses. She was at eye level with third-floor office workers in the buildings they passed, yet no one seemed to raise an eyebrow. Either the truck was invisible or New Yorkers had become really seriously jaded.

"Wheee," said Caroline, sticking her feet out the door.

"Magic enough for ya?" said Barkis, whistling the theme song from a kiddie movie. Caroline smiled. Barkis really seemed to believe in things, in his harmless, soybean-sized working-stiff's brain.

That's when she saw herself below, lying on the sidewalk surrounded by tourists. Up the block, one tourist was filming the homeless guy who lived under the overhang of the Belle Connerie building. A hand emerged from the pile of filthy clothes to make a go-away gesture at the guy with the camera, who shut off his video gadget and wandered over to join the crowd clustered around Caroline, who was still out cold on the sidewalk. He turned the camera back on and began to record just as she started to regain consciousness. The HumBug that had pulled a U-turn on Forty-second Street was barely visible to the west, still speeding up.

"One of those tourists was filming me," Caroline said to Barkis. "But why was he filming that homeless guy?"

Barkis shrugged. "Mysteries, mysteries."

"Seriously, I was nearly killed yesterday," she said. "In traffic. I still don't know what happened. One minute I was collapsing in the street with a miniature SUV about to run me over, and the next minute I was back on the sidewalk, unconscious."

"Yeah?" said Barkis.

"I wonder if that guy with the camera saw what happ—"

The sentence was cut cleanly in two by what Caroline saw up ahead. Her own office window, high above Forty-second Street. In it loomed Arabella Allen, excitedly looking around the office, redecorating tools in her eyes. She was talking with evident delight and much waving of arms on her cell phone. Caroline could hear every word as if she was right there in the room.

"My daughter would be a perfect candidate to replace this loser we just axed," Arabella was saying. "No, I didn't have a clue where to place her! I was just hoping that after I started sniffing around the office, someone would commit career suicide. And someone did! The accessories director! It was so marvelous the way she imploded. She literally burned her career to the ground! Of course I told Page Six about it. I'll make a few phone calls over the holidays just to make doubly sure she never works in this town again. I do mean that literally. I've put the word out at Belle Connerie. And I know simply everyone at Time Inc., Hachette, Hearst, all the magazine companies. None of them will hire her after I speak to them. She won't be able to find work answering phones at *Road & Track*. I will chase that girl off this island. She'll be lucky to get work in New Jersey."

Caroline was already feeling not well when Barkis banked the wheel hard again. Her stomach moved with it. This time they were speeding by one of the new superswank all-amenities buildings that had popped up not far south of Times Square. Caroline saw two faces she knew. Anyone could have seen them, since they had twelve-foot picture windows and a stunning view. Just a couple like any other getting a head start on Christmas, exchanging exquisitely tiny packages. Behind them stood a Christmas tree underdecorated to perfection. The girl had a large head, a tiny body, and a dazzling underbite. It was Miss January *Vogue* cover, Eddie Granger, all English, all supermodel. The one who was rumored to be dating Belle Connerie's owner. Except maybe not. Because here she was on Christmas Eve, holding a glass of champagne in her picture window like a billboard for the good life, two hundred feet above the ground-level swarm. She picked up the bottle of champagne and topped off the glass of her companion, a man with big white actor's teeth and longish wavy hair. It was certainly not Trot. It could not be Trot. It was Trot.

The two of them clinked glasses ever so gently, yet just firmly enough to shatter something inside Caroline.

Trot and Eddie. No. But that would explain why Trot had acted so weird this morning. And why he had carried a copy of *Vogue*. He probably got a thrill out of buying a copy at the newsstand, right in the Belle Connerie building's lobby. Caroline wondered whether Paul Dombey knew what Eddie was up to.

Barkis zoomed past the building. Caroline stretched around to look behind her as the truck sailed by. No doubt about it. Either they were a devoted couple or they were giving each other mouth-to-mouth.

"Whoo!" said Barkis as he banked sharply on Twenty-fourth Street, heading west.

"I think I'm going to be sick," said Caroline.

"How's dat?" said Barkis.

"I just saw a guy I know tongue wrestling with a super-model."

"A supermodel? I'd hit dat. They're good kissers."

Caroline lowered her head and groaned. She sounded like a sheep. "What man is ever going to marry me?" she wailed.

Barkis shrugged. "Barkis is willin'," he said.

"What man who isn't a truck driver is ever going to marry me?"

"Your loss," said Barkis. "I may drive a truck, but I got style."

As he said the words he spun the wheel, threw the parking brake and made the truck fall suddenly to earth. It was perfectly positioned over the closest thing to a parking space in sight, which was a spot occupied by a HumBug. There was a crunchy noise as Barkis landed the truck on top of it.

"Those new HumBug mini-SUVs?" Barkis said, more in sorrow than in anger. "Unsafe in a collision."

Disoriented as she was by what Arabella Allen had said, by Trot and Eddie, by Barkis's driving, and most of all by Barkis's parking, Caroline still had enough of her self left to automatically check her hair in the side-view mirror: not good.

"Heah we are, everybawdy out, ladies first," said Barkis.

Barkis hopped out of the car. Then he came around to Caroline's side and helped her step down. Which was decent of him. Her boots weren't made for leaping.

"Here's the part I love," he said, going around in back and yanking open the cargo bay. Inside were neat stacks of brown paper packages. He took out a handcart and propped it up on the sidewalk next to the truck. He checked his handheld computer, selected fifteen or so boxes, loaded them carefully on his handcart, and secured them with an elastic cord. Caroline looked around: New York City Housing Authority Chelsea Houses, said a faded and peeling sign. Empty plastic bags bounced over the ground; more were stuck in the naked talons of the trees that clawed at the sky overhead. The sidewalks sparkled with tiny bits of broken glass, ground almost to dust. Someone had covered a rusted fence with handbills for a band called Tom All Alone's.

"Oh dear," said Caroline. "Could I just wait in the truck?"

"Ya won't wanna miss this," said Barkis. "Here ya go. This one's yours."

He stood the handcart up in front of Caroline. "Oh, ha ha," she said without laughing. "Thanks but no thanks. You must have me confused with a manual laborer."

"Ya have to do what I say," Barkis said, as he loaded up a second handcart for himself. "I'm a ghost."

Caroline turned her back on the handcart. "Ordinarily I'd be thrilled, but I just had my nails done," she said.

Barkis fixed up his handcart just so and tipped it back on its wheels. "Race ya," he said.

"I am not doing this," she said as she tipped the handcart back. "I am totally against this. What am I doing?" she began to push the cart forward. She was breaking into a jog.

"You know how in a dream you can't control what you do?" Barkis said, as he jogged behind her on the sidewalk, pushing his cart effortlessly.

"I guess," said Caroline, who was huffing a little. Normally she only breathed heavily in the company of highly paid fitness instructors who trained her how to move oxygen in and out of her lungs.

"That's the best part of dreams, ain't it?" Barkis said. "You're totally out of control."

"I'm totally out of control," Caroline said, still picking up speed.

"That's the spirit," Barkis said.

"No," Caroline said, out of breath, her cheeks going in and out madly in a hunt for air that wasn't coming. "I mean, I'm *totally out of control*." Her cart got the better of her and she found herself just hanging on as it sped down a small hill and crashed into a mailbox.

"It's okay," said Barkis. "I didn't give ya anything fragile, so we're good heah."

"Aren't these projects dangerous?" Caroline said as the two of them started pushing their carts down a little footpath toward one of the towers.

"You'll see," said Barkis.

At the entryway to the building, a depressing twenty-two-story people shed of dirty yellowish brick, a girl of about twelve was sitting on the step combing her younger sister's hair with a big pink plastic comb.

"Hey, Mr. UPS man!" said the smaller girl.

"Got anything for me?" said the older one.

"That depends," said Barkis. "Do you live in Fifteen-G?"

"Yeah," said both girls.

"That's too bad," he said. "Because I have a lot of stuff for Five-D."

The older girl shook her head and smiled. "We live there, too," said the smaller girl hopefully. Her sister smacked the top of her head with the comb.

"All right," said Barkis, winking at her. "I guess I'll see ya up there."

Caroline smiled and pushed her way up a cement ramp as Barkis held the door.

"First stop, Three-C," Barkis said on the elevator. "Neck-ett. Nice lady."

Caroline and Barkis pushed their handcarts off the elevator to 3C. Mr. Barkis pressed the door buzzer. Inside, there was a TV, a mysterious thumping, and a whole lot of boiling cabbage. "Who is it?" came a voice. Something slid behind the peephole. Caroline wondered how fat she looked through a fish-eye lens.

"United Parcel Service," said Barkis, winking at Caroline next to him.

There was a sliding of a bolt, and the door flew open. A tired-looking girl of about seventeen stood before them with a toddler squirming under one arm and a hairy, wriggling animal under the other one. It appeared to be an untamed dog, or possibly a warthog. In the background, a seemingly limitless series of small children was racing up to the highest point of the couch in the living room and jumping off it. Thump, thump, thump. The tired teen smiled at Barkis.

"Oh, Mr. UPS man, how can I thank you?"

"By giving me your autograph, Miz Neckett," said Barkis, touching a button on his handheld computer and handing it over to her.

"Please, call me Charlonda." She put her toddler down on the floor, signed with the blunt plastic pen, then took the package in her arms and hugged it.

"What is it?" Caroline whispered, nudging Barkis.

Barkis just chuckled. The woman looked back at Caroline, smiled, and started to say something. But Barkis stopped her.

"That's okay, Miz Neckett," he said. "We don't need ta know. A Merry Christmas to ya."

"Thank you," said the girl, giving the box a squeeze. "You have a merry one too, Mr. UPS man."

When the door shut, Caroline was incensed. "Where's the payoff?" she said. "You stopped her from answering my question. If I'm going to be your little helper, I need something to keep me going. What was in the package?"

"Ya never ask what's in the package," Barkis said, as he led the way back to the elevator. "Never, ever." He pushed the up button and waited. This time he was whistling a theme that Caroline recognized as a formerly cool techno dance song that had become utterly ruined when it had turned up in a paper towel commercial.

"Why?" she said.

"You make the next delivery," he said.

At 4J, Barkis stood next to her as Caroline pressed the buzzer above the name reading "Johanna." Nothing. No sound from within. It was spooky.

"No one's home," Caroline said. "Who's next?"

"How would ya like it if ya didn't get your collection of next fall's Jimmy Choos because I came by while ya were in the bathroom?" Barkis said.

"You know Jimmy Choos?" she said.

"I know him like I know my cousin Jimmy. Only he's Jimmy Santangelo, and instead of making stiletto heels, he delivers fish."

"So, great analogy, then," Caroline said. "I thought you were going to say he makes cement shoes."

"What are you, thick?" Barkis said. "That's not a full-time gig."

There was a creaking sound in the room, then a lock on the door slid back, and the great metal door began to creak open. A tiny, gray-haired lady sat there in a wheelchair fumbling with an inhaler, which she stuck in her mouth and squeezed. "Oh, hello, UPS man, I'm so slow, I know. Mr. Jaggers was on my lap, and it took a minute to get him off."

"Howzit goin' Miz Johanna?" Barkis nudged Caroline, who was having a hard time envisioning anything male getting near this woman's lap.

"My friends call me Jo," said the woman in the wheelchair, reaching out gently to grasp Barkis's hand.

"Hi!" said Caroline, glancing around the small apartment. "I love what you've done with the place. Early modern slum, am I right? Sort of a Bombay-meets-ninth-circle-of-hell thing."

"You can call me Ms. Johanna," said the woman in the wheelchair.

"Well, try to pick up the pace next time, Ms. Johanna," Caroline said, "or we might not bother to deliver your next package. Would you mind signing this doohickey here? Cause I have got to jet."

With an infinitude of slow and tiny movements, Johanna put her inhaler in the pocket of her quilted nightie and reached out for the handheld computer whose readout showed her name and address and had a blank box for her signature.

"Dear me," said the lady, adjusting her glasses. "I've never seen one of these objects before. How does it work?"

"You take this plastic thing here," said Caroline, "and you use it like a pen. And you sign your name right in this space. You can write, right? I mean, do we accept an X?" she said, turning to Barkis. He frowned at her and wagged his large square head no. "We don't?" said Caroline.

"You're offending me, young lady," said the old woman, her hand shaking as she signed with the little plastic stick.

Caroline tore the electronic doodad out of the woman's hands and gave her the box on top of the cart. "Here ya go," she said. "Have fun with it."

The old woman smiled gratefully and read the return label on the box. Then she hugged it to her chest. "Oh, my," she said. "Oh, my. Thank you very much, young lady, and I hope you get some manners in your stocking."

As the woman let go of the door, it swung a few inches and then seemed too tired to continue. It hesitated on the linoleum, out of ideas, gaping.

"Look at that," whispered Barkis as an enormous gray cat the size of an ottoman came softly out of the kitchen and rubbed its roly-poliness against the wheelchair. "That's the biggest cat I've ever seen. It's like a furry hippo."

"Hey," Caroline called out. "You want us to shut your door?"

The woman smiled feebly. "Yes, thank you," she said.

Caroline touched the doorknob, hesitated, looked at Barkis. Should she? Could she?

Barkis was pulling faces at the fat animal, making little cat-beckoning noises.

"Hey lady," said Caroline. "What's in the package?"

Barkis looked up and glared at her. To Jo he said, "You don't—"

Johanna, though, was happy to answer. "Cat food," she said.

"Sorry ta have bothered ya, ma'am," said Barkis, yanking Caroline out of the doorway.

Caroline was giggling as they pushed their carts to the elevator. "That was worth this whole trip downtown," she said. "Wasn't that hilarious? She went all weepy-eyed with joy and emotion and love, and what's in the box? Cat food."

"That's why ya never ask what's in the box," Barkis said.

"But it was priceless!" Caroline said.

Barkis pushed the button for the elevator. "It was ta her. But it's always nothing ta you. That's why ya never ask the question. Ya never ask what's in the box. Before we knew what was in it, coulda been a pot a gold in there, for all ya know. Coulda been a cloud or a planet or a dream. It's not knowing that makes it all these things. Once ya find out what's in it, it's just a thing that somebody bought in a store. Or didn't. Could be some used underwear or boring old legal papers. If ya don't know, it's still magic," he said. "Ya know what makes Christmas great? The month of thinkin' about it before it happens."

The elevator door opened. Caroline was finding it awkward to look Barkis in the eye. They wheeled their carts into the elevator and Barkis pressed the button for the next floor. "I don't know about you," he said, "but I want ta deliver magic, not cat food."

While they finished making their deliveries to the building, Caroline didn't once ask what was in the box. The two of them met excited children, worn-out but basically content-looking mothers, even a few furled teenagers on stairways who unbent themselves smartly and signed their names with kiddie eagerness when the UPS man called their names. Barkis was called Santa by at least ten different jazzed-up kids, and somebody gave Caroline a tip. The tip was that her roots were showing.

"Lesson learned," Caroline said, climbing up into the passenger side of the UPS truck. "Christmas means something to the lower orders. Got it. So it's home for me, then. I've got presents to open. From my favorite person."

"Not quite," said Barkis, pulling out into traffic. He drove around the corner and headed north. Caroline was waiting for liftoff, but all four tires seemed to be stuck to the pavement. They moved into traffic, which wasn't moving at all.

"Where are we going?"

Barkis didn't answer.

"How much longer are you going to keep me here?"

Barkis said nothing.

"What am I supposed to be learning?"

Barkis delivered a few lusty honks to add to the general noise and confusion, and then he turned to her. "I'm not gonna tell ya what's in the box," he said.

The truck crawled up toward Lincoln Center and stopped at a fashionable building. The two of them walked right by the doorman into the building.

They popped through walls and floors and into a somewhat cramped two-bedroom. It was not tidy. It needed a woman's touch. In fact, it needed a human's touch. It looked like a Doritos factory after a herd of water buffalo had stampeded through. In the center of a wine-colored, beer-stained couch sat a large, large man. He was crying so much that the people in the apartment underneath his were about to have a flooding problem.

"Hulking loser?" said Caroline. "That's what you brought me here to see?"

"You don't recanize this guy?" said Barkis. "I do. All a New York does."

Caroline looked again. Barkis was right. The man on the couch was no one other than "Tiny" Tim Kitsch, the 6' 7" Zen kicker. He was sitting hunched over a tabloid newspaper in his full New York Jets football uniform, including his helmet, while reading a story about his seven-week string of missed kicks. On his last kick, during a road game in Indianapolis, he had missed the ball completely, blaming a sudden gust of wind. Commentators did not hesitate to point out that the stadium was domed. Tim had responded with a series of broken sentences and gestures that seemed to postulate that an unpredictable crosswind had been created by a combination of air-conditioning and the breeze kicked up by fans waving giant novelty foam fingers. If that Zen thing about God being the sound of one hand clapping was true, then He must have been using His other hand to slap this schmuck in the face.

Tiny Tim finished reading the newspaper story, whose front-page headline contained a horrifying close-up of his face beneath the legend, PUBLIC ENEMY NO. 1, and picked up another tabloid, one that took a somewhat less kind view of his athletic endeavors. Both papers recommended that the team release him, although one specified that he be released into the shark tank at the New York Aquarium.

"Do I have to watch this?" said Caroline. "I think I've had my recommended daily dose of pathetic."

"Wait," said Barkis as Tim sat oblivious to their conversation below. On cue, the door opened. And Tim was joined by someone else Caroline knew: Krystyna.

"Come on," Caroline said. "This is unbelievable. He's dating her?"

"Jealous a her?" said Barkis.

"No, I'm just kind of revolted," Caroline said. "I don't want my cleaning woman to associate with known losers. I mean, she might track minute particles of failure DNA into my apartment."

"They ain't datin'," said Barkis.

"Color me relieved," said Caroline.

"They're brotha and sista."

"They're—huh?"

Caroline saw in a moment that it was true. Krystyna hugged her brother, gave him a peck on the helmet, and set about picking up the papers and snacks. Then she gently went to the closet to get a mop for his tears.

"Dint you go out wit him?" said Barkis to Caroline.

"Go out with him? I rejected him."

Krystyna was saying, "We have must to clean this place ready for tomorrow, Tim. I not believing the mess you make. I go, three, four hours and it look like the bad part of Kroplochnich all over again."

"I know, I'm a loser baby, why don't you kill me?" said Tim. "I no kick good no more. But is no matter at end, you know? All that matter is, I fly like an eel above all this. Then I achieve enlightenment and become bodhisattva."

"In case that no work good, I have other idea," said Krystyna. "I achieve law degree and become owner of Park Avenue co-op."

Caroline whined, "She's going to law school? I need her to clean my apartment!"

Krystyna sat next to her brother and put a hand on his forearm. "Tim, you I want to get grip on yourself."

Tim hushed himself, sat quietly, and seemed to meditate about how to master the path of Not Acting Like a Complete Wussy.

"I was not so bad with the dating, was I?" Tim asked. "How I becoming loner of a homely heart?"

"Brother, you are going to be famous hugger of supermodels," said Krystyna.

"I not wanting the supermodels," said Tim. "I just want of her."

"No, now, you said you would no think about her until after the game," said Krystyna.

Things were switching on in Caroline's head like Christmas lights. "Of course!" she said. "Tim's real name is Krtzychzt! Like Krystyna's. Only my cleaning woman wasn't dumb enough to change her name to Kitsch. Who are they talking about, by the way?"

Barkis snorted.

"Not—?" Caroline grabbed him by the shoulder.

"Whadda you think?"

Caroline's thoughts were ping-ponging unpleasantly around her mind. "My cleaning woman is the brother of some loser I had one date with, and he's still talking about me?"

"Quel freakin' coincidence, huh?" said Barkis.

"So she wasn't really my—"

"Sure she was. Dint she do a good job?"

Caroline was turning bright red. If her face had been a lip gloss color, it would have been Seething Passion.

"She did the best job, that little spy!"

Tim had a wistful gleam in his eye. "Say to me all about uptown girl and her uptown whirl," he begged his sister.

"I have been saying everything," said Krystyna.

"Then telling me again," Tim said, like a child begging to hear *Goodnight Moon* again.

"She not eat," said Krystyna. "She not eating anything at all. She isn't swallow a single calorie of any food. Except pastries, candy bars, brownies, cupcakes, and cookies."

"Telling me—" Tim's eyes were dancing. "Telling me about the underwear."

"There were Oreos in her bra cups this morning," Krystyna said. "I find a little ebony jewelry box for earrings and stuff. Only it was fill with M&M's! She is the insane, you don't need her!"

Tim chuckled a little.

Caroline, feeling violated, held together the top of her coat and shivered. "That little wench," she said, remembering how she had first seen Krystyna, huddled shyly at the bus stop opposite the apartment, posting her hopeless little flyers that offered the first three cleanings free. How long had Krystyna been practicing her waifish lurk, waiting to ensnare Caroline? Caroline hadn't even suspected Krystyna would do a passable job on the cleaning. But free was her favorite price. And Krystyna had turned out to be so magnificent, such a genius of dirt—and candy—extermination that even now it was sickening to imagine life without her.

"You're fired!" Caroline screamed, pointlessly.

"She can't hear ya," Barkis reminded her. "We're in ghost mode here."

"Okay, can we put a little ghost message on the wall or something?" Caroline said. "Lipstick on the mirror, so it looks like blood?"

Barkis rolled his eyes. "Tack-y!"

"Buddha teach I need of learning morality, wisdom, and concentration," Tim said. "But since I be on dating with Caroline, I not be concentrating at all. All my concentrate on how she be knowing about extra-small pee-pee."

Caroline giggled. Barkis looked at her. "What, you told him he got a joint like a cocktail wienie?"

"He was acting like a total jerk," said Caroline. "I didn't know it was actually true. But in these cases, it usually is, you know?"

"I tell you some more times, okay?" said Krystyna to Tim. "That was just being a joke. Nobody is knowing that."

"Since then I being missing every field goal," said Tim. "I not even see straight because she not talk to me. She blinded me with silence."

"Is like her joke crippled you," said Krystyna.

"I say Lotus Sutra to myself, quiet, all the time, so no one hear, you know?" said Tim.

"I hear. You not being so quiet."

"Lotus Sutra tell of life being pain. Lotus Sutra is right."

"Maybe you should study less Lotus Sutra and study more how to be kicking better field goals?"

"I just being need of some confidence," said Tim. "Then will be super okay American again. You will see! I will being walking on moonshine."

"I having the confidence in you," said Krystyna. "But just in case tomorrow not be going so good, guess what, Mom call today and she say she already make your bed in Kroplochnich. She say she have nice big bowl of burshnika all hot and ready for you!"

"Can we get out of here already?" Caroline said to Barkis. "That girl is so fired. As soon as she trains somebody to take her place."

"Sure," said Barkis.

"We're done?" said Caroline.

"Here?" said Barkis. "Yup."

They slipped through the building and back into the UPS truck. Barkis started it up and pulled into traffic. Caroline felt slightly reassured going up Madison. This allowed her to do a quick eval of what was going on in the Roberto Cavalli and Valentino and Ralph Lauren windows. They weren't showing off anything Caroline didn't have already, which comforted her. Then the most familiar store of the entire gleaming designer boulevard came into Caroline's line of sight. As they were approaching, Barkis pulled over.

"Here we are," he said.

"But—here?" Caroline said. "I don't get it. What do you have to show me at the shop?"

"Unt-uh-uh," Barkis said. He got out of the driver's side and helped her down.

Caroline walked tentatively up to the huge slice of plate glass that faced out onto Madison on the south side of Seventy-seventh. The shop, as her mother had always called it, was a shop in much the same way that Buckingham Palace was a tool shed. It had always had a ghostly air but now it was positively eerie. Peering between the bars of the metal grille that had been zipped down over the window, Caroline gazed at the mannequins, standing in their wedding dresses with chic disdain, daring mere mortals to approach them in style or splendor. The dummies were tall, regal, and starved—well over six feet, Caroline knew, and her mother had once told her that each had an eighteen-inch waist. They looked even more elongated on the foot-high platforms that set them off from the rapt humans who would gaze up from below, fantasizing about how such a dress might be seized from the heavens and used as the central element in the happiest day of their lives. Even at its busiest times, the store was priced to be nearly empty. La disliked crowds. The shop was not Macy's. It was an exclusive salon for the discerning and the discreet. And if her artistry made people choke up, her price tags made them gag.

Caroline gave Barkis a pleading look.

"There's no one here," she said softly. "I don't really like this place. Please take me home."

"It's not over," said Barkis cheerfully. "Let's do this thing, huh?"

The two of them slipped through the windows and onto the shop floor among the mannequins, who snarled down at them, their business of posing for one another interrupted. Caroline gulped. Then she remembered the one comforting part of the shop. She turned. Over the entrance, there it was, the oil painting she had always liked. In the forefront, of course, sat a timeless bride. Her doting groom stood supportively behind her. Both had graceful smiles on their faces. They seemed as though they had always been there. Their classic clothes indicated any century, or even the future. Caroline was struck again by the groom in the picture, the way he looked honest but smart, the kind of man who kept his strength hidden at all times. She could not remember a time when this painting wasn't familiar to her. When she was a little girl she had secretly hoped the man really existed so she could marry him herself one day. She never told anyone this, but she liked to think she resembled the thin blond bride in the painting: the confident set of her mouth, the delicate arch of the brow, the eyes flashing with expectations of greatness. Caroline's glance drifted from the painting to one of the full-length mirrors that framed the entrance. She noticed that her eyebrows had fallen into worry and her mouth had twisted into uncertainty. She no longer looked like the picture bride.

As she looked in the mirror, though, she noticed a curious light. She turned again, standing perfectly still as her eyes searched the back of the shop. Still and empty as it was, it nevertheless suggested a presence.

Caroline walked down the grand center aisle to the back where the fitting rooms, offices, and cash register were. No cash or plastic ever changed hands on the main floor, of course; the necessary transactions were conducted privately, in back, so the mannequins wouldn't be embarrassed.

In La's office there were framed photographs of Heidi and Gisele and KK working the runways in La's creations. There were black-and-white pictures of La at a Bridgehampton polo match with Karl Lagerfeld, La sharing a joke with Valentino against a Mediterranean sunset. There was one in Milan of a dashing Tom Ford kissing La on the cheek, and one of a dinner at Per Se where La sat with Carolina Herrera, Marc Jacobs, the First Lady, and a couple of platinum-selling pop singers whose bashful looks suggested they knew they were in well over their heads. Caroline looked at these photos every time she was in the office, wondering why she had never met any of these people. It took her a moment to realize La was sitting at the desk toying with a silver and black gizmo.

"Mother?" she said, but her mother said nothing.

"Just watch," Barkis said, standing next to her. "It's almost over."

La pushed a button on the remote control and stared at the far corner, behind Caroline. Caroline tried to turn to watch but found herself frozen to the spot. She couldn't even look over her shoulder at the TV stand.

La pushed another button and the sound came up. The low hum of excited but subdued chatter. It was some kind of party, Caroline thought, but the kind of party where people are self-conscious about being too loud.

"What is she watching?" Caroline asked Barkis as she watched her mother light a cigarette.

"I can only show ya what I'm showing ya," Barkis said.

The party sounds died down and a piano began to play something classical but simple. The song reminded Caroline of spring. She focused intently on La's face. La's face would have to tell her everything.

La was smiling now, but gradually the pianist segued into the wedding march. There was a sound of people standing. Someone coughed. And La's smile slowly trickled out of her face, starting by emptying out of her eyes and ending by dripping off her formidable chin. Silently, La began to cry.

Sounds came from the TV. Strange sounds. There was a soft flopping noise, then the sound of women screaming. There was rustling and thumping. Someone called out, "Is there a doctor here?"

"This has to be a dream," Caroline said firmly to Barkis. "She never cries in real life."

Barkis shrugged.

"Six, fourteen, eighty," La said. "Six, fourteen, eighty. Is that all you have to say about this? We've got a plus-sized catastrophe on our hands, and you just keep flashing six, fourteen, eighty."

Caroline started to ask Barkis something again, but he cut her off with a pre-emptive shrug.

That's when La spoke again.

"Ted," she said, "you are the *in*finite schmuck."

Barkis this time crossed his arms and pointedly looked away.

"Please, Mr. Barkis," Caroline whispered. "Did she just say 'are,' as in, not 'were'?"

Barkis said nothing.

"Because Ted *was* my father's name," Caroline whispered again, pleading, grabbing at Barkis but coming up with air. "This is supposed to be Christmas Present, right? Not past? So, like, my mother could be watching TV right now? In New York? When she's supposed to be in Branson? Does that mean my father's alive? Or has she just lost it and gotten stuck in the past?"

Barkis's features became hazy and soft. His waistline expanded. His hair disappeared. His face lost all color. Barkis was losing his human form. He was turning into a pillow.

Caroline opened her eyes. She sat up in bed. It was too dark to see anything. She could hear her heart thumping crazily. She breathed and waited, breathed and waited. Her shades were drawn, so she couldn't tell whether it was day or night. Was it still Christmas Eve?

"Hello?" she whispered. "Any more ghosties out there?" She swung her feet onto the floor feeling both that she had just woken up and that she needed a nap of approximately twelve hours. "Leprechauns? Gremlins? Hobgoblins? Dwarves? Any sobbing football players or child actresses?"

The thought came like a craving for Milk Duds: *Under the bed.* She leaned over the edge of the bed and lifted up the bedskirt. "Hello?" she said, upside down, her blond hair falling on the carpet. Nothing there.

She slipped her feet into her slippers and went to try a closet door. Nothing. She tried another closet door. Nothing again. *Only six more closets to go,* she thought.

When she was done searching everywhere she could think of, she sat on the edge of her bed telling herself everything that had happened must have been a dream. So no Carly. No Nina. No Barkis.

And no Dad.

chapter ten

CARLY HAD SAID THERE WOULD BE VISITS FROM three spirits tonight, hadn't she? But Carly herself had been a spirit. Did she count? If so, that made three. This night was over. Celebration! Caroline instinctively reached into the hollow space between the box spring and the headboard and brought out a Ding Dong, which was in truth a little smushed and not the freshest but edible enough in an emergency snacking situation.

As she licked the sticky, chemically fabricated crème off the cellophane, she tried not to think about all the creepiness. Something was definitely happening. The apparition of Carly could have been a freak-out, true. The weird trips through the past and present with Nina Cru and Barkis could have been dreams. But still. Someone, or something, was trying to send a message.

Which didn't mean she had to listen. Look, there were lots of people out there in this city who had done worse things than Caroline. And anyway, her job title was Accessories Director, not Savior of the World.

Not that she had a job anymore. Possibly she could have handled that last day at the office a little differently. Maybe when Arabella Allen first got on the elevator, Caroline should have regarded her as a person instead of as a host organism for retarded footwear. There was also, from a certain point of view, an argument to be made that perhaps there was a possibility that setting fire to the Thing's—okay, Ursula's—sweater had been something Caroline should not have done. She was pretty sure there were experienced arsonists you could hire to do these sorts of things.

But as for the poor people in the housing projects? Not a lot Caroline could do about that, was there? And Tiny Tim—well, she didn't want to come right out and say what the guy was, but let's just say, um, a nonwinner? Again, fixing mental state of tormented Buddhist athlete guy: not on her list of duties.

Yet there was an unnerving feeling hanging over her. It was a feeling of . . . TK-ness.

In early drafts of magazine articles, when you didn't have the answer to something, you solved the problem elegantly with two letters: TK. "This handbag sells for $TK." "Available colors include TK, TK and TK." TK stood for "to come"—intentionally misspelled so it would stand out in the copy and be sure to get fixed before it made it into print—but what it meant was, Not my problem. With two deft keystrokes, Caroline could pass the buck to whatever assistant or fact-checker was assigned to fix up the holes in the story before it closed.

Caroline sat with waitingness clutching her throat like a too-small turtleneck. TK was in the air. But here there were no underlings to do the dirty work. The TK was all on her.

As she sat wondering where she had hidden the last pack of Hostess Sno Balls, there was the faintest clicking noise in the corner, over by the Louis XIV–style wing chair she used exclusively for putting on shoes. There appeared to be some kind of garment draped over the chair. Her heart sped up. Blood whooshed through her ears. There was so much noise in her head that she wasn't entirely sure she wasn't imagining the clicking sounds.

She tried to flick on the lamp by her bed but the lightbulb must have been dead. There was only a weak stream of street light leaking through her curtains. Without taking her eyes off the chair she opened a drawer in her bedside table and groped for a weapon. She came up with Junior Mints. Krystyna was really, unbelievably fired, she thought, as she shook out a handful of candy and stuffed her mouth. The box slipped out of her hand. Precious nuggets were rolling around on the floor. Caroline quietly got down on her hands and knees and started rounding up the minty chocolate treats before they could escape. She looked back up at the chair, and there it was: a gaunt form with a hood concealing its face.

Caroline's shriek escaped her before she realized what she was seeing. The creature silently raised one arm in front of Caroline's open mouth. Caroline, still screaming, peered into the sleeve but could see nothing. A gruesome, wraithlike hand emerged, an assemblage of long gray bones that creaked with a dry, blood-chilling sound as a withered gray forefinger curled into a beckoning motion. Caroline found herself silenced. She stood up. She was taller than the creature, whose black hooded garment reached all the way to the floor, falling around its invisible feet in soft folds like a train.

"Hello?" said Caroline. But the thing just stood there. Not moving. Not speaking. Just watching from deep within its hoodie mystery.

Caroline looked at the Junior Mints in her hand and decided that the spirit, being too rude to answer, did not deserve a treat. A different approach was called for.

"The hoodie thing is totally over, in case you hadn't heard," Caroline said.

No answer.

Caroline sat down carefully on the bed. This, it appeared, was the third phantom, the main event, the wrap-up ghost that would provide all of the necessary exposition for everything that had happened. Except the creature was mute. After a few minutes of staring into the nothingness framed by the hood, Caroline got up out of boredom, walked up to the spirit, and ran a thumb and forefinger over its garment just to see if it was as cheap as it looked. At that moment she felt her feet leaving the floor and the bed sinking away beneath her.

"Sure," said Caroline. "Waft me away. See if I care." She felt glumly confident that this was the Ghost of Christmas TK.

Over schools and churches and parks they flew, past suburban culs-de-sac, over the roar and brawl of the interstate highways, past boarded-up stores and empty fenced lots where cola cans and burger wrappers stopped running and settled in to cuddle up against the chain-link. The Ghost of Christmas TK slowed a bit as they came up over a weed-choked cemetery that was visited only by anxious teenagers telling one another they were the first ones ever to think of consuming canned beer among dead people.

"Oh," said Caroline, "is this the graveyard routine? Like, you're going to point at a gravestone with your nasty old finger and it's going to have my name on it? Because, see, let me point out something: since everybody winds up six feet under, that's a pretty juiceless threat, isn't it? It's not like I didn't know that already, so it's not actually going to scare me, is it?"

Inside its hoodie, the phantom made no sign of having heard Caroline. But the two kept moving, floating over mile upon mile of concrete wasteland. A dirty green highway sign loomed ahead. Caroline tried to suss out its awful warning, its creepy hint of the underworld.

WELCOME TO OHIO!

The two of them drifted to earth at a strip mall containing a grotesque check-cashing joint, a Laundromat catering to T-shirted students and freshly divorced dads, one of those combination Chinese/Thai takeout places rather cumbersomely called I Want to Wok and Roll All Night and Satay Every Day, and a place where poor women came to have poorer women slave over their nails.

The spirit led Caroline into the nails store, whose door was topped with a set of those pathetic a-client-has-arrived sleigh bells even though everyone in the room could see everyone else in the room. A woman in a burnt orange sweater vest and a green turtleneck covered with sparkly appliqués asked Caroline and the hooded figure to kindly wait until the next certified service technician became available.

Caroline could feel the vinyl sticking to her thighs even before she sat down. The Ghost of Christmas TK sat beside her, leafing through a three-year-old copy of *TV Guide*.

"So, what TV shows do you like?" Caroline said pleasantly.

The ghost turned its hood toward her and wagged a single bony finger. These spirits were pretty tough to trick. You had to admire the way they stayed on message.

The ghost put down its magazine, reached into its cloak of sorrows, and took something out. It was soft yet had two sinister metal rods poking out of it. Caroline wondered if it was some horrible multicolored torture device—a gag, perhaps, or a blindfold. Actually it was a tea cozy. Unfinished. With its skeleton fingers the ghost plucked the knitting needles out of the fabric and began to knit some stitches. The horrible fingers working, working.

So Caroline picked up a magazine. It was a trashy member of the *Glamopolitan* family stuffed with blaring candy-colored articles on sex, dieting, and lip gloss, plus more pictures of top-heavy women with impossibly slender waists than you would find in any copy of *Playboy*.

Caroline leafed through in disgust, pausing only briefly at a ridiculous headline styled in all-lower-case orange and pink letters:

**be a better
friend,
girlfriend
and daughter
today!!!**

Caroline's glance—glare, really—trailed lazily through the obligatory made-up opening anecdote ("Sabrina, twenty-three, was having a sucky week") to the nut-graf jibber-jabber about how "Thanks to these tips from *Glamopolitan*'s panel of experts, you **will** be a better friend, girlfriend, and daughter!" Cue eye-roll.

"We're ready for you now," said the reception lady. Looking up, Caroline tried to nod while averting her eyes from the glare at the same time. That orange was really too much, even for a bad dream. And weren't dreams supposed to be in black-and-white anyway? She found herself looking down at the magazine again. But as she turned the page, the nasty skele-fingers of the hooded spirit ripped the whole rag out of her hands.

"Okay, okay!" Caroline said, and got up.

The spirit seemed to glare from within its empty hood. It raised its index bone to the ceiling then made a swooping motion that ended in a severe point to the floor. Caroline looked down. The ghost had torn the magazine out of her hands so abruptly that the page Caroline had been turning had fallen out.

"I'm picking it up, see?" said Caroline, crumpling the page into a ball as she did so. "I wouldn't want to spoil the pristine natural beauty of a strip mall in Ohio."

Caroline and the spirit took their seats, side by side at a little table whose edges were covered with various nail-cleaning solvents and polishes and emery boards and cuticle scissors and pumice stones. Call it a strange dream, call it a hideous fantasy, call it a supernatural visit: Caroline still liked having her nails done. She placidly splayed out her fingers on the stained purple velvet.

But the ghost was a step ahead. All ten horrifying skeleton bones were laid out daintily for the manicurist to try to fix.

"Well, hmm, let's see," said the girl, whose voice carried the mannish throatiness of prolonged cigarette abuse. "When was your last manicure? Maybe never?"

The spirit's hood didn't move.

"Okay, never mind, I talk too much anyway," said the girl, opening a drawer and taking out a piece of nicotine gum, which she added to the big bolus she was already chewing away at. Then she continued to talk, though entirely to herself. "From out of town? Mmmm-hmmm. I see. I'll just take a pumice stone to these hands, try to soften them up a little? Mmmm-hmmm. Okay, maybe a little emery board. My, these nails are long! You know, they say they keep growing after you . . . well, never you mind that, I'll just take out my little scissors and trim them down a little bit. There, isn't that nice? A little clear polish first, okay, then what do you say to something festive like tangerine? O-kay! Let's go for it!"

The longer Caroline looked at the poor girl, with her ill-fitting pink fuzzy pullover, her denim jumper and glow-in-the-dark white tights, her haystack of hair that hadn't been teased so much as downright abused, splotchy skin that looked like it was treated with a nightly application of motor oil, the clownlike circles of blush on each cheek, the thick crumbly too-red dry lipstick, the costume jewelry around her neck, the big dangly white plastic earrings and the baby blue eye shadow, the more alarmed she became. No, she thought, no.

The girl was just finishing up on the spirit's left pinky when she said, "I like your all-black look, you know. We can't wear that here in Ohio, people just think you're weird. You know, I used to live in New York. You can't believe it, right? It's cause I blend in here so well, Taffy always tells me that, she says, I swear you'd think you's an Ohioan, born and bred. I've just been here so long I can barely remember what you're all like back in New York. But there was a time, I swear there was, when I worked at this really fashionable magazine. . . ."

"Stop!" said Caroline, tugging the ghost by its enormous black sleeve. "Get me out of here! What is this place? Is this hell?"

"Uh-uh," said the girl as she applied polka dots of sparkly royal blue nail polish to the tangerine base on the ghost's pinky. "It's Akron!"

A horrifying image lurched out of Caroline's subconscious. It was Arabella Allen, with her furry boots and her secret Caroline-extermination plan. The words she'd shouted into her cell phone as Caroline and Barkis had flown by in the UPS truck: *I know simply everyone at Time Inc., Hachette, Hearst. I will chase that girl off this island. She'll be lucky to get work in New Jersey.*

The Caroline of the future would not be lucky and would not get a job in New Jersey. She would be chased into the hinterland, jettisoned with the hopelessly uncool, the way New

York's excess garbage was sold to dumps hundreds of miles away, to be parked forever in schmuck states grateful for the business.

"Take me back to the graveyard, spirit," Caroline pleaded. "I haven't been that bad. I don't deserve this. Burn me, bury me, make me go to a party at Alexander McQueen's wearing a Talbots pantsuit. But not this. What you're doing to me, it's not fair, it's not fair, it's not. . . ."

chapter eleven

FAIR. CAROLINE OPENED HER EYES AND STARED AT the ceiling. Her ceiling. In her apartment, all snuggly and warm. She pinched herself. Ow. Reassuring. She distinctly remembered not pinching herself during any of her weird ghosty dreams. So this was reality and the other things weren't. Probably. Plus, maybe, she thought with a little thrill of hope, the night was over. Maybe nothing had actually happened to her except a four-part nightmare.

If so, nothing had changed. She was still Caroline. Everything could go on as before. Except. She was pretty sure that the getting fired part had not been a dream. But come on. Akron? There were a lot of jobs in New York for pretty magazine girls, no matter who they might have, completely innocently, made lifelong enemies with. Weren't there? Akron? Come on. Caroline had not up and flown halfway across the continent last night. It was impossible. Also, the last ghost hadn't said a single word to her, hadn't told her what she had to do to avoid the awful fate that had been shown to her. So the whole thing was out of Caroline's hands, right? It wasn't like there was any kind of lesson she was going to be quizzed on later. Anyway, in the event—the preposterous event—that Arabella Allen really had succeeded in blackballing her from the island of Manhattan, there was nothing she could do about it now. And of course all four ghosts had only been episodes of one long dream. Of course.

Then why was she wearing her Burberry overcoat while lying here in bed? Tentatively, she reached a hand into her right coat pocket. With a dull, defeated feeling, she found something there that had a shape and texture she couldn't identify.

Caroline took the item out of her pocket and looked at it. A balled-up piece of paper. Smoothing it out, she read:

**be a better
friend,
girlfriend
and daughter
today!!!**

Her eyes skipped to the third graf again: "Today—yes, to-day!—is the most exciting day of your life! Thanks to these tips from *Glamopolitan*'s panel of experts, you **will** be a better friend, girlfriend, and daughter—before midnight tonight!" Before midnight tonight? Caroline didn't recall seeing those words the first time she read the article. They were the last words on the page. To be continued. So Caroline flipped it over: a Maybelline ad was on the other side.

Today. Before midnight tonight. Be a better friend, girl-friend, and daughter. The page wasn't an advice column. It was Caroline's set of orders from the final spirit. All of this had to be done today. Before midnight. Or it was a nail shop in Akron for her.

If you believed in that sort of thing. It was possible the torn-out page had been in her pocket for weeks, in which case she'd merely dreamt about something she had come across long ago.

But what day was it? How long had she been asleep? Caroline walked over to the window and pulled up the shades. There was a splash of sun on the nearby buildings. Daylight!

She pulled up the sash of the window and held her pajama top tight around her neck as the chill burst into her apartment. The city below was in motion. The snow had stopped, and the streets were dappled with bright sunshine. Was it still Christmas? Or had she slept the day away and missed the whole thing?

"Does anyone know what day it is?" Caroline called out.

A guy in a parka who was standing next to a bagel cart said, "What, you mean today?"

A spectacularly dressed woman hurrying across the street with two little girls dressed like pages 1–150 of the Prada catalog said, "Sorry, I have no time for this."

A guy selling paper bags of roasting chestnuts for a dollar said something that sounded like, "No entiendo lo que usted significa."

A woman who was struggling to keep herself from tripping

over the leashes of the eight dogs she was walking said, "Saturday, I think. Either that or Wednesday."

A teenager in a puffy coat took off his Yankees hat, made a sweeping gesture, nudged another teenager he was walking with, and called out, "The first day of the rest of your life."

A grinning fellow in a thin denim jacket who was standing on the corner rattling a coffee cup full of change called, "Throw me down a dollar, and I'll tell you. No, two dollars."

A guy in a Brooks Brothers overcoat who was trying to hail a cab said, "The fourth of July."

And a woman in a fuzzy pink beret who was walking with a huge guy in a green ski cap with some sort of logo on it looked up and smiled. "Hi, Miss Caroline!" said Krystyna. "Is Christmas Day! Come down and be having at dinner with us! I mean, not dinner, but. Some carrot sticks and Pellegrino?"

Christmas! Caroline smiled. Maybe she still had a chance. "Hang on," she said. "Be down in thirty seconds."

Forty minutes later, Caroline stepped out of the elevator into the lobby wearing a cashmere sweater, her comfy jeans, and an absolutely minimal amount of base, concealer, eyeliner, and lip gloss. Christmas or not, standards had to be upheld. On her feet were a pair of furry boots that she had rescued from the darkest, dustiest corner of her shoe closet. The boots had been dead for at least two years. But she, Caroline, did not care. They were fun. She was going to bring them back to life.

Krystyna was sitting in the lobby talking to the guy with the ski cap pulled down to his eyebrows. It was the Zen kicker, Tiny Tim Kitsch himself.

"Hi Krystyna!" Caroline said, looking uneasily at Tim. In

her dream Tim and Krystyna had been brother and sister. But that had just been a dream, right?

"Um, I think you are knowing my brother, Tim?" Krystyna said sheepishly.

"Oh. Tim," Caroline said. And everyone paused to observe a moment of awkwardness. It was all part of my subconscious, Caroline thought. I knew all along that they were siblings. The dream just brought out what I sort of knew already. This doesn't prove anything.

Tim's glance swished all over the lobby, focusing on nothing. His mouth twitched slightly. It must be said that his look was improved by the absence of a football helmet. But he still looked like a 6' 7" rabbit.

"Okay!" said Caroline. "Quel coincidence that Krystyna became my cleaning woman right after my date with you! Small world, huh?"

Krystyna and Tim seemed to relax a little.

"Tim," Caroline said, "I've been meaning to call you. I had a nice time on our date."

"Really?" Tim said.

"Yeah. It's just that, I've sort of got this old flame, you know? An ex of mine. He just kind of, um, reheated."

Tim looked at Krystyna. Krystyna shrugged.

"The only thing that surprises me," Caroline said to Krystyna, "is that your brother's a professional football player and you still clean houses for a living."

Tim looked at his size sixteen feet. "I not being a very good football player, maybe you not hear."

Krystyna shrugged. "I study for law degree. At night. Is not clear how long Tim's football career is going. But come with us! We go to Tim's house of Christmas dinner."

Caroline agreed to show up later in the afternoon, but that gave her a few hours off. Which was perfect, because she needed some quiet time. She needed a new approach to what kind of person she had become. Most of all, she needed a doughnut.

Yum, she thought as she waved good-bye to Tim and Krystyna: behind them, the round yellow and blue sign reading "Just out of the oven" was lit up.

Inside the store the radio was, mercifully, tuned not to one of the Christmas carol stations but to classic rock. Caroline smiled at the first vaguely cool song she had heard in weeks. Da-dump. Da-dump. Da-dumpity-dump-dump-dump: *We are spirits in the material world.*

Caroline didn't wait for the girl behind the counter to give her a Merry Christmas. Caroline just went ahead and gave one to her. Free of charge.

"Merry Christmas to you, too," said the girl, who looked as if her shift had begun on Labor Day.

"Can I have a Boston crème, please?" said Caroline. "And whatever your strongest coffee is."

The girl at the counter put the doughnut in a bag, then reached for the coffee. "Oops," she said, swirling the remains of the pot. "We'll have to make you some fresh. This stuff has been sitting here for a while. Kinda looks like sludge."

Good sign. "Sludge me," Caroline said.

As she sat there with her doughnut and a cup of what to a casual observer might have appeared to be Pennzoil 10W-40, Caroline went over a few things in her head. The caffeine was lighting up her circuits. Random notions came twittering through the wires:

Child stars always thought they were hot until puberty struck.

She no longer had a job.

She might have a father.

Eddie Granger and Trot were totally wrong for each other.

Or she might not.

The middle part of the country? Even worse than you'd think.

She had spent time in an orphanage.

Her mother had a lot of explaining to do.

No one could possibly wear a size [-2]. It was impossible.

Did that mean she was an orphan?

Still no date for New Year's.

Her mother was in Branson—or maybe not?

She, Caroline, had been a horrible person for most of her life.

UPS trucks had extremely inadequate seat cushioning.

She, Caroline, had been a horrible person for most of her life.

✍ ✍ ✍

THE MORE SHE THOUGHT about the night full of dreams or visits from spiritland or whatever that had just passed, the more she kept returning to a phrase that Summer had once used on her: To explain is not to excuse. Caroline saw where this collection of experience and thoughts and values she called her self had come from and where it was heading. She realized that everything can be a lesson if you pay attention. She sensed how someone who appeared to be there for you might not actually be there, and how someone who was not really there could sort of be there, in a way, after all. She saw why she was lonely.

But all of this didn't change the fact that to explain is not to excuse. Self-understanding was neither a crutch nor a weapon. It was just something that could be kind of useful if you were actually inclined to try to make yourself a little bit better.

Caroline went back to the counter. The girl was leaning on her elbows, her gum-crushing jaw the only part of her in motion as she watched a tiny portable TV. A boy newscaster with a square bland face was going on and on about some kind of "Christmas miracle on Forty-second Street," and the mocha-colored lady co-anchor with the frozen black hairdo added that it was "a Christmas mystery, too." Then she segued into "sad news from Washington: Senator Christopher Casby died tonight after a long illness. The Senate's senior statesman was eighty-four." The boy anchor read a condolence statement issued by President Cuttle's office.

Casby's death made Caroline a little sad, although she hadn't actually realized he was still alive. She was a little thrown by the coincidence, too. Casby wasn't a guy she thought about a lot, and yet she had just come across him twice, sort of, in one night. In a back closet of her mind, there might have been other coincidences, too.

"Hi," Caroline said to the counter girl. "One just wasn't enough."

The girl looked at Caroline as though she recognized her. "Hey," she said, "Aren't you—?"

Caroline waited, puzzled.

The girl lost interest in her thought. "Never mind. We got some specials," she said. "Blueberry, cinnamon banana, strawberry-glazed, chocolate fudge overdrive, caramel custard."

"I'll take a dozen," said Caroline.

The girl took a flat piece of cardboard and folded it into a box. "Dozen of which?"

"All of 'em," said Caroline.

Staggering up the avenue, it didn't take long for Caroline to find enough takers curled up in sleeping bags under alcoves or rummaging through trash bins. Because really, who doesn't love a doughnut? Caroline found a few tired-looking housecleaners waiting for buses back to the Bronx and a few nannies hurrying into the neighborhood to spend Christmas morning spoon-feeding the infants of the overclass, and she gave each of them a doughnut, too. She was waiting to cross Eighty-eighth when a cab pulled up next to her and the cabbie rolled down his window.

"No, no," she said, waving him on. "No cab. I'm walking."

"Sweet lady!" said the cab driver. "A Merry Christmas to you!"

Caroline looked at him. "Mabouelezz Khalid?" she said. She wanted to wish him a happy holiday too, but what annual event did this guy most look forward to? Taking a shower?

"I give you a ride somewhere? Free of charge, fabulous lady!" he said.

"No thanks, I'm just heading over there," she said, pointing back to the doughnut shop. "Hey, have a doughnut!" And with that she gave him the very last one. It was great the way this time his face didn't change into Carly's at all. He just continued to look like a ragged, unwashed, pockmarked, hairy foreigner. "Oh, and by the way, I didn't really tip you enough yesterday morning," she added. "Consider this back payment." She slipped him a twenty.

"You are most generous, wonder lady," said Mabouelezz. "Your beauty is payment enough. But I take this anyway."

"Say, Mabouelezz," said Caroline. "Do I look changed at all? Since yesterday morning?"

Mabouelezz narrowed his eyes and chewed thoughtfully on his beard. "Most definitely. Even more beautiful than before."

"Why?" said Caroline as the light changed and Mabouelezz shifted back into gear.

He shrugged. "You look more . . . nice," he said, and slipped her a card with his phone number on it. As he pulled away, he held his right hand up to his ear and extended his pinky and his thumb in a little "call me" gesture.

So cute, Caroline thought, waving good-bye. Hard-working guys like Mabouelezz were what New York was all about. They made the city function, and their positive attitude was always catching. Then she ripped the card into many tiny pieces and let them fall to the sidewalk like snowflakes.

She headed straight back to the shop, ordered herself a chocolate glazed with sprinkles and a cup of coffee with whole milk and three sugars, and plopped herself down in a booth with a contented sigh.

After the first bite into this perfect chocolatey cloud of goo, Caroline contemplated her rigorous life of fabulosity and wondered silently if it was worth it. All the starvation and the control-top undergarments and the pinchy shoes? All the cajoling of designers, all the marching into the front rows of the fall shows as flashes exploded in her face? All the trying on of six different pairs of pants to find just the right size followed by the inevitable episode two years later when you throw away those same pants unworn? The three-hour haircuts, the eyebrow dyeing, the rip of the wax as it removes the hair from the ouchiest areas? Was it really worth the full-time, lifelong dedication it took, just to look fantastic?

Of course it is, she thought. But starting now, there would be room in her life for the occasional doughnut also.

"Bliss," she said aloud, and took the next soft, scrumptious bite.

"Thank you," said a man's voice.

Caroline looked up. Two booths across from her a guy of about her age had slipped in without her noticing. In front of him he had three trays heaped with doughnuts, no two of them the same variety. He was taking one bite of each doughnut, making a few notes on a yellow legal pad, and dropping the rest into a large white paper bag. He smiled at her as he tasted what looked like a raspberry-filled. At the crown of his head a single lock of chestnut brown hair sprouted tall and defiant.

Caroline hadn't seen him in more than five years.

"You," said Caroline. "What are you doing here?"

"I work here," Philip said.

"You *own* here, Philly," Caroline said.

"Shhhh," Philip said, turning around to make sure the girl at the counter hadn't heard. "Undercover agent. Doughnut police. Quality control. By the way, it's Philip, now."

"It's Christmas morning, and you are in one of the hundreds of branches of a doughnut chain you own making sure everything's up to standard? I thought you were a billionaire."

"I'm not in it for the money," he said, grabbing another doughnut and taking a slow, luxurious bite. "I'm in it for the chocolate."

Caroline asked him to join her, so Philip and his trays of doughnuts came and sat down in her booth. The two of them did some more scientific tests so Philip could write down such intricately detailed notes such as "HEAVEN WITH A HOLE IN THE MIDDLE!!!" Philip wondered aloud whether he should start offering a line of low-fat doughnuts, and Caroline politely replied that he was absolutely freakin' out of his mind.

"I didn't even know you lived in New York," said Caroline, nibbling on a powdered apple-cinnamon.

Philip picked up a napkin and gently wiped some fluffy white sugar off her chin. Caroline looked horrified. "Am I a total slob?" she said.

"You are perfectly charming," he said. "I just moved back East recently. I broke in out West because there aren't as many doughnut chains to compete with out there, but I always wanted to come back here. We finally opened our first Connecticut store this year."

"Connecticut," she said. "I was mean to you in Connecticut."

"You were just being you," he said.

"I'm not anymore," she said.

Philip laughed. "Then who are you?"

"I think I'm becoming somebody else. I'm not sure." She shook her head and turned around as the doorbell jangled. Two hip-looking girls in their twenties were walking in. As soon as they saw Caroline, one turned to the other and whispered something mean. Then the other one giggled. But Caroline didn't care. She was off duty. It was Christmas.

"I'm talking crazy talk," she said. "Anyway, I won't know until I talk to my shrink. But I'm sorry I was mean to you in school. It's just that when you're a girl, everyone's after you, you know?"

Caroline paused as the two girls came up to their booth and begged Philip to take a picture with them. They handed Caroline their cell phone camera. She snapped their picture, took a look at it, and deleted. It wasn't very flattering. She took the picture again.

"There ya go," she said. "Nice meeting you."

Caroline handed back the cell phone and the girls squealed.

"I never met a billionaire before," said one of them. "When is your IPO?"

"Maybe next year," said Philip with a wink. "But you never know."

"My dad says it's going to be the hottest offering on Wall Street," said the other girl.

"As Philip's attorney, I must advise him not to discuss any proprietary or nonpublic information in the quiet period that precedes a public offering," Caroline said. (Where did *that* come from?)

"I think my lawyer is trying to tell you to scram," Philip told the girls. "Sorry about that."

The girls smiled, wished Philip well, and went giggling to the counter.

"What were you saying about when you and I were kids?" said Philip.

"It's just that you get so used to being pursued by boys, and yet it comes at the exact time in your life when you especially don't think too highly of yourself. So if you think you're basically a loser, you think anyone who likes you too much must also be a loser. So I kinda only dated guys who were jerks to me."

"I guess I see that," said Philip.

"It was so cute of you, though," said Caroline.

"What?" said Philip.

"The little love notes. Every year at Christmas."

"Hmm?" said Philip, taking a sip of his coffee. "I never sent you any notes."

"Come on," said Caroline, covering his hand with one of her own. "Fess up."

Philip shrugged. "Sorry," he said.

Caroline let it go. When they'd had enough doughnuts and coffee, Philip threw away the parts they hadn't eaten.

"Do you have to be somewhere?" Caroline asked as they dawdled on the sidewalk, the bright circular "Pip's Doughnuts" sign lit up behind them. She didn't exactly want to go home, but she didn't really know Philip either, only an outdated version of him. She wondered if it was possible to reknow someone you already sort of knew.

"Not really," he said.

"Come on," she said, tugging him by the wrist. "I have an idea."

"Where are we going?" he said.

"Follow me," she said. "We have a couple of errands to run."

॰ॐ ॰ॐ ॰ॐ

BACK IN THE LOBBY of her apartment, the doorman was doing nothing about as well as it could possibly be done. As he sat behind the desk guarding the building's cosseted residents from predators, stalkers, creeps, perverts, burglars, murderers, and the guys who slid Chinese food menus under your door, he was asleep. Snoring, even. Behind him a row of gleaming brass baggage carts stood at attention.

"Hey, doorguy," Caroline said. "Wake up!"

The doorman didn't quite take to the concept until she yanked on the hand that was holding up his chin. The guy's skull jostled like a bobble-head doll.

"Yes, ma'am?" said the doorman.

"You were asleep," she said. "Do you know what that means?"

"What?" he said, wiping the sleep out of his eyes and taking a sip of a cold cup of coffee that had a little slick of souring milk on top. "I can't be demoted."

"It means you get a bonus," she said, dropping a $100 bill in front of him.

"Nice tip," he said. "That's about ten bucks a year."

Caroline shrugged off the ingratitude. "He's a foreigner," she said to Philip.

"I'm from New Jersey," said the doorman.

"Exactly," said Caroline. "So, anyway, Randy."

"Uh," the doorman said. "It's Rudy."

"Let me ask you something. Do you know a lot of other doormen who are getting off shift?"

"Seven or eight," he said.

"Any of them want to make a hundred bucks for two hours' work?"

"Undoubtedly," he said.

"Call them," she said, and turned to Philip.

"What do you think of that?" she said.

"I think," he said, "that I'm about to be asked to loan somebody about a thousand bucks."

"How nice of you to offer," Caroline said.

chapter twelve

THE PEOPLE WHO WAIT FOR A TRAIN AT THE
Eighty-sixth Street and Lexington Avenue subway
station in the dismal silence of a Christmas morning are as follows: People who guard things. People
who clean things. People who sell things to the people who
guard and clean things. On this particular Christmas morning,
a Filipino chemical engineer who spoke six languages was selling cigarettes and breath mints. A woman pushed a baby carriage full of empty soda cans. A few homeless men in bulky
coats slept contorted on benches specifically built to defeat nap-
pers. And a size zero blond woman in a vintage Chanel coat
skipped down the stairs clapping her hands and shouting instructions. Behind her came a guy about her own age, struggling to keep up with her, then a rolling, squeaking mob of
nine doormen, each of them working a slightly different Central American dictator look, each of them pulling a six-foot
brass clothing and baggage rack of the kind that expensive

hotels and apartment buildings keep in their lobbies to help guests and residents move their possessions.

"Come on, Dashu," said Caroline. "And Dantzler and Pransser and—Rudy, can you guide these people? You know what you're doing, you should be in front."

The people waiting for a train at the Eighty-sixth Street and Lexington Avenue subway platform were surprised to see the luggage carts slowly being pulled down the stairs, bumpity-bump, but they were even more surprised when the small blond woman with the wide smile started approaching each of them and handing them a gorgeously wrapped gift.

"Oooh, here's the train!" said the blond woman. "Hold the door, Philip. Everybody on. Come on Blitstein, you're going to miss the train."

And in a moment the people waiting for the train were on the train with the pretty lady, the man she called Philip, and the nine helpers with their overloaded baggage carts.

"So," said Caroline, hanging on to a silver pole, "this is the subway!"

Philip noted that it was a reliable form of transportation used by many New Yorkers each day.

"I'm not sure about the s-m-e-l-l, though, are you?" she said, whispering the last few letters.

Eighteen pairs of tired eyes—night watchmen's eyes, newsstand operators', churchgoers' and traffic cops' and short-order cooks' eyes—were directed at Caroline from under their winter hats and above their scarves.

"They're not deaf," said Philip. "Just sleepy."

Caroline addressed the entire train. "Ladies and gentlemen,

my name is Caroline. Merry Christmas. Now who's first?" she said as she picked up the first package, a small box wrapped in golden paper and tied up with a green bow. She shook it gently as the crowd formed around her. "I think this one's an iPod. You, ma'am!" she said, handing it to a woman in a worn gray checked coat.

The woman shook her package. "You got an Xbox instead?"

"Excuse me, not a store!" said Caroline. "Just a Samaritan. No returns." She raised her voice so the whole train could hear. "If you don't like what you get, trade with your neighbor. Next!"

Minutes later, when the floor of the train was littered with wrapping paper and everyone was buzzing and smiling and bragging about their new high-tech hair dryers and impossible-to-get handbags and cashmere scarves and cappuccino machines, the train pulled in to another station. Caroline and Philip hopped out of it and ran into the next car of the train to see how Rudy was doing with his load. All eyes were upon him as he stood between the doors with his cart full of boxes and bags.

"How are we doing?" said Caroline.

"Okay," said Rudy. "What are we supposed to do with all this stuff?"

"Drop it like it's hot," said Caroline. "Hey everybody," she said, calling out. "It's Christmas. Step right up and get some, one to a customer." As passengers swarmed around her saying, "I can't believe it" and "What have you got?" and "Are we on TV?" and "You one crazy lady," she and Philip handed out boxes and smiled.

"Hey," said a hipster with a patch of hair on his chin, an eyebrow piercing, and a vintage Smiths T-shirt from which he had just removed the tags, "what am I supposed to do with this?" He held up an adorable but tiny sweater.

"For this one time only, I'll take it back," Caroline said, and handed him a small box in trade. He opened it in seconds, shredding the paper like a five-year-old. "Sephora?" he said when he got down to the box. He took off the cover. "Pump Up the Volume Waterproof Black Mascara and Lash Builder?" he said. "Cool."

Meanwhile two enormous women sitting side by side held up their gifts for each other to inspect. One was a size-zero red and black teddy, the other a baby-doll T-shirt that did not appear big enough to cover any part of either woman's ample form.

By the time the train pulled into the next station, it was time to hop off the car and onto the next one. Caroline stuffed the cutesy little sweater into her bag. "Do you have a little person in your family I don't know about?" Philip asked her.

"Wait and see," Caroline said, then called out to the train. "Ladies and gentlemen, this train is no longer the 6 train. Today and today only, it's the love train."

Everyone groaned. One guy yanked open the connecting door at the end of the car and fled into the next one.

Caroline hurried on. "So, these presents are for you. One each, everybody gets one."

This crowd was out of their seats instantly. Caroline was swarmed.

"You are not the girl you used to be," Philip said.

"Oh yeah?" she said. "Well, you used to be a pudgy geek who liked to bake. Let's get a cab."

When all the presents were gone, Caroline sent the doormen away. She and Philip emerged from the subway and Caroline hailed a cab. When she told the driver where to go, Philip didn't recognize the address, but he sat next to her, smiling anyway.

"So what's the big plan?" he said. "Saving the world?"

"Please," she said. "I can't even save my skin from the winter air. But I just thought of a really stylish gesture."

"Oh yeah?"

"You're familiar with Coco Chanel, right?"

"Not so much," he said.

"She said a lot of totally wise things, you know? I mean, I practically have everything she said memorized. There was one thing I kinda always didn't really get, though. I mean, I misinterpreted it, or something."

When the cab pulled up in front of the Chelsea projects, Philip paid the driver and Caroline led the way to the building in the back.

"Come on, what'd Coco say?" Philip prodded.

"I'm not sure exactly how the quote goes," Caroline said, "but it's something like this. 'There are people who have money, and people who are rich.'"

The elevator was out. So they walked up the stairs to 4J, where the nameplate still said "Johanna."

"Hi," said Caroline, when the door opened.

The lonely apartment looked exactly as it had in the dream. The woman in the wheelchair looked exactly as she had in the dream. What was not the same as in the dream was the tiny portable radio that sat on top of a three-legged coffee table blaring "Grandma Got Run Over by a Reindeer."

Caroline caught her breath and instinctively took a step backward with a look of dismay suggesting a vampire who has awakened in Malibu on a July afternoon. If she had had a cape, she would have flung it over herself. Counting the dream about the nurse in the orphanage, it was the forty-seventh time she had heard the song this season. A new record.

The woman in the wheelchair eyed Caroline suspiciously. With feeble, trembling movements, she took an inhaler out of her shirt pocket and stuck it defiantly up her right nostril as if to say, "Checkmate, sister."

Caroline bit her lip and tried to concentrate. There was nothing in this room, she thought, except a sweet old lady. And just a slight touch of reindeer nausea.

"Good morning," said Caroline as the song went into its refrain.

The woman in the wheelchair said nothing.

"Maybe you don't know me," Caroline said.

The woman in the wheelchair said nothing.

Caroline took a deep breath and held it. *The song isn't happening. The air is clean. I will survive this.* "It's just that I had this dream where you said you wanted Santa to bring me some manners in my stocking," Caroline said, pushing the sound away from her. "And in my dream, anyway, I was rude to you,

Ms. Johanna. Is any of this ringing a bell? Because possibly I'm just crazy. Except, you look exactly like the person who lived in this apartment in my dream."

No sound emerged from the woman in the wheelchair except that of a single nostril in action.

Philip had questions. But he just stood there with a look of amusement on his face.

"So, anyhoo, I brought you this." She reached into her Longchamp bag and brought out the tiny sweater. "I thought, um, Mr. Jaggers? Might like it?"

A smile seeped into Johanna's face, then spread rapidly. "Oh my," she said. "Mr. Jaggers!"

The dream had been real, then. The enormous ottoman-sized cat, which if anything looked slightly larger than it had when Caroline and the spirit of Mr. Barkis had visited, thundered his way into the room and began sniffing around the wheelchair. When Johanna reached down to rub her thumb and index fingers together, the mammoth beast gratefully rubbed his cheek against her knuckles and began a purr that sounded like a boiler room on a cruise ship.

"Look, Mr. Jaggers," said Johanna. "A sweater just for you." She held it up for Mr. Jaggers to examine. The cat sniffed delicately at the little hem.

"I think it'll stretch out a little," said Caroline. "Anyway, Merry Christmas, Ms. Johanna!"

The cat, humming noisily, did figure eights around and around Caroline's furry boots as the reindeer song reached its final, demented key change.

"Young lady," said the old lady, looking back and forth from Caroline to Philip, "You can call me Jo."

When the door closed, Philip and Caroline exchanged a look. "I really hate that song," said Philip, and Caroline gave him a little hug.

"Let's bolt," he said, and they ran giggling down the stairs. The flat-soled furry boots provided surprising traction advantages over Blahniks or Choos.

In the cab back uptown, Philip checked his watch. "It was great to see you again," he said. "Can you drop me at Park and Seventy-sixth?"

"Swank, very swank," said Caroline. "Hosting a big Christmas do, are you?"

"Sort of," he said. "A few family members coming over. My Uncle Joe, you remember him? A couple of others. Not a big deal. I'm not the one doing the cooking, though," he said. "Um, I'm not sure I'm allowed to invite anyone, but—"

"Oh, no, no, that's okay," said Caroline. "I have plans already. My cleaning lady, Krystyna, invited me over to her brother Tim Kitsch's place for Christmas dinner."

"You know Tim Kitsch, the Zen kicker?" Philip said. "I'm jealous. What a character. Everyone's talking about that guy on sports radio. It's make or break for him today."

"Actually," said Caroline, checking her watch, "I'm supposed to be there now. It's on the West Side, so I guess I get off first."

"Not a problem," Philip said. "Best day of the year for a drive around town. Hardly any traffic. And all the decorations, I can't get enough of 'em. Look at this one," he said, as they passed a store with two candy canes crossed over its entrance like swords. "Know where those come from?"

"Ugh. The land of perpetually stale hard candy?"

"It's a Christian symbol," he said. "You know the routine about how 'The lord is my shepherd'? The candy cane is in the shape of a shepherd's crook. And the holly, that's to symbolize the thorns Jesus wore. And the red berries are like the drops of his blood."

"Interesting. Pointless, maybe, but interesting."

"And Christmas trees are evergreens because Christianity promises everlasting life," he said, as the cab pulled up in front of Tim's building across from Lincoln Center. "Kind of comforting, isn't it? I mean, regardless of whether you believe. It's nice just to know that everything means something."

"Okay," said Caroline, who was smiling with her mouth but not with her eyes. And even her mouth wasn't smiling with dental exposure. It was the get-me-outta-here smile.

"Oh, don't give me that look," Philip said. "I'm not trying to sell you on anything. I'm not much of a churchgoer. I just check in on Easter and Christmas."

"The blockbuster holidays," she said.

"Exactly," he said. "And you know why I go? Not because I believe a Styrofoam cookie is the Body of Christ or because I get off on the smell of incense or because I believe all the fairy tales about people rising from the dead. I go to reassure myself on one point. One point only."

"So give it up," said Caroline.

"That there's always someone looking out for us."

"Which corner?" said the cab driver.

"Right here is fine," Philip said, and opened the door.

Caroline, at that moment, didn't feel particularly tough. In fact she was already starting to cry.

"I know who you are," she said, her voice a near whisper. It was embarrassing and painful to get the words out. She leaned into him, "You're . . . Nemo."

Philip drew back. "I hope not," he said.

"Why?" she said, a little startled.

"Nemo, if my Latin holds up, means 'nobody,'" he said.

Caroline sensed that he was just teasing her. Even so, he had ruined her moment. If the long night of ghosty dreams, or dreamy ghosts, had only helped her figure out who in the Chelsea projects was most deserving of a cat sweater, it hadn't really been a raging success, had it?

"Sorry, Caroline," he said as she got out. "I hope you find your Nemo."

Still feeling weirded out, Caroline walked into a brass-and-marble lobby and took the elevator up to Tim's place, a two-bedroom apartment filled with a herd of babbling Kroplochnichians. While Tim was wrestling with the turkey and singing, "I still haven't found who I'm cooking for" and Krystyna was whipping potatoes, Caroline started looking through the cabinets. She found all the stuff she needed to make brownies, chocolate pudding, crème caramel, and snickerdoodles. All the baked goods recipes that lurked in some reptilian node of her mind came back to her effortlessly.

After dinner, when every one of the dozen or so guests had stuffed themselves with one forkful of Tim's turkey, some vegetables, and four or five desserts each, there was general agreement that the meal had been a success. While it was true that Krystyna's mashed potatoes were bland and Tim's bird was not a triumph—the diners politely differed on whether it tasted more like scorched bark or a cremated tire factory—everyone agreed that they had been lusting for Caroline's selection of desserts from the moment the first gooey pan went in the oven and the odor had lazily wafted into the living room, as though approaching each of the guests in turn, politely tapping them on the shoulder and saying, "Excuse me, have we met? I'm brownies."

"Honestly, Krystyna," Caroline said, "I never realized how beautiful you were before. I don't think I've ever seen you with your hair down."

"Oh, is not true," said Krystyna, and blushed anyway.

"No, it is true," Caroline said. "In fact, you look kind of like Julie Christie in the sixties. Do you have a boyfriend?"

"No," Krystyna said, too quietly. "Is too hard to find time," she added, remembering the reason she had no time. "Work is more important!"

"I know someone who loves demure, soft-spoken, fair-haired types. He'd be the perfect man for you," Caroline said benevolently.

"What his name?"

"Nic," said Caroline. It felt good to be generous at Christmastime.

"Does he have a girlfriend already?"

"Not one as pretty as you," said Caroline.

All of the guests but Caroline had left when she was getting up to serve Tim and Krystyna a third cup of coffee.

"What you usually have for Christmas dinner, Caroline?" said Krystyna.

"Me?" Caroline ran through last year's Christmas feast in her mind: no-calorie organic matter loaf, roughage salad, cream of nothing soup. "I don't usually have turkey, much. You know, you don't have to go along with what everyone else does, anyway. You can have ham for Christmas. Or duck. Or pizza." She sat back down.

"Pizza?" Tim said dreamily, his pupils like pepperoni. "Is okay for Christmas?"

"Pizza would be the weird option," said Caroline. "But this is a weird country. Be as weird as you want. People will love you for it."

"I always like that song," Tim said. "But it scare me about being weird. You know it? 'Everybody Wants to Rule the Weird?'"

"Ah," said Caroline. "But you've got that wrong. It's really, 'Everybody Wants to Room with Weird.' It means everyone wants to be with you when you're strange."

"I think before you didn't like me, that I was too weird."

"Not at all," said Caroline. "I really liked you."

"Liked me?" said Tim. "What you liked about me?"

Tim was pushing his luck by asking for details but Caroline mentally ran through the list of his attributes in search of some that were less gross than others.

She couldn't think of any. They were all pretty heinous.

Tim seemed to be waiting for an answer. There was a certain stillness around the table.

"Your smile," she said, thinking instead about the reasons

she liked Philip. "Your sense of humor. Your intelligence. Your spirit. The way you never give up. Your quirkiness."

"Quirkiness?" said Tim.

"The way you are completely comfortable being yourself," she said, trying to put out of her mind that ludicrous image of a giant in a plastic helmet ordering twelve California rolls.

"Do you want to go out with me for New Year's?" said Tim.

"I'm so sorry, I can't," said Caroline. "The truth is, I already have plans. With this guy I really like. And the thing with you is, um, big men? Kind of scare me. I never go out with anyone over six feet. So I liked you but you were just the wrong type for me, you know?"

Tim looked quite pleased with himself then. He winked at Krystyna as though no one else could see. He leaned back in his chair, interlaced his fingers behind his head and chuckled softly.

"She like me the whole time," he said. "I her biggie man."

As he went off to the bathroom repeating these words, Krystyna and Caroline looked at each other like sisters. The ego of a man, even a giant, is a tiny, shivering thing, and Caroline had just taken this wounded little hamster and nursed him back to life.

"Is about that time," Krystyna said, getting up to clear the last dessert things off the table.

"Wrapping up so soon?" Caroline said. "But it's kind of nice to just sit around and chat."

"Oh, didn't you know?" said Krystyna. "Tim has game to-day. In New Jersey. We have to go to Meadowlands by five o'clock."

"What time is the game?" said Caroline.

"Eight-thirty. Is important game. If they win, they being in playoffs. Tim has lot of pressure on him, you know? He miss eleven field goals this year and if he miss another, he is being cut. You know what this means in football? It means they not have to pay you anymore, not one zlinkty. That's why I work so hard for you. I worry about him. Only skill he is having is to kick this strange-shape American football. He can't run with ball, or throw it. He cannot even kick a round ball."

"I see where that could limit his marketability," said Caroline.

When they said good-bye, Tim came up to Caroline, bent down, and gave her a big hug. When he stood up straight again her feet dangled helplessly in the breeze.

"I thought about what you said," he whispered in her ear. "Weird. From now on I am being a weirder shade of pal."

"Go weird!" she said, gasping for air. She looked down at her feet, which were at about the height of his waist.

Krystyna and Tim went off to the game together as Caroline took a cab across the park. She was exhausted when she got home, and found herself taking a nice tryptophan nap. When she woke up it was dark. The apartment was too quiet, and she had too many questions. So she got dressed and got in a cab. Something was pulling her to the shop.

When she got to Madison and Seventy-seventh, there he was. Twice in one day. You might have said that fate wanted Caroline and Philip together, except that this time he and a devastatingly pretty brunette were standing very close together gazing at the wedding dresses. Holding hands. Which kinda wrapped up the whole Philip matter and put a tidy little bow on it.

"Stop the car," Caroline told the driver. "I want to enjoy this."

"Enjoy what?" said the cabbie.

"My punishment."

As Caroline watched, Philip and the brunette looked straight into each other's eyes and exchanged a few words, as though they had just that second agreed to a wedding date. Caroline set her jaw and forced herself to watch as the two fell into a long, deep hug. The hug of two people who have known each other for years and intend to know each other for many more. Then the brunette got in a cab. Philip smiled and waved as Caroline's cab sat idling ten feet behind him.

There really was not a single single man left in this town. Thinking of all those fifty-minute hours spent with Summer, she admitted to herself: it may be true that I have some issues. There may be some areas in which a little improvement would not be unwelcome. This is where a man comes in. Just a guy with a set of problems different from mine would be nice, she thought, so that when we averaged our problems out, everything would fall in the normal zone. She wasn't asking for a guy who outshone the sun. If she could just find someone who had as much fizz and sparkle as the average can of Fresca, she figured she'd be fine. Why couldn't she find him?

Plus which, Caroline didn't have a job. She didn't have a date for New Year's, and soon she would no longer have a shrink named Summer, who, when you really thought about things, was kinda her best friend. Why fight the truth? New

York had been fun to flirt with all these years, but in the end it had just refused to commit to her. There was no need to wait any longer. She wondered when the next plane left for Ohio. Fate was fate.

At that moment, Philip turned around. At first he had a glassy, lost look in his eye. But then he spotted Caroline and gave her a big smile.

Caroline zapped her window, which, like most taxicab rear windows, came down about two inches and stopped, apparently to prevent passengers from getting any relief from the thick bodily funk that strangled the air inside.

"Hi!" said Caroline, trying too hard to be cheerful.

"You again?" said Philip, opening her door. "Come out of there."

"I was just heading home," Caroline said. "I know you've got family to get back to."

"Nonsense," Philip said. "We're just winding up. In fact, you can meet some of them. Come over for some coffee."

Caroline found herself being pulled out of the car. Philip even paid for the cab, which was considerate of him. She would have preferred that he declare his love, but if not, then spending $9.70 on her was also cool.

"It's a short walk, right this way," Philip said, leading her east on Seventy-seventh.

The opportunity, when you combined it with the questions Caroline still had from flitting around with the three spirits last night, was just too much to pass up. So she stopped.

"This is my mother's shop, you know," Caroline said.

"Everyone knows that," Philip said. "She's only the best wedding dress designer in the business."

Caroline paused and waited for the confession. Perhaps Philip would tell her all about his upcoming wedding. Perhaps he would tell her about his gorgeous brunette bride. Perhaps Caroline would manage not to gag, although that part was not something you'd want to bet on.

None of this was coming out of Philip's mouth. He didn't say anything at all. So it was left to Caroline to make the proposition.

"How would you feel," Caroline said, "about a little petty crime?"

"What do you mean?" said Philip. His face was equal parts interest and fear.

Caroline dug in her Jil Sander bag and dug out a fistful of keys. "It's not breaking and entering if you have keys, right?"

She stepped up to the gray unmarked steel door and started unlocking its several deadbolts. "The thing is," she said, "I had this strange dream last night. It was too real not to be believed, if you know what I mean. And it showed me some things about my mother and this store."

Philip nodded slowly. "I understand," he said.

"Really?" said Caroline.

"No," said Philip.

"Never mind," Caroline said. "I just want to check out a couple of things. Won't take but a sec." And with that she popped open the door.

But in the service entryway there was a new device Caroline

had never seen before: a small white square, maybe the size of two credit cards, with a number keypad, an Enter key, a Cancel key, a Delete key, and a digital readout that was counting down backward from 30.

"Uh-oh," said Caroline.

"We have one of these at our headquarters," Philip said. "You need to know the security code."

24. 23. 22.

"Or else what?" Caroline said.

"Or else the alarm goes out to the police."

18. 17. 16.

"What about if we just skip the whole thing, lock this baby up and run?" Caroline said.

"Won't work," Philip said. "The alarm's been activated. It's usually a six-digit number, got any guesses?"

"My birthday!" Caroline said. She entered the day, month, and year. The only response to these digits was an electronic gonging sound.

12. 11. 10.

"I don't think that worked," Philip said.

"Thanks for the obvious," said Caroline.

8. 7. 6.

"Try something else, quick," Philip said.

"Mom's birthday," Caroline said. And punched in six more digits. Which were met with another game-show buzz sound effect.

"Try something. Anything," Philip said.

Caroline's mind clicked back to the dream about her mother watching something on TV and saying six, fourteen, eighty.

She guessed at once that her mother had been watching a video, and this had been the date stamped on it.

3. 2. 1.

Frantically Caroline punched in 06-14-80. The timer hit zero, then stopped. There was no buzzing sound. No nothing. Caroline shrugged. Philip shrugged. Then she led the way to the end of the corridor, unlocked the door to the office in the rear of the store, and took a deep breath. She was conscious, vaguely, of Philip squeezing her hand. She pushed the door open.

When she had been a little girl, Caroline had been very completely freaked out by the back room of the shop. It was like a bridal slaughterhouse. Everywhere you looked there were headless dummies, disembodied arms, legs lying in stacks. If the main floor of the shop looked like what happened to the wedding princesses, this dark little nook was damned by chopped-up spinster mannequins forever waiting, waiting, waiting for a wedding day. A single light was lit, a pathetic little fluorescent tube in the desk lamp. It cast a cold white spot of light.

La was slumped on the floor next to a dress, smoking a cigarette. Surrounding her were veils, sashes, trains, and wedding dresses, all taken out of their boxes and strewn everywhere in heaps. Cigarette butts with the life crushed out of them still glowed feebly on the cold cement floor. A TV flickered weakly in the corner. A VCR was turned off beneath it. Channel 7 news was doing Accu-Weather.

"Mother," said Caroline gently. "I thought you were in Missouri."

"Daddy and I broke up," La said, sniffling.

"Mother, a man you've been dating for eight months could hardly be my father," she said. She pulled up a chair next to her mother and thought about putting an arm around the older woman's shoulders. She thought about it, but she didn't do it.

"Mother," said Caroline, "this is Philip."

La strangled Philip with her eyes. "I remember you," she said. "That little boy from school, right, the one who smelled like cookies? With plastic boots? Born to go into the lucrative field of heavy-equipment operating? Do you really think you're suitable for my daughter?"

"Mother, what happened?" Caroline said.

"Eugene Wrayburn and I broke up a month ago," La said.

"But I thought it was going well," Caroline said.

La shook her head. "He told me I wasn't curing his boredom. He went off to chase some little tramp named Lizzie. I was too ashamed to tell you. So I made up that ridiculous story about spending Christmas in Branson. You didn't really think I'd gone hick on you, did you?" La crushed out her cigarette on a $4000 white lace bodice that lay crumpled at her feet. It looked like the life's work of a million silkworms.

"I guess that's a relief," Caroline said. "But if you had had a good time there, I wouldn't have cared. After the shock wore off."

"I'm the number one wedding brand on the East Coast. I've been involved in more than ten thousand weddings. But never as the star."

"You have high standards," Caroline said.

"I scare them away," La said. "Weddings, weddings, weddings, it's all I talk about. It's not actually a suitable topic for a first date."

"Don't be unfair to yourself, Mother," Caroline said. "You've had some of the most eligible bachelors in the world romancing you for periods of up to ten months."

"It's your father's fault," La said.

"Tell me about him," Caroline said. "Please."

La exhaled. "He loved you very much, did I ever tell you that? Maybe I didn't use those exact words."

"The exact words you used were that he couldn't stand the sight of me."

"That was an exaggeration," La said. "What he actually couldn't stand was your being out of his sight."

"So it was sorta more like a lie," Caroline said.

"Darling, Mother's telling a story. Don't interrupt. Anyway, I was crushed. When he, died?"

Caroline waited, growing impatient.

"I didn't want you to see me like this," La said. She paused theatrically and took a Bette Davis drag. Really, the woman's every gesture was stolen.

"Enough," Caroline said. "I know what you're doing. I saw it all in a dream. You've been doing it to me forever."

"Fine," said La. "But do you have any idea what it's like being me? To know, to really know, deep in my soul where the truth lives, that I'm still juicy and ravishing? Only to have to stand there every morning and take it while the mirror lies to my face?"

"It's a little late in the day for you to start with this act," said Caroline.

"What act?" La said, fumbling for the TV remote and squeezing the volume button as if to hide Caroline behind the news chatter.

"The human act. It's a stretch for you. You should stick to playing autobiographical parts, like gargoyles or Dracula."

The weatherman gestured wildly and talked about the incoming snow flurries as though warning of Martian invasion.

"It's you, you know," La said. "I was never the same after you were born. I spent my youth on you."

"You got off cheap. You certainly didn't spend any love on me. You saved it all for yourself."

"That is *so* not true," said La. "I loved you more than I loved myself."

Caroline pondered this sentence for a moment. Was her mother making an absurd claim of low self-esteem or a ridiculous declaration of maternal tenderness?

"I did and do," La said firmly.

"Look, if you're winding up for a big speech, can you just e-mail it to me instead? In an attachment? That way you can get all your feelings worded just exactly the way you want. You can write it as long as you want. And I can ignore it."

"I made the decisions I thought were best for you," said La. "I made the decision to put you through the best schools because I wanted you to be better than me. I made the decision to dress you in the best clothes because I wanted you to be prettier than me."

"I'm just waiting for you to get to your decision to attend that Cowgirls and Construction Workers theme party in a dormant Hawaiian volcano on my tenth birthday. Without me."

"Darling, you had birthdays every year. That party was a once-in-a-decade event."

"I'm out of here," said Caroline, standing up. "Give my re-gards to Missouri."

It was a bluff. But it worked.

"Wait," said her mother. "I tried to find a man who could support you. Well, and me. But mainly you. Darling, I knew with my lavish lifestyle—"

"Lavish?" Caroline scoffed. "Lavish is Marie Antoinette. Lavish is Graceland. What you are doesn't have a word."

"Just so!" said La. "With all my faults, I wanted to find a husband who was perfect. For me."

"Before I got married, is that it?" said Caroline.

La didn't say anything.

"None of my boyfriends were good enough for you," Caro-line said. "Because you couldn't stand the idea that I might get married before you."

La picked up a book of matches from Bemelman's Bar, struck one of them, and waved it out listlessly.

Philip heard the sirens first. "Uh-oh," he said.

"What happened to my father?" Caroline demanded. But there wasn't time to answer before the place started swimming in flashing blue lights.

A man was yelling through a bullhorn. "This is the New York City Police," he said. "Come out immediately. Put your hands where we can see them."

When Philip and Caroline and La came out into the Sev-enty-seventh Street night, a man was standing by the entrance to the shop with his hands raised, quietly presenting himself to two cops getting out of a parked cruiser with its roof lights flashing. The man with his hands in the air had longish, tousled blondish-brown hair, piercing blue eyes, and a delicate jaw line. There was something strange about this stranger, and what was strangest was that he wasn't all that strange. Caroline thought she recognized him from somewhere, some underlit corner of yesterday or last night's dreamscape.

The cops took their time approaching. The first one, whose nametag read DUBBLEY, had a body that looked as though it was expanding with equal urgency in every direction, topped by a head that was as round as an orange. He was clearly in charge of the situation, and his forehead was clearly in charge of him. It pushed his brown hair back until the two of them, the hair and the forehead, agreed to a temporary space-sharing truce on the crown of his head. Pushing off in the other direction, the forehead seemed to have squeezed Dubbley's eyebrows down too low over his tiny, widely-set eyes, placing the face in a permanent squint. He looked dangerous and soft at the same time, like an exceptionally fierce stuffed animal.

Behind him, or rather above and behind him, stood his partner, a hulking specimen of hairiness whose nametag read GRUMMER. The tangled furrows of his curly black eyebrows were so deep and so high above sea level that robins could have nested in them. He walked in slow, jerky, uncertain steps, like a 1930s movie monster. His thumbs were hooked carefully into his belt, a gesture perhaps intended to keep his hands centrally stored and therefore easy to locate in an emergency.

Officer Dubbley had a bullhorn in one hand and a long, heavy silver flashlight in the other, looking like an actor who has emerged onstage for his big scene with entirely the wrong props. But putting them back in the car would have looked like an admission of something, so Dubbley held tight to these two objects and sought to work them into his routine whenever possible.

"Somebody wanna tell me what happened here?" said Dubbley, his mustache continuing to move even after he had finished speaking. He aimed the unlit, unwieldy flashlight at the stranger as though it emitted a powerful truth beam. Then he scratched his ear with the bullhorn in a gesture he did not quite succeed in making look casual.

Grummer, the taller cop, frisked the suspect. "He's clean, Dave."

"What's the problem, officers?" said Philip.

Dubbley swung the still-unlit flashlight Philip's way. After a second, he also pointed the bullhorn at him, for extra seriousness. "We got an alarm sent by this address."

"Break-in," said Grummer.

"Someone's in trouble," said Dubbley.

Caroline bit her lower lip and looked up at Philip. He squeezed her hand. "It's okay," he told her. Caroline opened her mouth.

"It was me," the stranger blurted. "I did it."

Caroline was puzzled. "No, I did it," she said. "This is my mother's shop. I was trying to break in."

A feeble gray-haired lady walked by with a dachshund that paused briefly to sniff at a parking meter on the other side of the street.

Dubbley, snapping into action, turned around and switched

on the megaphone with his thumb. "Stand back," he said through the megaphone.

The dachshund and its elderly chaperone looked equally surprised, being forty feet away. Grummer went into the squad car, rummaged for a moment, and emerged with a spool of yellow crime scene tape. For a moment he appeared to consider wrapping the woman and her dog in it, but the two of them had moved on to another parking meter.

Dubbley faced the suspects again. He held his bullhorn by his side, still switched on, just in case. "Who's the mother here?"

"That would be me," said La. "I know I don't look it."

Dubbley looked at Grummer. Grummer looked at Dubbley. "We better go inside and untangle this," Dubbley said.

There was much checking of IDs inside the office, where a TV voice was promising, "We'll give you the latest on the Christmas storm heading our way right after this." Slowly, as befitting public servants drawing overtime, Grummer and Dubbley agreed that La Havisham was indeed the owner of La Havisham Weddings, and Caroline her daughter. The strange man, though, refused to give his name or provide identification. He seemed indifferent to punishment, which was starting to annoy the cops.

"And who are you?" Grummer said, turning to Philip.

"Philip Pirrip," he said.

"Funny name," Grummer said, suspicious.

"Maybe you're a comedian," said Dubbley, whose glare suggested dire consequences for anyone committing unauthorized acts of comedy.

"I'm a doughnut maker," said Philip. "I have some stores. Pip's Doughnuts? Maybe you've seen them around town." He smiled hopefully.

Dubbley looked at Grummer. Grummer looked at Dubbley. Dubbley put his bullhorn on a credenza.

"You," Dubbley said, pointing an index finger the thickness of a spring roll at the stranger. "Enough foolin' around. I wanna know who you are and where you live. You," he said, indicating Caroline, "I want to know why you were breaking into your own mother's store on Christmas Day. You," he said, indicating Philip, "I want to know how you get those apple-cinnamon fritters so tasty."

Grummer whispered something in Dubbley's ear. Dubbley nodded. "*And* the blueberry-filled," Dubbley said.

"Well," said Caroline, "as I said, I was trying to sneak in without my mother knowing. I know it was wrong, but I do have a key to the place. She won't press charges." Caroline lightly tossed a smile at her mother, but La's eyes were out of position to receive. La was busy staring down the strange man, who met her gaze like a gunfighter.

"You can take me down to the station," the strange man told the police. "I'll tell you everything there. But this young lady didn't do anything wrong."

"Both of you, be quiet," said Dubbley. "Don't interrupt me. We're going to take this in a logical order. Nobody speaks until spoken to." As the room went satisfyingly still, he took out a notebook and a pen. "Now," he said, "First things first. We'll keep it simple, everybody, okay? We need to know what new flavors you'll be introducing this year, doughnut guy.

Also, I need the exact locations of any and all new Pip's branches."

"There aren't any near Chinatown," Grummer pointed out.

"Yeah, and there isn't a single one above Ninety-sixth," said Dubbley. "Do you know you can't get a decent doughnut in all a Staten Island? I oughta arrest you for that."

"What is this?" said La. "Bad cop, bad cop?"

Dubbley gave her a sneer that was perhaps meant to be terrifying but was in fact peevish. His pale round face turned rosy at times of high excitement. He looked as hard as strawberry yogurt.

"I seen Pip's Doughnuts are all over the Upper East Side," said Dubbley.

"Your wealthier neighborhoods," said Grummer.

"I'd hate to find out you were violating federal discrimination laws," said Dubbley.

"We're doing our best," Philip said. "But to answer all these kinds of detailed questions"—he took out a cell phone—"let me make one call."

"No, no," said Dubbley, attempting a smile. "No need to call your lawyer."

"We're just talking here," said Grummer.

"I'm gonna need you to leave the lawyer out of it," said Dubbley, breaking with the tradition in which police advised citizens under questioning that they had a right to legal counsel. He clicked his pen, many times. He tried to scratch under his mustache with his flashlight, but the apparatus proved bulky, and he ended up squashing the tip of his nose with it.

"Or maybe you want we should do our talking down at the

station," said Grummer, pulling his upper lip back and baring an array of mismatched teeth.

"On what charge?" Caroline said. "Excessive deliciousness?"

"They're in cahoots," said Grummer.

"A regular Bonnie and Clyde," said Dubbley.

"But as the owner of the company," said Philip, "I just don't know the details about all these questions."

"That's okay," said Grummer.

"It's fine," said Dubbley.

" 'Cause we got all night," said Grummer. And both of them sat down and crossed their arms.

The strange man cleared his throat. "Since I don't seem to be a target of this line of questioning, can I go?"

Dubbley looked at Grummer. Grummer looked at Dubbley.

"Shuddup," said Grummer.

"You're interfering with police work," said Dubbley.

"Obstructing justice," said Grummer.

"Perverting the legitimate aims of a law enforcement investigation," said Dubbley.

"Unless *you* cooperate," said Grummer.

"Turn state's evidence," said Dubbley.

"What do you mean?" said the stranger.

"Do you know anything about what new flavors they're cooking up at Pip's, or don't you?" said Dubbley.

"I don't know anything about doughnuts," said the stranger. "I can't stand them, actually."

"Would you swear to that?" said Grummer.

"I guess," said the stranger.

Grummer nodded at Dubbley. Dubbley nodded at Grummer.

"They always turn on each other in the end," said Grummer.

Caroline was losing interest. Her mother lit up a cigarette, her fingers shaking uncharacteristically as she looked at the pile of shredded wedding dresses all around her. Channel 7 news was still on TV in the corner. As Caroline watched, a familiar face popped up on the screen.

Caroline made a high-pitched squeak and lunged at her mother to snatch the remote out of her hands. Her mother dropped the cigarette onto her lap, where it made a smoldering black spot. La patted out the spark and yelped.

On TV, Caroline was stepping into the street, strands of hair dangling in limp watery tangles. A HumBug 3000 was heading straight for her, at a speed more than sufficient to squash a Kodiak bear, much less a fashion editor. As Caroline watched herself collapse in the middle of Forty-second Street, the anchorman was saying, "—yesterday's Christmas Eve Midtown miracle. A German tourist shot this amazing video of an unknown woman falling in front of oncoming traffic."

The tape went into slow motion. Behind Caroline you could see a man springing out of a ragpile next to the entrance to the Belle Connerie building. With amazing speed, the man dashed into the street, picked up Caroline, and dragged her to the sidewalk. He listened quickly to her breathing as a crowd started to form. Then he stole away, went back to his rags and buried himself under them from head to toe. The video zoomed in on Caroline, lying flat out unconscious on the sidewalk. Her eyes flickered to life and the tape ended.

"If you have any information on the good Samaritan," the anchorman was saying, "or the poor woman who was nearly killed in the Midtown miracle, please call our news desk."

Caroline had information on both. Because she had seen the guy who had rescued her recently. Very recently. He was standing about ten feet away.

chapter thirteen

"IT WAS YOU," CAROLINE SAID TO THE STRANGER, stunned. "You saved me. Who are you?"

La stood and clamped a warning claw on Caroline's shoulder. "I know who he is," she said, her tongue fully forked. "He's a very dangerous man. Officers," she said to the two cops as she stretched out her arm and pointed her cigarette at the stranger, "I think you will find there is an outstanding restraining order on this man. He is forbidden from coming within five hundred feet of me or my daughter."

Dubbley looked at Grummer. Grummer looked at Dubbley.

"Is this true?" Dubbley asked the stranger.

The sad man nodded. "Take me down to the station. I'll explain everything."

Dubbley began handcuffing the stranger. Grummer nodded with satisfaction. He looked at Philip. "This is what happens to people who don't cooperate with the police, you know," he said. "Don't leave this place until we tell you to."

"Look," said Philip, getting out a cell phone, "let me make one call." He punched a few numbers. "Sam," he said. "Desperate situation here. What store has the hottest, freshest doughnuts right now? Uh-huh." He held his hand over the receiver. "Ten minutes from now they'll be coming out of the oven at Fiftieth and Rockefeller Plaza," he told the cops. Then to the phone he said, "Go there, my man. Make haste." He snapped off his phone. "Sam's going to bring back some doughnuts. Then everyone will be in a little better mood, no?"

Dubbley looked at Grummer. Grummer looked at Dubbley. "You'd better hope they get here fast," Grummer said. "Otherwise we might have a lot more questions for you."

On TV the anchorman was reading a canned obit about the passing of a proud public servant, an honest American, a symbol of democracy. "Senator Christopher Casby died today in a Washington hospital," said the anchorman.

"What?" said the stranger. He turned around and looked at the TV in disbelief. "Did they say Casby's dead?" He looked at La.

"Yeah," said Caroline. "I heard it earlier on the news."

The stranger looked at La. "Well then."

"Well what?" La snapped.

"Your eighty-four-year-old boy toy is gone," the stranger said.

Caroline looked back and forth from La to the stranger. La looked faint. She put a hand up to her forehead and collapsed into a chair. But elegantly, so elegantly.

"It's over, La," said the strange man. "You couldn't win forever."

La's eyes were closed. "Officers," she said, "let him go."

Dubbley poked the strange man. "Not if he doesn't tell us who he is."

"The only picture ID I have," the stranger said, "is in the next room."

In the main showroom, Caroline stood next to Philip. Philip slipped a hand around her waist, and she felt herself leaning toward him automatically. But she swatted his hand away. She didn't need comforting gestures from an engaged man. Not an hour ago, he had been looking longingly in the window of this very shop with his fiancée.

The stranger pointed up at the oil painting hanging over the entrance. It was him. The man in the painting, the timeless, classically handsome groom, was the man standing next to Caroline in handcuffs. The man said a few words, La gave a stiff nod, and the police uncuffed him.

La was standing next to the stranger. Caroline looked from them to the painting. The bride in the picture was so young, so carefree, so fresh that Caroline had never noticed it before. It was her mother. She gazed at the strange man, her eyes full of questions and longing.

"Why?" Caroline said to both of them. Philip stroked her hair a little.

"I—" said the stranger.

Caroline held up a hand. "First," she said, "I want to hear from her. Mother?"

"Come look at the tape," La said. "You'll understand."

Everyone returned to the back office, where La turned on the video machine and hit play.

Superimposed over one corner of the image was a graphic reading 06-14-80. The camera took up a position near the front, where a minister was standing, then swung back in the direction of the trellis behind the guests, where the groom was arriving. He had longish, tousled blondish-brown hair, piercing blue eyes, and a delicate jaw line, but his most noticeable feature was his nervous smile. It was the brave act of a little boy dying of an infectious disease as his sports hero shows up in the hospital with an autographed uniform. The groom on the tape glanced around at the guests sending a weak little beam of joy in every direction, then paused to remove a handkerchief from his pocket and apply it to his face. He folded the handkerchief again and gripped it tightly in one hand for future use. He walked as directed, one slow step in advance, then a step to bring his feet in line. Then he shoved off on another step, with effort. The ground was perfectly level but the groom's efforts suggested a hike up a Himalaya.

As he passed the back row of guests, they started to look worried. Women whispered in their husbands' ears. The husbands nodded gravely and patted them on the forearms. The groom got closer to the camera. As he did so, his red face seemed to surge with pimples. The groom stopped walking again, touched his soaked handkerchief to his forehead again, smiled at everyone, then teetered forward a bit and toppled face-first onto the grass. Guests rushed around him. The camera jerked around wildly for a few seconds, then the image went blank.

"Buffoon," said La, and stopped the tape. She turned to

Caroline. "Because your father failed the walking-and-standing portion of the ceremony, we had to cancel."

"My father is—?" Caroline looked at the stranger. She looked at her mother. La didn't say anything.

"Not dead," said the man, finally.

Caroline was enraged. "You told me my father died when I was just a little girl," she said. "How could you do that?"

"Why didn't you just wake him up with some smelling salts, give him a glass of water, and go ahead with it?" said Grummer.

"Because you just can't fit all the guests into the back of an ambulance, darling. He had to be sped off to the hospital for observation. Ver-ry dramatic. Ted Leeford was quite the little object of attention, weren't you?" La said, casting a spiteful glance at the stranger. "Except, news flash, the bride must always be the star of the wedding."

Ted shook his head.

"We lost the reservation," La continued. "The place was booked solid for months. And of course I couldn't wait months. Because. . . ."

"Because of me?"

La nodded. "I wasn't showing the day we were supposed to have the wedding. After you came along, we were going to get married as soon as I could fit into my dress again. No big deal, right? But let me tell you about the dark days before personal trainers. It took longer than I'd expected. There were mood swings. Hormones. They couldn't be ignored, they had to be treated. That treatment involved powerful doses of hot fudge sauce and maraschino cherries. And something happened to your father in just those few months."

"Was he hurt? Did he run away?" Caroline felt some unwanted action going on in her eyes. "Did he leave me?"

As she looked at Ted, she knew it couldn't be true.

"Leave you? He could barely look away from you. He quit his job—a rather promising one, too. The man was a cinch to make partner at his law firm. He said he couldn't stand the long hours when he knew you were at home. His world was you."

"This is a problem?" Caroline said.

La glared at her. "I didn't exist. All he could talk about was you. All he did was spoil you. I was . . ."—she searched for a word, making clawing motions in the air—"demoted."

"So where did you go, Daddy?" Caroline said. The word seemed strange, exhilarating.

Ted looked at her kindly. "I had to go away," he said.

"Actually, I sent him away," said La. "He didn't really have a choice."

"What do you mean?"

"Christopher Casby was exceptionally fond of me, darling, as who wouldn't be? He was already a highly important judge when you were born. I met him at the Met's Costume Ball. Such a flirt! And he helped me cut a few corners when it came to evidence."

"Evidence?" said Caroline, whose compassion was turning rapidly into alarm. "What are you talking about? Was there some sort of crime?"

"Not really," said La. "But you don't really need to prove anything when it comes to restraining orders."

"Restraining order? Against who?"

"Against me," Ted said.

"Let me tell it my way," said La. "Caroline, I'm sorry. I admit it. I was jealous of you. I was jealous of the way he treated you. One of you had to go."

"And at first," said Caroline, catching on, "it was me."

La nodded. "At first it was you. I sent you to an orphanage to prove I meant business. He couldn't believe it. He tried to use the courts of law, but—"

"The law is an ass," grumbled Caroline's father.

"You have it backward," she said, and ran a hand from her waist down to her tiny, hard, never-say-die butt. "This. This is the law. So: after I hit Ted with the restraining order that kept him five hundred feet away from you and me at all times, your father finally agreed to let me raise you by myself, and not to interfere or see you or try to contact you. It was either that or allow you to be raised by strangers."

"So that's why you got me back from the orphanage?" Caroline said. "Because my father promised not to be around anymore?"

"Darling," said La. "He didn't have a choice, did he? I had Judge Casby, then Senator Casby, in my pocket. Occasionally I'd have exciting little affairs with Chris, just to keep him interested. Men are like goldfish. Sprinkle a little something close enough so that they can get a taste, they stay happy for quite a while."

"Twenty-something years," said Ted. In old jeans and brown work shoes, he was more weathered than the kind of guys you normally met in Manhattan. Office guys. His face looked like it had seen more sunshine than fluorescent lighting. "But not forever."

"I was happy to get you back," La said. "It was so chic to be a single mother at the time. You were completely on trend as an accessory."

"Caroline," said Ted, "you have to believe me. I loved you more than anything. She wouldn't let you see me. But she couldn't stop me from seeing you."

La froze. "What?"

"I ignored the restraining order," he said. "I learned how to disguise myself. Caroline, I was there. Not all the time but a lot of the time. And definitely every Christmas. You spent a Christmas Eve at the orphanage. You almost fell out of your crib."

Caroline felt the tears. She held onto them. Clutched them tightly in the corners of her eyes.

"But you didn't," Ted said, "because I had a job sweeping floors at the orphanage. I was looking out for you. I was there. That time in Washington when that guy ran away with your purse. I was there to stop him, dressed as a cop. Yesterday on Forty-second Street you almost got killed. But you didn't. Because I was there. I pulled you out of traffic, and then I went right back to my post."

"Your post?" Caroline said.

"Outside the Belle Connerie building. First heap on the right." He pulled his coat over his head, reached into his pocket, and took out a bottle of the Koelner in its retro-futuristic silver bottle. " 'Been sitting here a long time,' remember?"

Caroline blinked off the tears. She was memorizing his

face, but it didn't take much effort. The oil painting had always been with her. "You did all that for me?"

"Caroline," Ted said, "I sent you Christmas cards every year. I signed them Nemo. It means 'no one.' Because I felt like no one without you. But I've always been looking out for you. And I'll always be there. Until the day I give you away." He smiled at Philip.

Caroline felt a blush coming on. She tried not to look at Philip, but she couldn't help it. Which made her blush a little more.

"Um, he's engaged," said Caroline.

Philip had a funny look on his face. He was about to say something, but just then his phone buzzed.

"What?" he said to the phone. "I can't believe it. These cops aren't going to let me leave until they get what they want. Why didn't you tell the cab to wait? Never mind. I've got no time for one of your anecdotes, Sam." He held his hand over the receiver and told the cops, "Look, there's going to be a little delay on the doughnuts. There's some sort of free pop concert at the Rockefeller Center Christmas tree. Massive gridlock. No cabs."

"Where is he?" said Grummer.

"Fiftieth and Rockefeller Plaza," said Philip.

"May we suggest alternative forms of transportation?' said Dubbley.

Grummer was speaking into his radio. "All Midtown North units, all Midtown North units," he was saying.

Caroline shook her head sadly at Philip and moved on. "And anyway, Mother has kind of won, hasn't she? I mean, I got—a little bit—fired—yesterday."

Caroline may have learned a lot overnight, but she was still broke, with no idea how she was going to make a living. Her beloved Shoeseum was farther out of reach than ever. What seemed very much in reach was a strip mall job buffing Ohio's nastiest nails. "And with all the time you spent hanging around me, you couldn't have had a real job, could you?"

"That's true," he said, smiling a wicked little smile that suggested his next word was going to be "but."

La lit another cigarette, her hands shaking. "Do we have to listen to this?" she said. The hands always give you away. Hers looked like a dead person's. "I'd rather be in Branson."

"The only way I can picture you earning a living," Caroline said to Ted, "is if you could somehow profit from work done by other people without doing much yourself."

"Exactly," he said. "That's why I became a talent agent."

"Really? For who?"

"I got a couple of authors who never wrote a book anyone ever wore out. Couple of filmmakers who made movies you've never seen."

"Oh," said Caroline, losing hope again.

"Had a couple of blond cookies who went from waitress to pop star to waitress in five years flat," Ted continued. "When you put out your shingle, you never know what's going to come in. Most of it's bad, and the rest is worse. But all you need is one thing that works, and you'll never have to punch a time card again."

Caroline had not failed to notice that it had been a weird two days. Lots of strange little coincidences. Patterns.

"So what worked?"

"I was at the track in Belmont one day watching the ponies go around and around, pouring my money away twelve ounces at a time. Happened to meet a horse veterinarian. Guy's name was Elmo."

"But he probably didn't actually win any races, I'm guessing. Not being a horse himself."

"No, but he played in a bluegrass band. Said he needed a little help."

"With what?"

"Dealing with the radio stations. I didn't know anything about radio. So naturally I became Elmo's agent."

"That's nice, Daddy. It doesn't really matter, though. I don't care if you have a cent to your name."

"He introduced me to his friend Randy Brooks. So I took him on, too."

"Not exactly Lennon and McCartney, though," Caroline said, poking him in the waist.

"I brought their record to a radio programmer, friend of a friend, in San Francisco. It started to get some airplay. Regional hit, nothing special. We didn't make any money off it, but it was nice to be in business. I was poor but excited. I began to drink less. A few years later, when you were just a toddler, we put together a video. Unbelievably low-budget. But there was this brand-new cable channel that had twenty-four hours a day to fill, and they used to air the most amateurish stuff. They'd play anything so long as it had something to do with music. They played our song. It got bigger and bigger. Last year it earned millions in radio fees and publishing rights. The weird thing is that after all these years, it's still gaining in popularity."

"What song?" Caroline asked, with as pure a case of mixed feelings as has ever been recorded. She read the answer on his lips before the sound reached her ears.

"'Grandma Got Run Over by a Reindeer.'"

Her mother's "Ugh" was what did it. It set Caroline free. Free of the past, free of all the mistakes she had made, free of her fear of this tall smiling man with weather-beaten features. From now on, anything her mother liked was to be regarded with extreme dubiousness. Anything that annoyed her mother was cool. La took a huge angry puff of her cigarette and started digging in the pile of torn wedding dresses at her feet. She began to pick them up and toss veils and trains and bodices madly into the air with both hands. Even in her genuine misery, Caroline thought, she's still posing a little. As she heaved fabric this way and that, La didn't even put down the cigarette she held precariously between her second and third fingers.

"Oh Daddy," Caroline said, and as she rushed into his arms, she felt that she had known her father forever. "I knew there had to be a reason."

"For what?" he said, rocking her slowly back and forth.

"For all the suffering that song put me through," she said.

He laughed. "It was all for you," he whispered into her ear. "Everything I did. Every call I made. Every mall appearance I booked. Every night I stayed up studying contracts. But I didn't do it full-time. Because I had to get back to you. Your whole life, wherever you went, whatever you were doing, there was always someone looking out for you."

"I knew it," said Caroline, no longer succeeding in the tear management department. "I knew it all along." She pictured her father standing proudly beside her as they cut the ribbon in front of the Shoeseum. She would even name it after him! Ted's Shoeseum. Or, possibly, not.

That's when the sound came from the vicinity of La, the strangest sound Caroline had ever heard her mother make. It wasn't quite a bleat, nor yet a yell. It had in it the elements of a kamikaze war cry, but also of a small, cornered animal. It was the call of a woman who has just gone up in flames.

The cigarette was at the center of the flames, on top of the little mound of wedding dresses that were now burning like a bonfire to honor the gods of matrimony. Flames leaped several feet high. La's clothes were on fire, sparks glowing in her hair.

But Dubbley and Grummer moved fast. Each of them had found a fire extinguisher and neither of them was holding back. In seconds, the fire was out, smothered by a thick layer of white foam. So was La. From her pumps to her hair, frothy white gook covered her. She looked like the lead of a horror film called *The She-Creature from the Bubble Bath*.

"You wretches!" La said to the cops, enraged. "Look what you did to my dress, you pathetic yokels."

"What'd you want us to do?" said Grummer.

"You should," said La, quivering crazily in her foam, "you should," she said, rage nearly igniting her all over again, "*you should have let me burn.*"

Caroline was horrified. She buried her head in her father's chest. Ted held her tight.

"She'll be okay," Ted murmured, rocking her. "Stone doesn't burn."

Grummer was calling for "a bus" with his shoulder-mounted

walkie-talkie. Dubbley sprayed La a little more, just to make sure she didn't spontaneously combust.

The siren of the ambulance could already be heard outside on Madison.

"Lady—" said Dubbley.

"How dare you call me by my first name?" said La. "It's Ms. Havisham, to you."

"We're going to have to take you to the hospital," said Grummer.

"I'm not going," said La. "This is my shop, and I'm staying. I'm perfectly fine. I'll have your badges for this, you hicks. I know a very powerful senat—"

The end of the sentence never came. Caroline, still in her father's arms, giggled. Philip smiled. Even the cops looked happy as they dragged the shivering, foamy figure out the door and into the ambulance. Philip and Ted and Caroline, trailing along after her, watched in amused horror as they shivered in the chill on Seventy-seventh Street.

Philip's cell phone buzzed. He answered quickly, then flipped it closed. "It's a shame," he said.

"You got that right," said Caroline. "I'm not saying I want my mother roasted alive, but couldn't she have suffered just a light toasting?"

"I meant, shame about the cops leaving," said Philip. "Because the doughnuts are coming."

Grummer and Dubbley, who were stepping up into the back of the ambulance, halted so quickly that they nearly twanged. Grummer looked at Dubbley. Dubbley looked at Grummer.

Then it all came roaring in: the sirens, the flashing blue

lights, the whine of the motorcycles, the clopping of the hooves. In front were three motorcycle cops, making a quantity of noise and fuss befitting a simultaneous visit from the President of the United States, the Queen of England, and the winner of *American Idol*. Then came the police cruiser, its lights whirling in a blue fever. It was followed by the alternative form of transportation: a white horse-drawn carriage, its noble steed racing up the middle of Madison at full gallop, busting through red lights as ordinary vehicles scattered. Behind the cart were three more police cruisers fully blasting their sirens and giving their lights a workout.

Inside the horse-drawn carriage was a rumpled man in an overcoat, corduroys and a sweater that did not quite conceal the long sleeves of his pajama top, holding onto two towering stacks of blue and yellow boxes labeled Pip's Doughnuts.

"Ladies and gentlemen," said Philip, "my long-suffering but faithful deputy, Sam Weller."

Grummer and Dubbley jumped down off the ambulance and slammed the door. There was another emergency to deal with, this time in their stomachs.

Grummer and Dubbley led the organizational effort as the motorcycles and police cars lined themselves up along Madison and Seventy-seventh in splendid array. One cop hopped off his motorcycle and directed traffic. One took charge of parking operations. The other thirteen personally supervised the off-loading, carrying, and safe delivery of the doughnuts. Dubbley rediscovered his megaphone and eagerly yelled, "Stand back!" to two elm trees and a mailbox.

Inside La's office the doughnut boxes were opened and

spread out on desks and tables and a credenza. Some of them were still so warm that the doughnuts' steamy essence rose out of the boxes and climbed back to heaven where it came from. A chorus of manly praise greeted the display. There was an embarrassing moment when several officers noticed, or thought they noticed, a tear in Dubbley's eye. "It's a Christmas miracle," one of them said. Several officers crossed themselves.

"Stand back!" Philip whispered to Caroline. She giggled as the officers went to work. There were chocolate iced with sprinkles, apple-cinnamon twists, powdered strawberry-filled, double-glazed chocolate crème-filled, maple iced, chocolate-glazed crullers, powdered blueberry-filled and traditional chocolate cake with chocolate icing and chocolate sprinkles. It was moments before all units on hand were munching away, their eyes triple-glazed with joy. Caroline found herself collapsing naturally into her father's arms.

"To me you are the best daughter there ever was," Ted murmured in her ear. Caroline knew this meant something—a bell went *ding* in her head—but before she could process it she was distracted by a voice in the hall with a manufactured-sounding Southern accent.

"Yoo-hoo!" said the voice. "Is this place open?"

Philip and Caroline looked at each other.

"In here," said Philip.

Ursula Heep slithered into the room with Nic close behind her, as if on an invisible leash, and began dramatically removing her gloves. The left one first, of course.

"Cold out there!" she said. "Good thing I brought my gloves!"

The stone on her engagement ring was about the size of a chandelier. Normally Caroline made a point of not noticing girls showing off their rocks, but she was in a good mood.

"Nice," Caroline said. "Did you two get engaged? I'm so happy for you." And she even gave Ursula a hug, though not more than five percent of the two women's bodies actually came in contact with each other. It was like watching porcupines mate.

"What a night!" Ursula said. "Nic was acting so nervous on the way to the airport, weren't you, sugar?"

Nic looked bashfully at Caroline.

"Then we got bumped from the flight and I was going to make a big fuss and everything but Nic went to the l'il boys room and I was looking through his bag for a cough drop and right there! I found it! This ring!"

"Right at the bottom of the bag," Nic said.

"The sweetie was going to propose to me on the plane!" Ursula said. "I was so excited, I said, let's stay up all night and have a wild romantic New York Christmas. Then tonight we thought—"

"She thought," said Nic, with partial good humor.

"We'd just stop by here and, you know, kind of check out the selection of dresses. I mean, obviously, I won't let him see the dress I actually get married in, but just to get some ideas. I've always loved your work, uh"—she looked for the store's absent proprietor, momentarily registered the unexplained presence of fifteen hungry policemen and foam all over the floor, then hurried on so as not to lose the room. "I just thought it would be so romantic! Of course, mine *must* be custom-designed," she said to Nic. "I can pay for it myself. I'm expecting this big promotion at, uh, work." Her eyes met Caroline's for half a second. Caroline was picturing the smoking remains of what had once been Ursula's work station. Both of them smiled sarcastically.

Then Caroline smiled a more general smile and picked up a big yummy box of temptation. "So," she said. "I guess it's time to celebrate."

Ursula shot Nic a wild, daredevil look. "I know I shouldn't," she said. "But I'm getting married, after all. Why not let go a little?" And with that she popped about two thirds of a powdered blueberry-filled into her mouth. A puff of white confectioners' sugar wafted over her chin and settled there.

"One of our most popular choices," said Philip.

"Really?" said Ursula. "Oh, my, I've never tasted such manna." She put the rest of the doughnut in her mouth. "What else is good?"

"Here's my personal favorite," Philip said, picking up the maxed-out chocolate number. "I named it after an uncle of mine. I think you'll like it. It's called Barnaby fudge," he said. Caroline caught his eye.

Ursula gobbled it down and started pushing through the cops to get to the rest. "Oh my," she said, taking a huge bite of another doughnut. "Lemon-filled." A drunken expression crossed her features.

Grummer took a quick break from his apple fritter to ask Caroline, "Hey, can you turn it to channel two? The Jets game is on."

Dubbley swallowed a bite of a chocolate iced and checked

his watch. "Should be near the end. I hope it doesn't come down to that Zen kicker again."

Channel 2 showed a lonely-looking football player jogging onto the snowy field. It was Tiny Tim. A graphic in the corner of the screen said "Jets 14. Dolphins 16. 4th. 0:04." The announcers were excited. The crowd was screaming. And Tiny Tim, now demonstrably insane, was barefoot. What a doofus, Caroline thought. She had tried to help the guy, she really had.

"Four ticks left in the game and this is a whole new flavor of weird, Bob," said one announcer. "Tiny Tim is going to kick barefoot? Never done it before, not in his entire career. We haven't seen a barefoot kicker in this league in about twenty years. And I've never seen a guy go barefoot on his nonkicking foot as well as his kicking foot. Especially on a frozen Christmas Day in the Meadowlands."

"Troy," said Bob the Announcer, "the snow is starting to fall, and the field is slick, but I support this call a hundred and ten percent. The man has to do something to shake himself out of his slump."

"So this is it," said Troy. "If he makes it, the Jets advance to the playoffs. If he misses it, I hope he can afford a ticket back to his home country, because he'll be done in this one."

"It'll be ugly," said Bob. "The fans'll be chasing him into the night with pitchforks and lanterns. It'll be like something out of *Frankenstein*."

"Nic," said Caroline, "I'd like you to meet my friend Philip, the world's greatest doughnut maker. You two have lots in common."

Nic and Philip shook hands. And Nic gave a worried little glance at Ursula, who was doing to a maple walnut iced what Godzilla did to Tokyo.

"What do you mean?" said Philip.

"Oh, come on," said Caroline. "I saw you and your girlfriend looking at wedding dresses. It's okay. You don't need to hide it."

"My girlfriend?" said Philip. "That was Biddy. Friend of the family. She's marrying my Uncle Joe. I'm very happy for her."

Caroline looked at Nic. "Can you excuse us for a second?" she said.

"No problem," said Nic. "I think I'll just slip out and get Ursula a gross of napkins. It's nice to see you again, Caroline."

Philip and Caroline watched as Nic went back to Ursula and whispered something to her. Ursula nodded, then picked up a caramel crème crunch. Nic did not look pleased.

"Biddy is the woman I saw you looking in the window of the shop with?" Caroline said. "I could have sworn you were in love with her."

"I've known her for years," Philip said. "She's been working with my Uncle Joe for a long time."

This answer wasn't good enough for any woman, and certainly not for Caroline. She waited.

"Okay," said Philip. "I was a little bit in love with her, once. But I wasn't ready for her, or anyone. I went through a lot of rough patches when I was trying to start a business. I didn't like myself, sometimes. I had to learn a few things. But that's all over now. I really am looking forward to the wedding. Joe is a great guy and they're perfect for each other."

Caroline closed her eyes and shook her head. Relief, was the word. "Listen," she said. "I'm not usually this forward, but do you have plans for New Year's Eve? Because I've got nothing lined up. Zero."

"Is that a fact?" said Philip.

The cops burst into a cheer. Dubbley and Grummer were dancing around madly, arm in arm. Caroline's dad was exchanging high fives with each of them as they spun each other around. Her dad was a high-fiver? What other ugly facts had he hidden from her?

Caroline glanced at the TV: Jets 17. Dolphins 16. Final.

"Come on," she said, nudging Philip a little. "The past twenty-four hours have been pretty weird. Don't make it weirder."

"Shhh," Philip said. He was also looking at the TV. "I want to hear the Zen kicker."

Tiny Tim was being swarmed by guys with cameras. A reporter in a fur bucket hat was sticking a microphone in his face. "Tim," she said, "with your Jets' season and your career on the line, what made you decide to kick the game-winning field goal barefoot? You've never kicked barefoot before. And why would you go barefoot on both feet?"

"I been holding back team lately, you know?" said Tiny Tim. "All I am is dust in the windshield. But someone I know just convince me is okay to be weird." The fans continued to roar. The other players kept coming by to hug him and slap his butt. "Is okay to be weird! I am oddball! I am freak! But now I am super freak!"

The reporter nodded solemnly. "Tim, you came from a

poor part of Kroplochnich and now you're the hero of the biggest city in America. Any final thoughts on the most important day of your—"

A breathless young man ran up to the reporter and handed her a cell phone. The reporter frowned, touched her headset, and listened.

"Tim," said the reporter, "we've got someone special on the line who wants to congratulate you. We're going to patch in our audience so everyone can hear."

"Really?" said Tim, taking the phone with a trembling paw.

"Is that Tiny Tim?" said a boisterous voice. "It's Captain Cuttle here, how are ya, you crazy kicker?"

"Is Mr. President?" said Tim. "Sir, did you ever know that you're my hero? You are the wimp beneath my wings."

"Zip it, buddy, you're the hero today, I'm just a geezer sits behind a desk. I gotta tell you, the way you kicked today, I've been thinking: this country needs more wacky immigrants! There oughta be a law. And guess who signs 'em!"

"Mr. President," said Tim, "you are great man! Though I am not being understanding of your jokes."

"Never mind, never mind," said President Cuttle. "Listen buddy, I gotta run. But you did a terrific job out there today, and I'm here to tell you, just as a little token of my appreciation, tonight I'm gonna bomb the crap out of any small-to-medium-sized country of your choice. Gimmee a name. How about Denmark?"

"I am being confused," said Tim.

"It's a joke, son! Don't they have those in Kroplochnich? Gotta go!"

Tim handed the phone back to the sideline reporter, who hurried on. "Final thoughts, Tim, on this, the greatest day of your life?"

"I thank the President, my hunky tank wolfman," said Tiny Tim. "I thank my sister, I thank the fans, I thank most of all my good friend Caroline Havisham," said Tim. "And of course Buddha. Buddha bless us! Everyone!"

Good friend? Again the bell dinged in Caroline's head. But her dad was looking at her wonderingly. "I'm not a Havisham," she said quietly, but not too quietly. "I'm a Leeford."

Ted smiled.

"Looks like Tiny Tim is smitten with you," Philip said, nudging her. "There's your date for New Year's Eve."

"Oh please," said Caroline.

"I'm teasing," said Philip. "Hey, I should be off. You need to spend some time with your father without me getting in the way. I'm glad for you. And I can't tell you how lucky it was for me to run into you tonight." He made a little gesture toward the door with his head.

Caroline looked back at her father. He was smiling. He motioned for her to go with Philip.

Out on the street the city was perfectly still except for a few taxis on the prowl. The wind was whipping the snowflakes around crazily. Philip hailed a cab. The moment was awkward. Caroline leaned forward until the hug was inevitable. It wasn't particularly satisfying, at first. But then it was.

"So that's it," said Philip quietly. Caroline was pondering what exactly he meant by this when she noticed that he was kissing her. He felt warm, especially when he put his arms around her waist. He felt nice. He tasted nice. The wind settled down and the snow began merely drifting, elegant and slow.

"Good-bye, Caroline," he said, and broke off.

"Um, good-bye?" she said, trying to find something to do with her hands.

"Let's not do this again, huh?" he said, opening the door of the cab.

"Do what?" said Caroline. "The kissing part or the good-bye-ing part?"

"If I answered that," Philip said, "I'd be Mr. Obvious, wouldn't I?"

And as Philip got in and shut the door, the snow started coming down more heavily. Caroline frowned. This wasn't the right ending. She needed to resolve everything, now, today, Christmas Day. She knew her father was waiting for her, but she didn't feel like going back inside. She watched the cab roll carefully into the intersection, take a right, and head up Madison. At Seventy-ninth it stopped for a red light. Long day, she thought, and was suddenly, pleasantly sleepy. She put her hands in her coat pockets. And found something there.

She took out the crumpled page she'd found in a crappy women's magazine in Akron, Ohio. She smiled gently. She was a better daughter. To Ted. And as Tiny Tim had just told the world, she had become a valued friend to him. But was she a better girlfriend?

The answer was a great big nuh-uh. Not only wasn't she a better girlfriend, she wasn't anyone's girlfriend at all. Her only chance had just gotten in a cab. She looked at her watch: 12:01 AM. Time had run out. This Christmas was over. She had failed the test. Probably her Shoeseum idea would fail. She'd end up polishing nails in a strip mall in Akron. All because she hadn't made the most of this day. But it was okay. Because Christmas as an idea would always be there. It wasn't going away.

She looked at the clock that nestled in the curve of one of the classic bishop's crook street lights on Madison. Then she looked straight up into the black sky and felt the snow settle on her cheeks. A few flakes stuck to her eyelashes. She was shivering but glad of the cold. So she took a big breath of biting winter air and found it exhilarating. She glanced back at the clock: 11:56. Perfect. Christmas wasn't over yet. By now she was smiling, patiently waiting for the cab to turn right at the next light, go around the block, and head straight back to her.